RAVES FOR ELEANOR ROOSEVELT, SUPER-SLEUTH!

"TERRIFIC!"
Chicago Tribune

"PERFECTLY WONDERFUL!"
New York *Daily News*

"A PLEASURE!"
Richmond Times-Dispatch

"BRILLIANT!"
Seattle Post-Intelligencer

ELLIOTT ROOSEVELT

MURDER AT THE PALACE

AVON BOOKS ◆ NEW YORK

AVON BOOKS
A division of
The Hearst Corporation
1350 Avenue of the Americas
New York, New York 10019

Copyright © 1987 by Elliott Roosevelt
Published by arrangement with St. Martin's Press
Library of Congress Catalog Card Number: 87-27961
ISBN: 0-380-70405-6

First Avon Books Printing: June 1989

AVON TRADEMARK REG. U.S. PAT. OFF. AND IN OTHER COUNTRIES, MARCA REGISTRADA, HECHO EN CANADA.

Printed in Canada.

UNV   10   9   8   7   6   5   4

To my partner and loving wife, Patty

Author's Note

Once more I would like to thank my friend the novelist William Harrington, who has given me invaluable assistance with the First Lady mystery series. Both of us would like to thank Mr. Michael Shea, press secretary to Her Majesty Queen Elizabeth II, and Mr. Oliver Everett, librarian, Windsor Castle, for prompt and courteous response to inquiries about details of the Eleanor Roosevelt visit to Buckingham Palace in October 1942.

1

Looking out the big square window at what should have been a view of the blue skies, Mrs. Roosevelt saw nothing but a wall of gray. She glanced at her secretary, Malvina "Tommy" Thompson, who was still half asleep and comfortably relaxed in her leather chair. She decided not to tell her that the pilot was flying . . . What was the term? He was flying "blind" without being able to see the earth or the sky.

Across the Atlantic. That was the unrealistic element of it! They were flying across the Atlantic! Not only that, but nonstop! From New York to a landing in Ireland, the mammoth Pan American flying boat would be in the air twenty hours, flying only on the fuel it carried in what must be immense tanks. For— she glanced at her watch and counted the hours— some eighteen hours now, the four huge engines on the wings had been roaring synchronously, making a low, almost musical note that she guessed would remain in her ears long after they landed.

An officer who had spoken to her in the galley when she walked forward for a cup of coffee had told her that in a very real sense it was fortunate that they

1

were, as he put it, "in the soup" as they approached the Irish coast. Although the safety record for these flights was excellent and although the Royal Air Force would send out a flight of fighters to rendez-vous with the flying boat and escort them to their landing in Foynes, still they were now entering a part of the ocean within the range of some twin-engine Luftwaffe fighters, and it was just as well to be in cloud and fog.

That comment, too, she had kept to herself when she walked back to the suite in the rear of the flying boat, which she shared with Tommy and with Colonel Oveta Hobby and the colonel's aide Lieutenant Betty Bandel.

Her mind returned to past Atlantic crossings, always of course by liner. She recalled a conversation with Bernard Baruch, only a few years ago, on the occasion of the first transatlantic passenger flight, when they had wondered aloud if regular service was really practicable—or even useful. Well, it *was* useful, as it turned out. But it was also, she reflected as she stared into the gloom, an adventure.

Thinking of reaching England in only a few more hours, her thoughts went to the years she had spent at Allenswood School, just outside London. She had a special affection for England and the English people, and knew it would be painful to see London as it was now, damaged by Nazi bombs. She would meet Mr. Churchill yet again. She would see King George and Queen Elizabeth once more. And she would see her son, Elliott. That was important.

It had been Harry Hopkins's idea, she understood, that she make this flight to England. Mr. Churchill had spoken many times with the President about the prospect of his coming to England. Such a visit would be very useful, the Prime Minister had repeatedly said—as if he did not realize what toll such a journey would take on the President's energy. Franklin was, after all, sixty years old; and for him, traveling was a far more burdensome thing than it was for a man who could trot down a flight of stairs. Besides, the presidency in wartime imposed a greater load on a man than anyone could possibly imagine.

Harry understood. Anyway, it was he who had suggested, apparently, that she fly to England.

"I will do it, if you think it will be really useful," she had said to the President when he broached the subject.

The conversation had taken place in the Oval Office, between appointments, when Franklin had been eating his light lunch consisting of an apple and a tuna-salad sandwich.

"Babs," he had said, "it will be useful. Anyway, it will give you a chance to visit with Elliott."

"And give certain people a chance to carp that I flew to England at the nation's expense just to have a visit with our son."

"Fly at your own expense, then. Juan Trippe is maintaining regular transatlantic service for those who can afford it and those who have priority. I can arrange the priority."

"On what justification?" she had asked.

"Babs," the President had said, picking up his apple, "it is no secret to you—though it is to most of the world—that many of our boys in England are going to be loaded on ships in a matter of days for Operation Torch, the invasion of North Africa. I'd like to go to England, tour the camps, see as many of those boys as possible, shake their hands, talk with them. I can't. You can.''

"And I can come back and report to you of their morale.''

"Yes. Besides, you can do something useful about the alliance. The King and Queen were here in nineteen thirty-nine. You got on well with them. A return visit. . . . Also, make a point of visiting with the Queen Mother, Queen Mary. And the Duchess of Kent. Besides, there are some heads of governments-in-exile who would be honored and would be strengthened in their loyalty to the cause if you were to talk with them on my behalf. Queen Wilhelmina of the Netherlands. King Haakon of Norway. King George of Greece. President Beneš of Czechoslovakia. The President of Poland . . . Oh, there's enough work to keep you busy for a month over there.''

"Army camps. Air bases.''

"Yes. I'll try to make do without you for a few weeks.''

She had sighed and frowned. "You seriously believe it will be *useful*," she had insisted.

"I seriously believe it will be useful," he had said solemnly.

She had been briefed extensively: by the State Department, by the Department of the Army, by Harry Hopkins and Cordell Hull, and by the President. She had met twice with Lord Halifax, the British Ambassador to Washington. Finally, she had chosen Tommy to go with her, and they had submitted to the shots one had to have before venturing overseas; and on October 22 they had taken the train to New York and boarded the flying boat.

Colonel Hobby, the head of the Women's Army Corps (W.A.C.), was accompanying her, though not officially of her party. She and her aide, Lieutenant Bandel, were to study women's contributions to the British war effort, to learn what additional functions the W.A.C. could undertake for the United States.

The flight had been uneventful, actually. For most of it they had experienced clear weather and had been able to look down on the North Atlantic, day and night. At one point they had sighted a convoy—it had looked like a hundred ships—scurrying in anti-submarine zigzags across the calm surface of the ocean, looking like so many water bugs. An officer had come back and asked for their promise not to mention the convoy after they landed. The ships would not reach British harbors for many days, and any mention that they were out there could help the Germans locate and attack them.

His words had been a reminder of the grim reality of the war which they were flying toward at more than two hundred miles an hour. Someone wanted to sink those ships, to kill those men.

Colonel Hobby and Lieutenant Bandel came out of the women's lounge. They had changed into civilian clothes. Ireland was a neutral country, and if they landed there wearing the uniform of the United States Army, technically they could be impounded for the duration of the war.

"A grim prospect," Captain Willander had said. "It's bad enough we have to land in their damned country, much less risk staying there."

"I hold Ireland in a great deal of respect," Mrs. Roosevelt had said.

"I would hold the Irish in a good deal more respect if they would declare war on Hitler like every other democracy," the Captain had retorted.

Colonel Hobby stepped to the window and looked out. "Blind flying," she said. "They say it's safe."

Tommy Thompson roused herself and looked out. "Oh dear," she said.

"I warned you it would be an adventure," said Mrs. Roosevelt.

It soon became apparent that they had begun to descend. Although it was morning, the atmosphere became darker, the cloud cover thicker, and fat drops of rain began to spatter on the windows. From the sound of the engines they could tell that they were being throttled back. The huge flying boat eased cautiously downward.

"I will ask you to fasten your seat belts, ladies," said one of the stewards, who stuck his head into their compartment. "Captain says the Mouth of the Shannon is just ahead."

As a courtesy, the captain had shown Mrs. Roosevelt the charts. Their flight had been up Long Island Sound, across the water to Cape Cod, north over Newfoundland, then out across the broad expanse of the Atlantic. They would land at Foynes, in the estuary of the River Shannon, a few miles from Limerick. From there they would transfer to a British plane, which would fly them across the Irish Sea to Bristol, in Gloucester, then on by train from Bristol to London.

She had asked why they did not fly directly to London from Bristol, instead of taking the train. The answer had been: because the King and Queen never meet anyone at an *airport*. Tommy and Colonel Hobby had been annoyed by the response, but Mrs. Roosevelt thought it typically English, and more amusing than irksome. The English did not readily break with tradition, she remembered vividly, and perhaps their refusal to break with some traditions was a source of their strength in this war.

The mist outside their windows darkened more, and the rain became heavier. When at first she saw a dark-green patch through a wisp of cloud or fog, she did not recognize it. Then another patch appeared, and after that another, and she realized she was looking at green water; they were indeed descending from the low-hanging clouds and approaching a landing on the Shannon's long inlet from the ocean.

Tommy heaved an audible sigh of relief. Mrs. Roosevelt concealed her own relief, but she was glad to see the misty shores and the villages to the left of the flying boat. The long flight, spiced with an inescapable sense of hazard, was almost over. Franklin had never flown the Atlantic, but Elliott had, and it was an adventure she and her son would share with Franklin when they were together again.

Water is no soft landing field and the big flying boat bounced alarmingly on the choppy water, its hull banging as though it had landed on ice. Then it settled into the water and, in effect, changed from a flying machine to a boat. Its four engines roared as the captain turned and accelerated toward the shore, and the flying boat wallowed in the swells.

A stay in Ireland had been in no way anticipated, but the rain was so heavy on their landing that the English pilots who were to fly them to Bristol insisted it was not safe to fly across the Irish Sea. The party spent the night in an Irish home, and the next morning took off from a nearby airfield for the flight to Bristol.

Over Bristol they had their first sight of a bombed city, with block after block of streets without a single structure left standing. They were shocked. They had heard of the bombing, of course, and had seen pictures; but this was their first glimpse of a city, dull-gray in the weak red morning light, lying in ruins beneath their wings. It was odd to see life among the ruins, but streets had been cleared of rubble, vehicles hurried across the bombed-out parts, and people rode bicycles through the cold, bleak streets. Wisps of smoke rose here and there—not from new fires, apparently, but, as they guessed, from the heating and cooking of people who had reestablished their homes and lives in the cellars beneath the ruins.

Mrs. Roosevelt would have liked to tarry in Bristol, to evaluate the damage—see how its people lived, what they felt about the horror that had befallen them, what care they needed, how America could help—but the Prime Minister's special train waited for them, and United States Ambassador John G. Winant escorted them directly to the station.

The run from Bristol to London, on the fast, clean, efficient British rail service Mrs. Roosevelt remembered so well, took only two hours.

The four women in the American party—Mrs. Roosevelt, Tommy Thompson, Colonel Hobby, and Lieutenant Bandel—took advantage of the quiet travel west of London to refresh themselves and see to their clothes. They knew their train would be met by the King and Queen.

"Remember your promise," Tommy said to Mrs. Roosevelt as they entered the outskirts of the city.

"Promise . . . ?"

"To guide me through this thing at Buckingham Palace," said Tommy. "I can't tell you how much I dread it. I am sure I will call someone by the wrong name, curtsy to a maid, demand fresh towels from the Duchess of Something-or-Other, or—"

"Tommy," said Mrs. Roosevelt, "I am as apprehensive as you are. I've never visited a royal palace before and I have no idea what one does or says. I tried to get us out of it, but the gravest discourtesy would have been to decline the invitation. All I can say is, be yourself. You are always poised. Just be poised in the Palace, as you are in the White House. That's what I'm going to try to do."

"Maybe they won't be *too* formal," Tommy suggested. "It is wartime, after all, and they must have had to make some concessions."

"I am sure that is true," said Mrs. Roosevelt. "I rather think it will be *quite* informal."

She recognized the station, Paddington, even though it had been damaged by bombs and part of the roof was gone. She and Franklin had boarded a train at Paddington Station thirty-seven years before, when they traveled from London to be guests at a great country house for a terrifying weekend of deadening ceremony. That had been on their honeymoon, in 1905. Surely England was different now. She fervently hoped the English would have had to put ceremony aside for the duration.

Her thoughts were interrupted by a discreet knock on the door of their compartment.

"Come in."

"Ma'am."

The figure who stood in the door of their compartment was resplendent in velvet, lace, and gold. The Lord Mayor of London? The Lord Chamberlain? Tommy Thompson, quickly on her feet, curtsied awkwardly. Mrs. Roosevelt waited for a word.

"Welcome, ma'am, to Paddington Station," said the regally garbed man. "I am Andrew Hobbes, master of the station. May I escort you?"

Mrs. Roosevelt glanced at Tommy with a weak smile. She pulled on her black coat, draped her fox stole around her neck, and checked one last time in the mirror to be sure of the set of her feathered hat. She picked up the book she had been reading— *Abraham Lincoln and the Fifth Column*—and tucked it under her arm. "We are ready, Mr. Hobbes," she murmured.

The station master led them through the car to the exit on the side opposite their compartment. Unaware of the reception they were to be accorded, Mrs. Roosevelt was surprised by a glimpse of red carpet, and even more so by the sound of the American national anthem struck up by a band on the station platform.

King George VI stood on the red carpet, a small, shy, but handsome man, dressed in the light-blue uniform of a marshal of the Royal Air Force. Queen Elizabeth stood beside him in a black velvet coat and one of the hats that was characteristic of her. Underneath its broad brim, her comely, guileless face beamed a genuinely warm welcome. Mrs. Roosevelt, pausing before stepping down, also recognized Foreign Secretary Anthony Eden in the party, together with Lieutenant General Dwight Eisenhower and Admiral Harold Stark.

Everyone stood smiling at each other until the band finished. Then Mrs. Roosevelt stepped briskly down from the train, bowed to the King and took his hand, then took the outstretched hand of the Queen.

"I hope you left the President in good health," said King George.

"We welcome you with all our hearts," said the Queen.

"My husband only wishes he could have come himself," said Mrs. Roosevelt.

Anthony Eden stepped forward to shake her hand, followed by General Eisenhower and Admiral Stark. Mrs. Roosevelt then introduced Tommy Thompson, Colonel Hobby, and Lieutenant Bandel.

They were escorted to the royal automobiles. Mrs. Roosevelt and the King and Queen entered an immense Daimler, in which they were driven south to Bayswater Road, then around Hyde Park to Constitution Hill and Buckingham Palace. Signs of bombing were all around, though Mrs. Roosevelt knew the damage was not nearly as heavy here as it was in the East End. Huge ugly black piles of coal stood in the broad green fields of Hyde Park, and the long barrels of anti-aircraft guns rose all but indistinguishable from the black trunks of trees. Barrage balloons floated on the ends of their cables, visible from everywhere.

The procession of cars swept through the gates of the Palace, across the forecourt, and through the passageway into the quadrangle. Welcomed by the Master of the Household, Mrs. Roosevelt was escorted by the King and Queen themselves to the rooms she would occupy: the Queen's own bedroom and sitting room.

The rooms were magnificent. Yet—

"You must f-forgive us," said the King, his famous stutter interrupting him and causing him to blush faintly. "The Palace was hit by bombs, you probably recall. W-Windows blown out. We have not replaced most of them, as you can see."

She could see. Though the rooms were splendid, some of the windows were boarded up, while others were covered with cloudy isinglass. The King himself proceeded to show her how the blackout curtains worked and to warn her that the curtains *must* be closed at night.

"We regret, too," said the Queen, "that only one small fire will be lighted in your suite, in the sitting-room fireplace. Even for distinguished visitors, we do not keep the Palace warmer than people's homes. I am afraid you are accustomed to better in the United States."

Mrs. Roosevelt glanced around the sumptuous room, at the elegant furniture, the art, the priceless clock and vases, and reflected for a moment on the irony that the room was cold and would remain so. "I am sure," she said to the King and Queen, "I shall be quite comfortable."

"Then we will," said the Queen, "leave you to rest for a while. We hope you will join us for tea."

When the King and Queen were gone, Mrs. Roosevelt explored her rooms. As she examined the capacious wardrobes, she chuckled at the sight of her two battered leather suitcases—all she had been able to bring because of the weight limit on luggage that could be carried on the flying boat. In the bathroom

she found a huge tub, but a black line had been
painted around the inside, near the bottom, to indicate the amount of hot water one should draw for a
bath.

She sat down in her sitting room, realizing that it
really was cold. She had brought dresses, blouses,
suits with jackets, but only one sweater. She wondered if she would be able to buy a heavy wool
sweater, or would their clothes rationing—

A knock at the door.

She opened it. "Ah, Sir Alan! How *very* nice to
see you!"

The thin, hollow-cheeked man who stepped inside
was Sir Alan Burton, a senior inspector from Scotland Yard, the man who had been impersonated in
Washington in 1939 by the late felon Archibald Ad-
kins and the man who had served as a bodyguard to
Winston Churchill during his December 1941 visit to
the White House. He had helped solve the mystery of
the body found in Mrs. Nesbitt's pantry.

"Mrs. Rose-vult," he said. "My *dear* lady."

"Oh, do come in and sit down, Sir Alan," she
said.

He walked directly to the small fireplace in her
sitting room, poked at the fire with the brass poker,
made a wry face, and took a chair. He was the same
Sir Alan—yellowish-gray hair plastered down with
dressing, watery blue eyes, mobile red lips. He was
dressed in a brown tweed suit.

"The President is well, I hope?" he said.

"Quite well, thank you. And you?"

"Entirely fit," he said.

"Well, I am so pleased you came to see me."

"It is more than just a visit, dear lady," said Sir

Alan. "I am your official bodyguard during your
visit to England. Someone thought it would not distress you quite as much to be assigned a bodyguard if
it were I."

Mrs. Roosevelt smiled broadly. "Are you carrying
a pistol, Sir Alan?" she asked.

He raised his eyebrows. "No, as a matter of
fact."

"I shall enjoy your company, then," she said.
"As I did before."

"Let us hope," he said, "that we find no dead
bodies in Buckingham Palace, as we did in the White
House."

"I join you in that wish," she said.

The princesses took tea with their parents and Mrs.
Roosevelt. Princess Elizabeth was a pretty, serious
young woman of sixteen, and Princess Margaret Rose
was twelve, still childish, in fact impish.

"Will the people of America continue to resist
socialism?" Princess Elizabeth asked gravely when
she had a quiet moment aside with Mrs. Roosevelt.
"I mean, as a universal ideology."

Mrs. Roosevelt wondered what teaching had prompted
this question. "I think," she said gently, "that de-
pends on how we define socialism. If we describe it
as acceptance of public responsibility for the general
welfare of all people, then I would say Americans
accept it. If we define it as state ownership and
control of everything, then I think Americans do not
and will not accept it."

The Princess nodded and seemed to make some
mental note. "Will that sense of responsibility extend
to America's Negroes?" she asked.

"Definitely," said Mrs. Roosevelt.

When Princess Margaret Rose approached, her question was, "Do you know Mr. Humphrey Bogart?"

Mrs. Roosevelt laughed. "I do indeed. He and I, with some other Hollywood people, spent a strange weekend together, during which we solved a murder mystery! Mr. Bogart proved to be something of a detective—in real life, I mean."

"Do you like tea?" asked Princess Margaret Rose. "I mean, served with all this stiff formality." She pointed disapprovingly at the silver tea-service set out on heavy white linen. "I've heard that *Mr*. Roosevelt takes something very different from tea at teatime."

"With every bit as much formality," said Mrs. Roosevelt. "But many years ago I learned to love the English way of serving and drinking tea. I went to school in England as a girl. Allenswood. I learned and loved very many English customs."

"Do American labor unions support all the sacrifices involved in fighting the war?" asked Princess Elizabeth.

Tommy Thompson, who was housed on the floor above Mrs. Roosevelt and had taken tea with the ladies-in-waiting, arrived at Mrs. Roosevelt's suite after tea to take some dictation—letters and the "My Day" column—but their work was presently interrupted by the arrival of another guest. Tommy discreetly withdrew.

Mrs. Roosevelt stood in the doorway between the waiting room and her sitting room, clasping the hands of her son, Lieutenant Colonel Elliott Roosevelt. He was thirty-two years old and served in the United States Army Air Corps, in which he had enlisted long before Pearl Harbor. Elliott was a personable young man, considered impulsive by the family and sometimes a source of annoyance both to his father and mother; but of course she was overcome with joy to see him, and she embraced him, kissed him, and drew him after her into the extraordinary suite of rooms.

"Father is . . . ?" he asked.

"Is well, considering the burdens he bears. Every time someone suggests he is imposing too much on himself he says it is little compared to what American boys all over the world are bearing."

"Well," said Elliott, standing back from her and looking around the room, "you will never be comfortable in the White House again."

"I shall be comfortable the first day I return there," she said. "For I shall turn up the heat!"

Elliott sat down. "There is no heat in England," he said. "Nowhere. But don't suppose it's because of the war. Fifty degrees was considered a nice comfy room temperature before the war. Americans, they say, damage their health by overheating their homes. Anyway, I wear two suits of underwear; and I've brought you a sweater. It isn't handsome—olive-drab—but you can wear it to bed."

She laughed as he pulled the wool sweater from the bag he was carrying.

"When you drive past this place, it doesn't look so impressive," he said. "But . . . my Lord!"

"I feel as if I'm living in a museum," she said. "Anyway, the King and Queen could not have been nicer."

"Dear old things," he said.

"Old! Elliott, the Queen is forty-two years old. The King is forty-seven."

"She's not a bad-looking lady, is she? When she takes off those god-awful hats."

"Elliott. I want to hear nothing but the most circumspect conversation from you this evening."

"Mother," he said with a grin, "I shall be a true Anglophile. Even if they serve Brussels sprouts—which I warn you they will."

Sixteen gathered for dinner at eight-thirty. They assembled in a drawing room; then, promptly on the hour, led by the King and Queen, everyone entered the state dining room. King George and Queen Elizabeth were followed by Mrs. Roosevelt, who was followed by Lord and Lady Mountbatten, then Winant, the United States Ambassador, then the Prime Minister and Mrs. Churchill, followed by the Prime Minister of South Africa, Field Marshal Jan Christian Smuts, then Lieutenant Colonel Elliott Roosevelt, followed by Captain Jan Smuts, then Tommy Thompson, Countess Spencer, a lady-in-waiting, and the Master of the Household.

In the dining room, some of the art had obviously been removed, though several almost-life-size family portraits remained—King George III and Queen Charlotte, King George IV in Garter robes, and others. The meal was served on gold and in crystal, with excellent wines. It was, nevertheless, a simple wartime meal of three courses. The main course was venison, from a deer shot on one of the royal estates—served, as Elliott had predicted, with boiled Brussels sprouts.

Mrs. Roosevelt sat between the King and Prime Minister Churchill. Churchill seemed preoccupied. He glanced often at his watch, and twice he received messages brought to him by equerries. His preoccupation carried him to the point of rudeness, and she could not help but wonder what crisis was on the mind of this normally affable man. Shortly she found out.

"Your Majesty," he rumbled after he had received his second message. "Mrs. Roosevelt. I may now inform you—" He paused and looked at Mrs. Roosevelt. "—as I informed the President by wire dispatched only minutes ago— A major operation began this evening as we sat down for dinner. It may change the whole course of the war. At eight o'clock, London time, General Montgomery launched an offensive in Egypt. A thousand guns opened fire at that hour. Ten divisions are attacking. If we can break through the minefields, we may deliver Rommel a blow from which he will *never* recover."

"Near what town, Prime Minister?" the King asked.

"El Alamein," said Churchill.

After dinner, the gentlemen retired to a separate room for a few minutes with their port and cigars, then everyone assembled for the showing of Noel Coward's *In Which We Serve*, a film based in part on Lord Mountbatten's naval service. A bit after midnight Mrs. Roosevelt returned with Elliott to her suite, and they had time to sit down and talk.

"You understand, of course, the significance of the offensive at El Alamein," said Elliott when they were seated. He had poked a bit of life into the anemic fire, and she had begun to reflect on how long a day she had had.

"I believe I do," she said. "It is something we must not discuss."

"We can between ourselves," said Elliott. "Certainly not beyond this room. Every man in the army wonders—not to mention how very interesting the question must be to the German generals."

"Yes," said Mrs. Roosevelt, firmly confining herself to that one word.

"We will be going into North Africa," said Elliott. "It's the biggest secret of war right now."

"How do *you* know, Elliott?" she asked.

"The planes we fly," he said. "Our reconnaissance aircraft, the P-38s. If we were going to invade Norway, as one of the rumors has it, we couldn't use the P-38s; their superchargers would fail in arctic weather. They're going to give us trouble enough over the Sahara. I understand the ground troops are being issued cold-weather gear, as if they were going north. We're not. We're flying airplanes that are going *south.*"

"It is your duty to keep quiet," she said sternly.

"I have, except to you. The Commander-in-Chief knows. And *you* know. I know you do."

"Will you be in combat, Elliott?" she asked.

He nodded. "I expect to be."

"Then I will have four sons who will be in combat. You know, James could very justifiably have remained in Washington. Indeed, the Marines told him he would be more valuable at a desk than in combat." She shook her head. "He told Father he could not accept that."

"No. No, of course not. We all know what would be said."

She rose and stepped to the fire, trying in vain to enliven the smoldering coals with a poker. Magnificent though the room was, it was gloomy and alien now, dimly lighted, cold, with nothing but a thin stream of smoke rising from coals that generated little heat. In a moment of whimsy, she wondered if the shades of long-dead kings and queens, emperors and empresses hovered in this room. She wondered where the tragic Napoleon III and his beautiful Eugénie had slept. Perhaps in this suite—or had their visit been only to Windsor Castle? And who else? Queen Alexandra? Queen Victoria? Who? When the fires blazed bright in the fireplaces and a hundred candles burned, and women in gorgeous dresses and men in gold-braided uniforms—

"Mother."

"Elliott?"

"Not bad, is it, for a couple of Hudson Valley hicks?"

Mrs. Roosevelt, startled out of her reverie, smiled at her son. "Elliott," she said, "if your grandmother had heard that, she would have *thumped* you."

"I must go back to the base in the morning," he said. "But your tour does include us, doesn't it? I wouldn't be forgiven if you came and didn't visit my outfit."

"Of course— Excuse me. Is someone knocking?"

"Yes. Someone is. I'll go to the door."

Elliott left open the door between the sitting room and the waiting room, and when he opened the outer door she saw the visitor was Sir Alan Burton. Elliott didn't know him, and she rose to welcome him.

"At this hour, Sir Alan? Is there a reason?"

Sir Alan, still dressed in his afternoon tweeds, nodded somberly. "Forgive me, dear lady, for I have sinned," he said.

"What sin could you possibly have committed, Sir Alan?" she asked.

"Whilst in the White House," he said, "I was, as you may recall, slightly contemptuous that murder could have been committed when so eminent a guest as Winston was there. Now I am compelled to admit that tonight, whilst you are our guest in this house, there has been . . . a murder at the Palace."

2

"Unfortunately," said Sir Alan, "this murder renders it impossible for me to continue to act as your personal bodyguard during your visit."

"I quite understand," said Mrs. Roosevelt. "The investigation will require your complete attention."

"I am afraid," said Sir Alan sadly, "that is not the reason. You see, I am a suspect in the crime. Although . . ." He paused to chuckle. "Although the suspicion against me is not heavy, nonetheless, it would not be appropriate for a man under suspicion to be assigned to accompany and protect a distinguished visitor."

Mrs. Roosevelt glanced at Elliott. Sympathy and concern lined her forehead with a deep frown. "Sir Alan," she said. "If I may have any influence in the matter, I trust you completely and have no hesitation whatever about saying I want you to continue as my protector . . . and friend."

"The choice is not ours to make, dear lady," said Sir Alan. "Indeed, it may be a ministerial decision."

"Have the King and Queen been informed?"

"Well . . . of the murder, I suppose. Of nothing

else. His Majesty will be most distressed, I am sure. The victim of the crime, Sir Anthony Brooke-Hardinge, is one of His Majesty's equerries and has served faithfully for many years. The Brooke-Hardinges are one of the most distinguished old families in England. His death is a calamity.''

"And why are you suspected, Sir Alan?" asked Mrs. Roosevelt.

"I am not the only suspect," said Sir Alan. "There are others. It is supposed, however, that every one of us had reason to wish Sir Anthony ill. In spite of his family background and his secure place in His Majesty's regard, he had, I may say, a somewhat checkered career."

"How was he killed? And where?"

"Sir Anthony had a suite of rooms on the bedroom floor of the Palace. A sitting room, a small library, a small kitchen, a bedroom, a bath. All quite comfortable, though not terribly luxurious. There are two fireplaces in the suite. Sir Anthony was beaten to death with a poker from the fireplace in his library."

"When?" asked Mrs. Roosevelt.

"One would assume it was approximately the time when the state dinner was being served on the floor below. A group of us had been invited to a private cocktail party in Sir Anthony's suite, beginning at nine—which would have been after he had completed any duties he had with regard to the state dinner. We arrived, one by one, but Sir Anthony was not there. We waited for him, though, and eventually we—I, actually—discovered the body.''

"How long dead?" asked Mrs. Roosevelt.

"Mother," said Elliott. "Before you left Washington, did Father, or did Father not, exact from you a promise not to meddle in any murder mysteries you might encounter in England?''

"I shall not meddle," said she. "On the other hand, I am distressed to learn that Sir Alan is suspected." She sighed. "Is there any way I can help you, Sir Alan? Without meddling, that is.''

Sir Alan Burton spoke to Elliott, somewhat loftily. "Your dear lady mother has demonstrated a marked talent for logical analysis. I need hardly remind you that the beautiful Pamela Rush-Hodgeborne would have hanged for the murder of Philip Garber had not Mrs. Roosevelt so firmly believed in her innocence and so persistently pointed out the defects in what seemed to be a closed case."

Elliott laughed. "The President has called her 'the White House Sherlock Holmes.' ''

"Sir Alan," persisted Mrs. Roosevelt. "How can I help you? I was really so pleased to learn that you were to accompany me on my travels around England, and I am distressed to hear that you are not. Can I speak to anyone?''

"Well . . . Lord William Duncan is upstairs. He is my superior officer and the one who suggested I step aside. You understand, the investigation is continuing. People are still being interrogated. Indeed, the body has not been removed.''

"I should like to speak to this Lord William Duncan," she said.

"Mother—''

"Elliott, I am going to do this. You may wait for me or go on to bed, as you wish. Since your duties tomorrow require a rested officer, I suggest you get your sleep. I expect to return in a few minutes, but my 'meddling' may take a little longer.''

* * *

The corridors of Buckingham Palace, particularly now, when only dimly lit, seemed endless as Sir Alan led her from her suite to an elevator that carried them up to the bedroom floor. In the afternoon the Palace had struck her as a museum. But now, as they walked through corridors from which many beautiful things had been carried away to safety, it impressed her as a mausoleum. She tried to shrug off that feeling, but the vast cold emptiness of the place was disturbing.

She was still wearing the pale-green evening dress she had worn to the state dinner, adding to the incongruity of this expedition through the halls of the Palace in the middle of the night.

The suite that had been occupied by the late Sir Anthony Brooke-Hardinge was very unlike the rest of the Palace. It was warm—a strong fire burned in the fireplace. Lights burned brightly. Platters had been heaped with hors d'oeuvres, most of which had by now been eaten, leaving only tattered evidence of what had been there. The only concession to wartime that she could see was the heavy curtains drawn over the windows.

There seemed also to be no concession to the fact that a murder had been committed in the suite only a few hours ago, or to the fact that the body of Sir Anthony lay in an adjoining room. Detectives and suspects—and of course she did not yet know which was which—mingled in an almost festive mood, apparently enjoying the unexpected warmth, certainly enjoying the stock of wines and liquors displayed on a table.

"Mrs. Roosevelt!" exclaimed a short, ruddy-faced

man with bald head and thick white mustache. He strode across the room toward her. He wore a dark-blue suit with white handkerchief showing from the breast pocket, waistcoat, white shirt, a necktie she recognized as a regimental stripe. If her guess was not wrong, he was a retired officer—a colonel perhaps, maybe even a brigadier. "I am honored and pleased to see you," he said. "Yet I must confess I am astonished that Sir Alan would bring you up here."

"I insisted," said she.

"Ah, well then. Uh, in any event." He bowed. "I am Lord William Duncan, from the Home Office. I seem to find myself in charge of the investigation into the unhappy event of earlier this evening—of which I know Sir Alan has informed you."

"He has, of course. I am very sorry to learn that he is suspected."

"Oh, let us not exaggerate that, Mrs. Roosevelt," said Lord William. "Everyone who had motive and opportunity is a suspect, by definition. I am afraid Sir Alan does fall into that rather broad category, but I do not take very seriously the possibility that it was he who bludgeoned Sir Anthony. Uh . . . May I offer you a whisky? Sherry? Port?"

"A small sherry, please," she said.

"Uh . . . Martin," said Lord William, summoning an aide with a peremptory gesture. "A small sherry for Mrs. Roosevelt, please."

"I am afraid everyone in the room is staring at us," she said. "Perhaps you should introduce me."

"Yes, uh, well . . . yes. They are the suspects. We asked them all to remain whilst we did what we could to untangle their stories. To be altogether frank,

Mrs. Roosevelt, it is almost certain that one of the people you are about to meet is the person who murdered Sir Anthony Brooke-Hardinge. Uh . . . I could spare you that—''

"And the others . . . *didn't*," she said with a smile. "Please, Lord William."

Lord William turned to the group, who were in fact staring toward him, the First Lady, and Sir Alan Burton. "Uh, ladies and gentlemen," he said. "You all know that Mrs. Eleanor Roosevelt, the distinguished wife of the President of the United States, is a guest in Buckingham Palace. This is she. I will, uh, be pleased to introduce you. Uh, first, uh, perhaps Lady Letitia Brooke-Hardinge."

The woman who separated herself from the group and came across the room was handsome, about fifty years old, slender with sharp features, graying hair, an almost-empty glass of whisky in hand.

"I'm so very sorry," said Mrs. Roosevelt sympathetically. "You have my deepest sympathy."

"Don't waste your sympathy, please," said Lady Letitia. "I couldn't be happier. That's why I'm a suspect."

"Uh, Sir Anthony and Lady Letitia have been divorced for some years," explained Lord William.

"You cannot believe," said Lady Letitia, her voice thick with bitterness and whisky, "how glad I am the bastard is finally dead. And to have been beaten to death with a fireplace poker! Oh, I could almost accept hanging as a good price for knowing he died that way. I hope he suffered."

Mrs. Roosevelt glanced at Sir Alan, then said, "I believe I understand." In fact she didn't. It was beyond her to understand such hatred. She had never known anyone who deserved it, she thought. Anyway, she was incapable of it. It made this woman ugly. "It must be a difficult time, in any case."

"Yes," said Lady Letitia. "They may take me to gaol before the night is over."

"I think we won't do that," said Lord William scornfully. "Uh, Mrs. Roosevelt, let me present Mr. Jennings Duggs."

Duggs was a cherubic little old man, bow-legged, bald, with a cheerful countenance. His eyes swam behind the thick round lenses of his little gold-rimmed eyeglasses. "Mrs. Roosevelt!" he said with a warm smile. "The wife of the President of the United States! I am indeed honored."

"I am pleased to meet you, Mr. Duggs," she said. It was inconceivable that this elfin man could have killed Sir Anthony Brooke-Hardinge. "I am afraid you are having a distressing evening."

Duggs nodded. "Yes." He nodded. "They think I might have killed him."

"Sir Anthony was once Mr. Duggs's partner in business," said Lord William. "He took a great deal of money from him."

Duggs's eyebrows rose above the rims of his spectacles, and he turned down the corners of his mouth. "Tony was a liar, a cheat, and a thief," he said blandly. "If we tried to assemble all the people he cheated, we couldn't get them in Buckingham Palace, much less in this room. If he had been murdered on the streets, half the population of London would be suspects. I didn't kill him; but, try as I may, I can't find it in myself to be sorry he is dead. To regret his murder would be an exercise in Christian charity that I fear is beyond me. I should, of course, forgive him, but I am afraid he will have to seek his pardon from a higher source.''

"The houseboy killed him, plainly," said Lady Letitia. "God knows how Tony abused him."

"The houseboy is not here, oddly enough," said Lord William. "Chinese fellow. Metropolitan Police are looking for him."

"Is anything missing from the suite?" asked Mrs. Roosevelt. "I mean, stolen?"

"Apparently not," said Lord William. "We can't, of course, be sure. It may well be that Sir Anthony kept a large amount of money on hand."

"As an equerry he was not in residence in the Palace all the time, as I understand," said Mrs. Roosevelt.

"Oh, no," said Sir Alan. "He lived here only when he was actually on duty. He has a nice house in Belgravia and a country place in Kent."

Mrs. Roosevelt looked once more around the sitting room. It was cozy, furnished with rather heavy chairs and a sofa, upholstered with chintz in patterns of subdued colors. The polished parquet floor was partially covered by two beautiful Persian rugs. Two lighted glass-front cases, to either side of the fireplace, displayed a collection of glass and china pieces, some small sculptures, some pieces of brass. A painting of King William IV hung above the fireplace. The King faced a nude Diana on the opposite wall.

"Well," said Lord William. "There are two others to be introduced. Let me present Mr. David Desmond."

Desmond had been standing a pace back and now bowed and stepped forward to take Mrs. Roosevelt's hand. Here, she felt as his strong grip closed on her hand, was a man capable of beating another to death with a poker, at least if size and obvious vigor of manhood counted. He was six feet four, she estimated, and in every way powerful. Though his hair had receded, it was black and thick where it remained, and he sported a black mustache. He was wearing a tuxedo and black tie, with a red carnation in his buttonhole.

"Lord William will want to tell you why I am suspected of putting an end to our deceased friend Sir Tony," he said. He spoke with his tongue well forward in his mouth, his lips visibly forming his words, in a deep, smooth voice. "We were partners, he and I. Since Tony's death would cost the partnership a great deal of money, we insured his life for twenty thousand pounds. That is a not uncommon practice in partnerships, as I am sure you know. Because my partner is dead, I am entitled to collect twenty thousand pounds. That makes me a suspect."

"That plus the fact that you are here this evening, in Buckingham Palace, for the first time in your life," said Lord William. He turned to Mrs. Roosevelt. "Mr. Desmond is in the theater, a producer of plays and shows. Sir Anthony Brooke-Hardinge was an investor in some of Mr. Desmond's enterprises."

"I am afraid the relationship went a little further than that," said Desmond. "I said we were partners. Tony did not, perhaps, want that to be well known, in view of his family position and his status here at the Palace; but the fact is, he was a theatrical producer of some experience. He had a flair for it. He could see where a shilling was to be made."

"Not a disqualification for service as an equerry,"

commented Lord William, "but more than a bit unusual."

"He was a friend of the King when His Majesty was Duke of York. I suspect that was his chief qualification," said Desmond dryly.

Mrs. Roosevelt could not decide whether to like or dislike this man Desmond—or to withhold judgment until she knew him better, in accord with her lifelong habit. The trouble was, he was a man who seemed to invite judgment, to be liked or disliked, immediately. She suspected few people remained neutral about him.

"And you haven't met Laura," said Desmond. "Which is a shame. She is by far the most attractive of the suspects."

"Miss Laura Hodges," said Lord William. "That is she, there."

Laura Hodges was sitting on the couch that faced the fireplace, and alone of all the suspects she had not risen or approached Mrs. Roosevelt. She was a pretty young woman. Her face was flawless. Her mouth was narrow, but her lips were full, colored lightly with red lipstick. Her most striking feature was her eyes. They were deep blue; and, as Mrs. Roosevelt would discover, Laura fixed them on people with a solemn, penetrating gaze that could be quite disconcerting. Though she had heard Desmond mention her name, Laura Hodges did not come to be introduced to Mrs. Roosevelt. She glanced toward the group centered on Mrs. Roosevelt, rose from the couch, but instead of approaching them she went to the coal bucket and added another scoop to the already blazing fire.

"What was her relationship to the late Sir Anthony Brooke-Hardinge?" asked Mrs. Roosevelt quietly.

"She was a friend," said Lord William.

Though they had spoken quietly, Laura Hodges had overheard. She looked up and spoke to Mrs. Roosevelt. "I was his mistress," she said simply.

Mrs. Roosevelt walked over to the couch. "Forgive me for prying," she said with a sympathetic smile. "I am deeply concerned that my friend Sir Alan Burton should be a suspect, and I have asked a few questions."

Laura Hodges stood and extended her hand to Mrs. Roosevelt. Her straight, light-brown hair fell to the shoulders of her gray double-breasted jacket, which was exactly like a man's. She wore a blue-and-white striped shirt with necktie, also like a man's, and a slim, tailored gray skirt with a hemline that exposed her knees and exceptionally shapely legs.

"You are Mrs. Roosevelt," she said. "I am not surprised to find you here, asking questions about a murder. When Colleen Bingham was in London, playing in *Night Winds*, she told me how you helped her avoid being prosecuted for the murder of Benjamin Partridge."

"I didn't realize Colleen had become a stage actress," said Mrs. Roosevelt.

"I guess she isn't accepted as one in the States," said Laura, "but she has had very good notices and two long runs in the West End."

Laura Hodges was a small young woman, no more than five feet four, and it seemed highly unlikely to Mrs. Roosevelt that she could have bludgeoned a man to death with a fireplace poker.

"May I ask why *you* are a suspect? All the others,

except Sir Alan, had motive for killing Sir Anthony, but—''

"Sir Alan had his motive, too," said Laura. "Ask him. As for me . . . Well. Let us just say that Tony was capable of being abusive. That is well known. Also, I had the misfortune of being here when his body was found. It really is most likely that one of us, or Wen Yung, killed Tony.''

"Wen Yung?"

"His houseboy. He could have killed Tony before any of the rest of us got here.''

"I see," said Mrs. Roosevelt. She glanced at Sir Alan and Lord William, who were standing apart, letting her speak privately with Laura Hodges. Now they came nearer.

"Well, dear lady," said Sir Alan. "You see our problem. A wealth of suspects.''

"May I ask why you are included, Sir Alan? Everyone has confessed to a motive, and I understand you have one. I assume it's no secret.''

Sir Alan frowned at Lord William. "Well, I s'pose 't isn't," he said.

"Sir Alan risked his career many years ago," said Lord William. "And I suppose we could say—could we not, Sir Alan?—that he lost the gamble.''

"I am surprised to hear that he lost," said Mrs. Roosevelt. "I had supposed Sir Alan was highly respected at Scotland Yard.''

"He is," said Lord William. "He is indeed. But he might have become chief superintendent if not for—''

"If not for Sir Anthony Brooke-Hardinge," said Sir Alan peevishly.

"Sir Alan became convinced that Sir Anthony had abused a child," said Lord William.

"He *had,* damn it," growled Sir Alan. "Evidence was plain enough. The Walton Loo molester was Sir Anthony Brooke-Hardinge."

"It was plain enough to *you,* Sir Alan," said Lord William.

"Hah! Couldn't have been Sir Anthony, of course. A Brooke-Hardinge? No. Not a man of his background. I accused him. The charge was first hushed up, then dismissed. I was ridiculed."

"And every year," interjected Laura, "on October second, Tony sent Sir Alan a single pink rose."

"Why?" asked Mrs. Roosevelt.

"A crushed pink rose was evidence in the case," said Sir Alan. "October second was the date when the little girl was abused."

"And he sent you a pink rose every October second?" asked Mrs. Roosevelt.

"That was Tony's style," said Laura.

"Every year since nineteen thirty-four," said Sir Alan. "Well, I shan't get my rose on October second, nineteen forty-three, shall I?"

"That was Tony's style," Laura repeated. "That is why anyone in this room this evening might have killed him."

"I am curious," said Mrs. Roosevelt, "to know how it happened that five persons, all with strong motives to dislike, perhaps even to kill, Sir Anthony Brooke-Hardinge, should have been assembled in this apartment at one time."

"We all received invitations," said Sir Alan. He reached into his pocket. "Here is mine."

Mrs. Roosevelt took the typewritten invitation and read:

BUCKINGHAM PALACE

Wednesday, October 21, 1942

I should be grateful if you would do me the honor of being my guest, among a few other friends, for cocktails and a light supper, on the evening of Friday, October 23, 1942, from nine o'clock until late.

If you are unable to join me for the occasion, you need not respond. I shall understand that duties and obligations do sometimes interfere with social occasions.

I shall have arranged for your admission to the Palace through the Pimlico entrance. Simply show this invitation to the officer on duty.

Sir Anthony Brooke-Hardinge

"Is it customary for a signature to be omitted, for the name simply to be typed at the bottom like this?" asked Mrs. Roosevelt.

"It's not usual, I should think," said Sir Alan.

"Actually," said Laura, "he asked me to type them for him. And to speak to the duty officer about admitting his guests."

"Where did you type them?" asked Mrs. Roosevelt.

"Here," said Laura. "On his typewriter. It's in the library, where . . ."

"Where the body lies," said Lord William.

"Would I be meddling too much if I asked to see the scene of the crime?"

"Oh, Mrs. Roosevelt, I—"

"Mrs. Roosevelt has some little experience with matters of this nature," interjected Sir Alan. "She has seen the corpses of murder victims before, and I assure you she will not scream or faint." He spoke to Mrs. Roosevelt. "I must warn you, though, that this one is a bit messy."

"I don't mean to intermeddle," she said to Lord William, "but I have asked a great many questions already, and I do have an interest. After all, if Sir Alan remains a suspect, I may be deprived of the services of a good friend as my protector during the weeks I shall be in England."

"Irregular . . ." mused Lord William. "It is really most irregular." He sighed. "But I suppose one need not always stand on formality. You do understand, Mrs. Roosevelt, that we are not going to release to the public the fact that there has been a murder within the precincts of Buckingham Palace. Bad for morale, you know."

"I quite understand," said Mrs. Roosevelt. "We concealed the fact of two murders in the pantry of the White House last year."

"For the same reasons," said Sir Alan.

"Well then . . ." said Lord William. "I suppose we can go in the library."

As they walked across the room to the library door, Lady Letitia called after them. "I say, Lord William, are we to remain here all night? For my part, I should like either to go home or to be allowed to get some sleep on the bunk in a nice quiet gaol cell. If you are not going to send us to the nick, why can't you let us go?''

"In a few minutes, Lady Letitia," said Lord William smoothly. "In a few minutes."

One of Lord William's detectives—there were three in the sitting room—opened the solid oak door to the library. Looking back as she entered the library, Mrs. Roosevelt saw Lady Letitia and Desmond going to the bar for fresh drinks. Laura Hodges watched them resentfully.

The scene inside the library was ghastly, as Sir Alan had warned. The room was surrounded by glass-fronted bookshelves filled with leather-bound books. To the left as one entered was an open door into the bedroom. A small Regency desk with a little portable typewriter sat against the wall by the bedroom door. To the right there was a large black leather-upholstered couch facing another fireplace. The body of Sir Anthony Brooke-Hardinge was sprawled across the hearth.

He had died horribly; there was no question of that. The cause of death was also excruciatingly obvious—not just one or two blows to the head with the poker that lay nearby, but as many as a dozen blows. His blood had so widely stained his hair that it was difficult to tell what color it had been—black but graying. His scalp was split by a major wound at the top of his head and slightly to the rear; but he had taken other blows—to the forehead, to the face, and to the side of the head, where his right ear was all but torn off. His nose was smashed flat. One eye was ruptured. Both his wrists were marked with dark bruises, indicating that he had raised his arms to try to ward off the furious blows.

He was a man of fifty, maybe, though it was hard

to tell, with a bristly graying pencil mustache. He was slender, and one could picture a man of erect, perhaps military, bearing. His blood-soaked suit was a beautifully tailored blue wool, single-breasted, with the obligatory white handkerchief folded in the breast pocket. Gray ash was in evidence on his clothes—from the fireplace, of course. He had drawn up into the fetal position as he died and lay with his head close to the fire, which still smoldered.

"It is our supposition," said Lord William, "that the first blow was struck from behind. That weakened him for the struggle, then the killer beat him to death as he tried vainly to escape the deadly pummeling."

A team of forensic investigators was working quietly in the room, photographing, measuring, dusting for fingerprints, crawling about on the floor, looking under the furniture. All of them were men of gray years; presumably all the younger investigators were serving in the armed forces.

"Let us show you something," said Lord William, picking up from the little desk a white card printed with black ink. "Look."

The printing on the card said:

CALLED DOWNSTAIRS FOR A FEW MINUTES. BUZZER OUT OF ORDER. DOOR UNLOCKED. WALK IN.

"I was the first to arrive," said Sir Alan. "That card was attached to the door by a bit of tape. So I walked in. I sat down to wait, and shortly Lady Letitia arrived."

"There are no fingerprints on the card," said Lord William. "Or on the cellophane tape, which would certainly take fingerprints from anyone who touched it. That means someone wore gloves while taping the card to the door. What's significant is, of course, that Sir Anthony's fingerprints are not on the card or tape.''

"It would seem to me," said Mrs. Roosevelt, "that that circumstance absolves Sir Alan. Obviously Sir Anthony did not put the card on the door—"

"And the buzzer, in fact, does work," interrupted Lord William.

"Yes," she went on. "Sir Anthony would not have troubled to print the card and affix it to the door without leaving fingerprints, so obviously it was not put there by him. Who in fact but the murderer would take care to leave no fingerprints on the card and tape? If the card was on the door when Sir Alan arrived—"

"I could have put it there myself, actually," said Sir Alan.

"As could a number of others who arrived killed Sir Anthony, affixed the card, and left," said Mrs. Roosevelt. "Did the duty officer at the Pimlico entrance record the arrival of these people?"

"All but Miss Hodges," said Lord William. "Since she, in effect, lived with Sir Anthony, she had a key to a private entry, also on the Pimlico side of the Palace. While obviously Their Majesties were never told that Miss Hodges slept with Sir Anthony in his apartments in the Palace, a good many of the staff knew it. She was not an unfamiliar figure in some of the corridors and could come and go as she wished."

"As, for that matter, could I," said Sir Alan.

Mrs. Roosevelt smiled at Sir Alan Burton. "If you

persist in being so meticulously fair, you may well hang yourself," she said.

"We have the duty officer's record of arrivals," said Lord William. Another detective handed him the sheet. "Lady Letitia arrived at eight fifty-seven, David Desmond nine-oh-four, and Jennings Duggs at nine-oh-seven. Wen Yung, incidentally, left the Palace at six forty-eight."

"Which absolves him, does it not?" said Mrs. Roosevelt.

"I assume it does, unless he, too, had access to a private entry—and a key."

"The arrival times are not as significant as they may seem," said Sir Alan. "It is possible—only remotely possible, but nevertheless possible—that Sir Anthony was killed by one of us after we were assembled in his sitting room."

"How could that be?" asked Mrs. Roosevelt.

"P'raps," said Sir Alan, "we should step away from this grisly scene. Through that door is the bedroom. As you will see, you can enter the bathroom from the bedroom or from a door into a short hallway."

They walked into the bedroom. "Here," said Lord William, referring to a big sheet of paper lying on the bed, "is a chart one of our chaps has already made."

"We arrived one by one," said Sir Alan. "Eventually, all of us were assembled in the sitting room, curious as to where our beloved host might be. Since he had not appeared, we helped ourselves to the bottles on his bar and to the trays of hors d'oeuvres on the bar table. Miss Hodges put a record on his player and played some music. We expected him to come in at any minute."

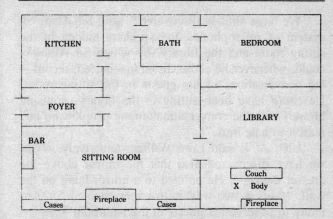

"Then how can you say that one of you could have killed him?" asked Mrs. Roosevelt. "Surely—"

"For a quarter of an hour, actually a little longer," said Sir Alan, "we sat here drinking and nibbling. Each of us, as I recall the period, left the room for a bit. One or two of us went to the bathroom. Duggs, as I recall, went to the kitchen for a glass of water with which to swallow a pill. Any one of us could have entered the library and bludgeoned Sir Anthony to death while the others sat here drinking, eating hors d'oeuvres, and listening to the rather modern swing music put on the player by Miss Hodges."

"Are you suggesting," asked Mrs. Roosevelt, "that Sir Anthony would have sat in the library, somehow amusing himself, while his guests assembled in the next room, wondering where he was?"

"Miss Hodges," said Lord William, "used the phrase 'that was Tony's style.' I am afraid it is entirely conceivable that Sir Anthony could have sat in the library, fully aware that his guests awaited him, and let them—"

"We have already discovered," said Sir Alan, "a system of microphones and speakers hidden in the sitting room and the library, by which Sir Anthony could, whenever he chose, listen to—indeed, record— the conversations of his guests in the sitting room. He *could* have been sitting in the library, amusing himself with the conversation among people who had reason to hate him."

"Uh . . . " said Lord William tentatively. "Uh, we have discovered also that the mirror above the dresser there—" He pointed to a mirror hung on the wall. "—is a two-way mirror that enabled Sir Anthony to observe his guests in the bathroom."

"Worse than that," said Sir Alan. "A locked drawer in his desk contained a number of photographs of female guests in his bathroom, in stages of undress, some of them performing the acts of nature."

"I am afraid some of us might almost be willing to accept the attitudes of some of the suspects here tonight," said Lord William. "I am afraid Sir Anthony was not the honorable gentleman His Majesty supposed."

"And assembled tonight in his apartment in Buckingham Palace," said Mrs. Roosevelt, "were the five people most likely to have wished his death."

"Is it unrealistic," asked Lord William, "to assume that one of those five killed him?"

"It is unrealistic, I believe," said Mrs. Roosevelt, "ever to believe than any specific human being killed another. Personally, I wait for the incontrovertible evidence."

3

"I have two alternatives," said Mrs. Roosevelt. "One is to return to my suite and rely on the unquestioned abilities of you gentlemen to discover who killed Sir Anthony. The other is to remain, stick my unofficial nose into your business, and see the matter through to a conclusion."

"Mrs. Roosevelt, my very dear and honored lady," said Lord William Duncan. With one finger he rubbed his big white mustache upward, fluffing the hair out. "You are welcome to remain with us and to participate in this inquiry in any way you may wish. I have some knowledge of your prowess as an unofficial investigator. My nephew, you may know, is smitten by the lovely Pamela Rush-Hodgeborne, who would today be serving a long sentence in an American prison, if she were not indeed dead by hanging, but for your devotion to her innocence. I should be happy to have your assistance in this inquiry—if your schedule of official duties permits it."

"It permits little, Lord William," she said. "I have a heavy schedule of appointments. I have nothing to do at the moment, however—but to go to bed."

Lord William Duncan smiled broadly, while conspicuously trying to subdue his smile. She could guess his thought: that the wife of the President of the United States, just come from a state banquet with the King and Queen and still dressed in her evening gown, proposed to remain at the scene of a brutal murder and offer her assistance to the expert and experienced investigators of Scotland Yard. The idea was so ludicrous that he had no idea how to respond, she supposed.

Yet, Sir Alan had told him she had a little experience in deciphering mysteries, bringing to the task a naive logic and an emotional sense of justice that often proved exactly right. She was modest about her abilities—as she had every reason to be—and still she had sometimes guessed right.

Yet it was odd. The hour was late, and she had sat down on Sir Anthony's undisturbed bed—where he would have slept tonight but for the circumstance that he lay beaten to death on the hearth in his library. She was tired, and it was difficult to care who had taken the life of this unattractive man—except that she could not bear the thought that the crime might be laid at the feet of Sir Alan Burton, or, for that matter, at those of the pretty young Laura Hodges.

What Elliott had suggested of his father was true. Franklin would say, *Don't meddle*. All right. She would *not* meddle. But she would remain here long enough to see at least another development or two in the inquiry into the death of Sir Anthony Brooke-Hardinge.

"All five of you arrived within not many minutes of each other," she said to Sir Alan. She remained sitting on the bed in Sir Anthony's bedroom. "So five suspects were in his sitting room, drinking from his bar, while either he lay dead in the library or for some reason waited there for his murderer to enter."

"Every one of us," said Sir Alan, "was absent from the room for a few minutes during the quarter hour or so before I entered the library and found the body. I don't remember the order, but I know I went into the bathroom during that fifteen minutes. As you will notice from the doors on the diagram, I could have entered the bedroom from the bathroom and the library from the bedroom and killed Sir Anthony with the poker."

"As could anyone who went to the bathroom," said Mrs. Roosevelt.

"Lady Letitia went, as I recall," said Sir Alan. "So did David Desmond. Jennings Duggs, as I definitely recall, went into the kitchen for a while, saying he needed a glass of water to take a pill. The diagram shows that one could easily slip across the hall from the kitchen to the bedroom, without being noticed from the sitting room—particularly from a group centered on the bar. Anyone who went to the kitchen or bathroom had opportunity."

"And Miss Hodges?" asked Lord William.

"I remember she went to the kitchen, or the toilet," said Sir Alan. "I really do believe every one of us had the opportunity to enter the library and kill Sir Anthony with the poker, while the rest of us enjoyed the party he called us to and never himself enjoyed."

"I find it curious," said Mrs. Roosevelt, "that someone could have killed Sir Anthony in that way without splattering himself or herself with blood. Sir Anthony's blood is on the floor, the walls, the sofa. . . . How could it not have splattered equally on the clothes of the person who committed the crime?''

"That *is* curious," said Lord William.

"What is more," said Mrs. Roosevelt, "the crime cannot have been committed quietly. Surely Sir Anthony screamed, or cried out, anyway. He cannot have died while the several of you were in the sitting room."

"That tends to limit the suspects to Miss Hodges and myself," said Sir Alan sepulchrally. "We alone could have been here before nine o'clock. The others passed the duty station, and their times of entry were recorded."

"Unless," said Mrs. Roosevelt, "the phonograph was being played so loudly that no one could hear a struggle in the adjoining room. I suppose that is hardly likely."

"I do not come to the same conclusion," said Lord William. "You may have noticed that the doors in these apartments are heavy and thick. If we close the door between us here in the bedroom and someone talking in the library, we will not hear anything. Buckingham Palace was not built by today's flimsy standards."

"And with the phonograph playing . . ." Mrs. Roosevelt mused.

"Sir Anthony would not necessarily have cried out very loudly," said Sir Alan. "Suppose the murderer crept up behind him with the poker, stunned him with one hard blow to the back of the head, and then beat him to death while he tried vainly to escape. He may not have screamed."

Mrs. Roosevelt walked to the window. Her impulse was to look out at what she supposed would be a view from the east front of Buckingham Palace, along The Mall toward Admiralty Arch; but she remembered the blackout and did not separate the curtains.

"It seems to me most unlikely that he was killed after the group assembled in the sitting room," she said. "Why would he invite five people to a cocktail party and then sit in the library alone after they arrived?"

"Oh, I can show you why," said Lord William. "I can show you, that is, if you don't mind returning to the library."

She nodded. "Not at all," she said.

Two men who had not been there before were now working in the library, kneeling on white cloths they had spread out around the body, which they were examining. It had not been moved before, but these two men handled it roughly, pulling at the clothing, emptying the pockets. Mrs. Roosevelt arrived in the room just in time to see one of them push a needle into the neck—apparently to extract a sample of blood. She turned her eyes away.

Lord William led her to the east wall, where she noticed for the first time the box for a small loudspeaker mounted beside the window. It was placed so that the curtain could easily be drawn back over it, concealing it from a casual visitor to the room. This was the eavesdropping system they had told her about.

"Listen," said Lord William. He touched a switch on the bottom of the loudspeaker box.

—". . . damned sick of sitting around here." This was the voice of Lady Letitia Brooke-Hardinge.

"If I drink one more glass of his whisky, I'm either going to be sick or go to sleep."

—"Patience, Letitia." This was the deep voice of David Desmond, speaking with that odd inflection that was characteristic of him.

—"I've never slept here. He never invited me to bed down with him in his Buck House digs."

—"Consider yourself lucky." The voice of Laura Hodges.

—"I don't know." The voice of Jennings Duggs. "It surely is nice and warm here."

Lord William flipped the switch, and the voices ceased.

"You see? He could sit here and listen to them talking. He invited five people who detested him, and he sat in here and listened to what they said about him. A possibility, anyway."

"He was capable of that, wasn't he?" said Mrs. Roosevelt. "Not a very nice man, was he?"

"He was not," agreed Lord William. "The blazing fires he kept, the warmth of this place, and the bright lights are all in complete violation of the rules His Majesty has made for the management of the Palace in wartime. It galls one to think of Sir Anthony sitting up here in cozy warmth, while Their Majesties shiver in the royal apartments to share in the national effort to save fuel."

"Another element," said Sir Alan, "of the Brooke-Hardinge 'style.' "

Mrs. Roosevelt glanced at the small wooden speaker box. "That thing," she said, "establishes the possibility that he sat in here after his guests arrived and eavesdropped on their talk. So it is quite possible that he was killed after they were assembled in the sitting room.''

"Suppose one of them came in here," said Lord William, "was infuriated by what he found, grabbed the poker, and—well, you can imagine."

"I will suggest to you, though," said Sir Alan, "that the killer must have surprised Sir Anthony. He was a strong man. If he saw the blow coming, he could have warded it off, I should think."

"Whoever killed him had to be a strong person," said Mrs. Roosevelt. "I mean, to beat a man to death with a fireplace poker would require a good deal of strength, I should think."

"Let us inquire of Dr. Hilliard about that," said Lord William. He turned to one of the men kneeling over the body. "A moment, Doctor?"

The short one of the two—a man with an unnaturally red complexion and bulging blue eyes—rose. "Lord William," he said.

"Allow me to present Dr. Henry Hilliard," said Lord William to Mrs. Roosevelt. "Doctor, this is Mrs. Eleanor Roosevelt, the wife of the President of the United States, who is a guest in the Palace. She is interested in this case and has a question."

Dr. Hilliard bowed to Mrs. Roosevelt. "Of course," he said.

"I should like to know, if you can tell, if the blows to the head of Sir Anthony Brooke-Hardinge were struck by a strong person."

Dr. Hilliard turned up the palms of his hands. He turned down the corners of his mouth. "One cannot be certain," he said. "I s'pose actually the blows were not terribly powerful. Come to think of it, uh . . .

Well, if, uh—My dear lady! It is not the sort of thing one would expect to describe to—''

"To a fifty-eight-year-old lady in the long dress she wore to a state dinner," said Mrs. Roosevelt. "Please, Doctor. I am not squeamish."

Dr. Hilliard glanced at Lord William and at Sir Alan. "Very well," he said. "On the basis of my initial examination, I would judge that Sir Anthony was first hit from behind. The deepest wound, the one that caused skull fracture and may well have weakened him beyond defending himself from further blows, was struck from behind and to the right. I would not, however, characterize it as a terribly strong blow. It was sufficient to do its destructive work, but a stronger blow might have rendered Sir Anthony unconscious, or indeed killed him instantly."

"Was the person taller or shorter than Sir Anthony? Can you tell?" she asked.

"One cannot tell," said Dr. Hilliard, "because almost certainly the blow was struck while he was seated. Otherwise the perpetrator must have been eight feet tall. The blow came down flat on the top of his head, to the rear and just to the right."

"He was certainly hit while seated," said Sir Alan. "Notice the ash. The poker had actually been used to poke the fire, and some ash had adhered to it. The shock of the blow shook much of the ash off. You notice it is on the right arm of his suit, and on the shoulder. But notice, too, that there is ash on the sofa, here at the right end of it. There is none elsewhere on the sofa. He was struck while he was seated here, perhaps with his arm up on the right arm of the sofa."

"By someone from whom he did not expect it,"

said Mrs. Roosevelt. "By someone who did not alarm him by picking up the poker."

"You know that because . . . ?"

"Because the poker was in front of him, in the rack by the side of the fireplace," she said. "It could not have been picked up without his noticing it. If he had anticipated an attack with it, he would have defended himself and would not have been struck while he was sitting."

"Precisely," said Lord William.

"I suppose there were no fingerprints on it?"

The question had been overheard by one of the detectives working in the room. "Wiped clean," he said.

"Of course," said Mrs. Roosevelt. "The killer would not have been wearing gloves. That, too, would have aroused suspicion."

"What you are describing does not suggest an angry confrontation," said Sir Alan, "but a casual conversation, during which the killer picked up the poker, actually stirred the fire—"

"Which would have allayed any suspicion Sir Anthony might have felt as to why the person picked up the poker," interrupted Mrs. Roosevelt.

"A calm, calculated murder," said Lord William Duncan.

Dr. Hilliard's assistant remained kneeling beside the body, his face down close to it, intently studying. He looked up. "This man was drinking at the time of death," he said. "Whisky, I should judge."

"Very much of it?" asked Mrs. Roosevelt. "Would you judge he was inebriated?"

"I couldn't say. The autopsy will tell us more about that."

"We—"

Someone knocked on the door between the library and the sitting room. When Lord William opened it, a uniformed officer of the Metropolitan Police was there, holding in custody a frightened-looking small man.

"Ah," said Sir Alan. "The Chinese houseboy, I imagine."

At Lord William's order, the policeman led the Chinese man into the library. He saw the body, threw his hands over his face, and trembled as though he were about to faint.

"Wen Yung," said Lord William sternly. "Tell us what you know about this."

The houseboy was wearing navy clothes, a dark-blue knit watch cap and a short, heavy wool jacket—over the white jacket and black trousers his job required. His shiny face was round and plump. He shook his head. "I know nothing of this," he said fearfully.

"When did you leave?"

"I leave about seven," he said. "New arrangements. Sir Anthony not require me to stay nights anymore. Go home nights now. Wife very happy."

"You used to stay overnight?"

Wen Yung nodded. "Always. For years."

Mrs. Roosevelt glanced around. "But . . . where did you sleep?" she asked.

The Chinese looked up into her face. He had no idea who she was, but the presence of a woman in evening clothes must have seemed ominous to him, for he shook his head again, this time in fright.

"I mean, there is but one bedroom here," she said.

"Sleep in kitchen," said Wen Yung. "Sometimes, cold night, sleep on warm hearth in sitting room."

"You had no bed?" she asked.

"Oh, no. Have blanket. Sleep on floor. Sir Anthony no permit sleep on sofas."

She glanced at Lord William. "Extraordinary," she said.

Lord William nodded. "There was a party here tonight, Wen Yung," he said. "Five guests. Wouldn't Sir Anthony usually have required you to stay here to serve?"

Wen Yung nodded. "No mention party," he said. "Strange."

"Did you prepare the food that was offered the guests? Trays of little sandwiches?"

Wen Yung shook his head. "No. No say make sandwiches for party. Very strange."

"Do you have a key to the private entrance to Buckingham Palace, Wen Yung?" asked Sir Alan. "Can you go in and out without passing the officers on duty?"

Wen Yung's eyes widened. "*Me?* Key to Buckingham Palace? Oh, no!" He smiled. "Wen Yung? Key to Buckingham Palace? You make funny joke, no, boss?"

"Yes," said Lord William dryly. "Very funny. I want you to look carefully around the apartments, Wen Yung, and tell me what's different. Is anything missing, or out of place? Will you do that?"

"Oh, one question before he begins looking," said Mrs. Roosevelt. "Who was here when you left?"

"Nobody," said the houseboy. He shook his head solemnly. "Place all quiet. Built up fires, so not go out before Sir Anthony return. Then go. Nobody here.''

"Was not Miss Hodges usually here?''

"No more. Only sometimes. New arrangements.''

"You mean,'' asked Lord William, ''that she used to live here with Sir Anthony but lately has been only an occasional visitor?''

Wen Yung nodded. "Not discreet to talk about,'' he said. "Sir Anthony very big on discreet.''

"Well, Sir Anthony is dead, and we are investigating his murder,'' said Lord William sharply. "Now, tell us—does Miss Hodges live here or does she not?''

"Depend on how you say,'' said Wen Yung. "Old time, she sleep here every night. New arrangement, she sleep here sometime. New young lady sleep here sometime.''

"What new young lady?''

The houseboy shrugged. "Sir Anthony not introduce guests to Wen Yung. New young lady very pretty, but not friendly. Miss Hodges very friendly, very kind. New young lady . . .'' He shrugged and shook his head.

"You don't know her name?''

He shook his head.

"Very well, Wen Yung. You go with the officer and look around the apartments. I want to know if everything is where it was when you left.''

As the Chinese walked away, Lord William nodded. "That explains something,'' he said. "Except for a few intimate items, Laura Hodges has no clothes here. In the drawer with Sir Anthony's handkerchiefs and gloves, a few undergarments, but nothing else.''

"Has anyone else mentioned the other woman?'' asked Mrs. Roosevelt.

"No," said Lord William. "An interesting development." He shrugged, showing a bit of weariness. "Well," he said. "It's a bit late, approaching two A.M. Perhaps you would like to go on to bed, Mrs. Roosevelt?"

"And spend the night tossing, mulling over the facts in this fascinating problem? No. Unless you should like to be relieved of my meddling, I should prefer to stay, Lord William."

"I am pleased to have you here," he said. "As for myself, I am going to have a glass of port. Will you allow me to pour you another sherry?"

"Perhaps one more," she said. "A small one."

In the sitting room, Lady Letitia no longer complained that she wanted to go to bed. She was asleep on the couch. David Desmond sat with his shoulders hunched, smoking cigarettes, while Laura Hodges paced the room. Jennings Duggs was in the kitchen making a pot of coffee.

"Ah! Ah!" shrieked Wen Yung. *"Gone!* Sir Anthony— There has been *thief!"*

"What is gone?" demanded Lord William. He put down his glass of port and turned to the excited man. "A thief, you say? What is gone?"

"Buddha!" cried Wen Yung. He pointed at the glass-fronted display case to the left of the fireplace. "Jade Buddha!"

Laura Hodges rushed to the case. "He's right!" she exclaimed. "It's missing. The jade Buddha!"

"All right," said Lord William as the others collected before the case. "Just what jade Buddha are we talking about?"

"Jade Buddha!" insisted Wen Yung.

"It is a carved figure," said Laura Hodges. "About, oh, eight inches high, maybe a little bigger, worth thousands of pounds, he always said. It sat . . . right there. Things have been moved in the cabinet, to hide the gap. But it sat right there."

"When did you see it last?" Lord William asked her.

"I . . . Well, I suppose I don't know, actually. It has always been there. It's one of those things you see so often in its usual place that you don't necessarily notice when it isn't. I don't remember when I last actually took notice of it."

"There today!" said Wen Yung. "Always see. Sir Anthony say him worth many pounds. Never touch. Never open glass. But—" The Chinese stopped and shook his head sadly. "Was very beautiful. No cheap jade. Very good. Very finest. Very old."

"I can add a bit of information about the jade Buddha," said Jennings Duggs quietly. "I remember when he bought it. He bought it from a fence, for a fraction of its value. It's a stolen piece, taken from a country estate in Warwickshire. He used to brag about owning it. Indeed, I suppose some of the other pieces in the case are stolen property. His other homes are full of the like. The administrators of his estate are going to have a fine time."

"I'm afraid it's true," said Laura sadly. "He did brag about that—about how he bought it cheap because it was stolen."

"Another element of his 'style'?" asked Sir Alan scornfully.

"Yes."

"Well," said Desmond, "I for one am willing to be searched."

"That won't be necessary," said Lord William irritably. "I believe, Mrs. Roosevelt and Sir Alan, we should return to the library."

"While we continue to wait, I suppose," said Desmond.

"Yes, if you don't mind. Feel free to drink some more of Sir Anthony's whisky."

"I believe I shall."

In the library, the two doctors had now covered the corpse of Sir Anthony Brooke-Hardinge with a white sheet. The contents of his pockets were laid out on his desk.

"Nothing unusual, I think," said one of the detectives.

Sir Alan frowned over the collection. "Fifteen pounds, uh, eight shillings, ten pence. Pack of Players cigarettes. Pocket cigarette lighter. Pen. Pencil. Note pad. Keys to a motor car. So."

"We should, perhaps, read the writing in the note pad," said Lord William.

"Indeed," said Sir Alan. He opened the little spiral-bound book. "We shall want to know whose telephone numbers these are."

"Other than that . . ." mused Lord William.

"That's curious there," suggested Mrs. Roosevelt, pointing to the sheet Sir Alan had just turned over.

It read:

THE DEADLY NIGHTSHADE
HATE
BEYOND FURY
UNFORGIVABLE
Damn!

"I wonder who he had in mind," said Sir Alan wryly.

"These are all the keys he was carrying, I suppose," said Mrs. Roosevelt, looking at the car keys. "Can anyone check the pockets of his overcoat? It must be hanging in the foyer. I would like to know if he was not carrying other keys."

Lord William nodded to one of the detectives. "Harrison, if you please."

"Yes," said Harrison, a white-haired man who was probably the oldest person in the apartments. "Before I do that, sir, I would like to point out the collection on the floor there. It is the contents of Sir Anthony's dustbin."

"Yes, thank you, Harrison. You think there's something interesting there?"

"I do, sir. There was another invitation to tonight's party—returned by the post office. Fingerprints have already been lifted from everything, so you can handle the papers."

Sir Alan knelt beside the collection of paper. Wadded papers had been unfolded, and the detectives had made a complete inventory.

"Ah, here," said Sir Alan. He picked up an envelope. "Addressed to Lionel Foster on South Audley Street in Mayfair. And returned stamped 'Addressee Deceased.' "

"Who do you suppose Lionel Foster was?" asked Lord William.

"Is that not an address book lying there?" asked Mrs. Roosevelt.

"So it is," said Lord William. "Let's see . . . Yes. Lionel Foster, South Audley Street. But no note as to who he was."

"Mr. Duggs might know," she suggested. "Or Mr. Desmond."

"Desmond is at the whisky again," said Sir Alan. "Let's ask Duggs." He opened the door to the sitting room. "Mr. Duggs," he said. "Would you mind stepping in here, please?"

Jennings Duggs came in, his eyes shifting nervously around the room, his lower lip held between his teeth. When his eyes fell on the covered corpse, his back stiffened.

"Mr. Duggs," said Lord William. "A question for you. Does the name Lionel Foster mean anything to you?"

Duggs nodded. "Indeed yes," he said in his soft little voice. "Yet another man who had reason to hate Tony."

"Why?"

"He went to prison because of Tony," said Duggs, still nodding. "For fraud. He was convicted of selling stock in a company that purportedly owned some valuable land in North Riding, when in fact it did not own it. The man behind the scheme was Sir Anthony Brooke-Hardinge, but his name was on nothing, and he had carefully avoided any open association with the company. When the scheme fell apart, it was Foster who was accused of crime. Tony's solicitors went to him and told him Tony was in a position to get him lenient treatment if he did not mention Tony's name—or far more severe treatment if he did. Foster testified that he was alone in the fraud and went to prison for it. Of course, Tony made no effort whatever to secure him leniency. Lionel Foster spent four years in prison and emerged a bitter man. He never ceased to hate Tony—which amused Tony immensely; he often bragged about it.''

"Foster is dead, though, is he not?" asked Lord William.

"Oh, yes. For some six or eight months, I should imagine.''

"Thank you, Mr. Duggs. Is your coffee ready?''

"Yes. Very good, too.''

"Save a cup or two for us, will you? Or make another pot?''

"Why, I should be happy to, Lord William. Do you like it strong, Mrs. Roosevelt?''

"I shall like it the way you make it, Mr. Duggs,'' she said.

When Jennings Duggs had left the room and the door was closed after him, Sir Alan smiled at Mrs. Roosevelt and said, "You can't imagine it was he, can you?''

"It would be like learning that Santa Claus had killed a man,'' she said.

"Haw! Yes! Quite good,'' laughed Lord William. Once more he used a finger to brush his mustache upward.

"Sir,'' said the detective Harrison. "There were no additional keys in the pockets of Sir Anthony's overcoat.''

"Thank you,'' said Mrs. Roosevelt.

"A bit more information, sir, if I may,'' said Harrison. "I am told now that the fingerprints on the liquor bottles in the sitting room are quite a jumble; everyone's been touching them. Except for one. The vodka bottle. It is absolutely clean of fingerprints. Wiped clean.''

"A suggestive fact,'' said Sir Alan. He ran his hand

across his yellow-gray hair. "I confess I cannot imagine what it suggests, but it is most irregular, is it not, for one liquor bottle to have been wiped clean. Most unusual."

"We are confronted with a substantial body of suggestive facts," said Mrs. Roosevelt. "Quite enough to solve the mystery, I imagine, if only we could explain them."

"It is quite a jumble," said Lord William, "and I see no way of putting them together. Do you, Sir Alan?"

"Not at the moment," said Sir Alan, his face sagging with fatigue.

"It sometimes helps," said Mrs. Roosevelt, "to sit down and review the facts, to look at them in a quiet, logical way. While I sip this excellent sherry and wait for a cup of Mr. Duggs's coffee, can we—?"

"Of course," said Lord William. "Perhaps in the bedroom, where we may have our privacy."

They sat down: Mrs. Roosevelt in the one armchair, Sir Alan on the dressing-table bench, Lord William on the bed.

"Now," said Mrs. Roosevelt. She paused for a small sip of her sherry. "Stop me if any of the following is not an established fact. First, Sir Anthony Brooke-Hardinge was a man with a substantial number of personal enemies. He led—dare I say it?—three lives. His public life was one of such probity that he earned the friendship of His Majesty King George and was appointed an equerry."

"Let us not suppose," said Lord William, "that complete probity is required to earn the friendship of members of the royal family. Such was imagined about Victoria . . . but there was Brown. I doubt that

His Majesty is so naive as to be wholly ignorant of
some of Sir Anthony's ventures into the kinds of
businesses that are not commonly engaged in by
members of the royal household.''

Mrs. Roosevelt nodded. ''In any event, he led also
a second life, that of an 'angel'; as we in the States
call one who invests in plays and shows. What is
more, in that life and in other business ventures he
engaged in what we might call sharp dealing.''

''He was a liar, a cheat, and a thief,'' said Sir
Alan.

''I have no doubt of it, Sir Alan. But because he
was well connected, there seems to have been some
hazard in trying to expose him. That hazard may
survive him.''

''I have been, as they say, once burned,'' admitted
Sir Alan gravely.

''And in still a third life,'' she continued, ''he
purchased stolen objets d'art from thieves, molested
at least one little girl, and abused his wife and mistress. I assume King George hadn't the slightest suspicion of any of that.''

''You assume correctly,'' said Lord William.

''Yes. Now, on Wednesday, Sir Anthony had Miss
Hodges send out invitations to—to how many? Let us
make a point of asking. Probably to more than the
five suspects who are here, plus the one who is
deceased. It is the kind of invitation many people
would ignore. At any rate, he invited people who had
some reason to dislike him intensely, so intensely
perhaps as to murder him.''

''And one of them did,'' said Lord William.

''Well, not necessarily, of course,'' said Mrs. Roosevelt. ''It *could* have been Wen Yung, and it could

have been, as the saying is, 'person or persons unknown.' "

"And, except for a vague reference to her being 'abused,' we know no reason why Miss Hodges should have wanted him dead," said Sir Alan.

"Except, of course, the fact that there was apparently another woman—'new arrangements,' as Wen Yung put it," said Lord William.

"Correct."

"They arrived one by one," Mrs. Roosevelt continued. "They found a note on the door saying that Sir Anthony had been called away for a few minutes and that they should enter. They did. They helped themselves to drinks and food—as well they might, considering their relationship with their host—and waited. Miss Hodges, being a young woman and perhaps bored, put music on the phonograph, at a rather loud volume, as is the custom among young people. One by one, each of them left the sitting room and was gone for long enough to have bludgeoned Sir Anthony to death, unless he was lying dead in the library already."

"Yes, but he had not been dead long," said Sir Alan. "I have seen many dead bodies in the course of my career. He had not been dead an hour, I should think."

"All right," said Mrs. Roosevelt. "Four people who hated him. Maybe five, maybe six, all of whom had motive and opportunity. All of this would be very neat, but for the fact that a valuable piece of jade is missing. Its theft constitutes, I suppose, another motive: robbery. But the remaining facts of Sir Anthony's death—that he was sitting on his couch, that someone picked up the poker as he watched"

—she paused and shook her head—"are inconsistent with robbery."

"By a stranger," added Sir Alan. "Not inconsistent with robbery by someone he knew."

"Then *someone not still here*," said Lord William. "None of them has the Buddha on his person. None of them has left the apartments—since they would have had to go out through the foyer, past the others."

"The fact," said Mrs. Roosevelt, "that no one still here has blood on his or her clothes corroborates that."

"Why did someone wipe the vodka bottle?" asked Sir Alan.

"And I believe someone said—did someone not?—" said Mrs. Roosevelt, "that the door buzzer was not in fact out of order, despite the note saying it was. What is more significant, the note and the tape used to affix it to the door bear no fingerprints."

"It does not look like robbery," said Sir Alan.

"We can be certain of one thing," said Mrs. Roosevelt. "The jade Buddha was not taken from the case after the guests arrived. The table bearing the liquor bottles stands in the same end of the room as the cabinet where the jade was kept. None of these people would have overlooked the lifting of a jade Buddha. None of them turned their eyes from those bottles for very long."

Sir Alan, who was only with difficulty subduing his deep concern about being a suspect in this murder, laughed weakly. He knew what Mrs. Roosevelt had not yet fully realized: that it was essential to his career in Scotland Yard for this murder to be resolved by clear evidence that laid the crime at someone else's door. It was not enough for him not to be charged; he must be completely exonerated.

"I would like to see the new young lady," said Lord William. "I mean the one who replaces Miss Hodges. I must say—please forgive me, Mrs. Roosevelt —that the young lady who replaces *her* must be a person of extraordinary qualities."

"Considering what has been established as the character of Sir Anthony," said Mrs. Roosevelt archly, "I would not be surprised to learn that the new young lady is a fan dancer from a country carnival."

Lord William Duncan ran his hand over his bald head and again pinched his white mustache. "Ah, Mrs. Roosevelt!" he exclaimed. "You are a witty woman!"

She glanced at Sir Alan, who she was not sure would similarly appraise her essay at mild wit. He seemed not to. He sat with pinched lips, his thoughts apparently elsewhere.

"We've got all night to conclude this matter, I suppose," she said. "In some way, a problem like this stimulates me and denies me sleep. The same may not be true of others. Shall we regard the night over, or have we more work to do?"

"Well . . ." ventured Lord William hesitantly. "At such an hour, we— Actually, we have not completed interviews with each of the suspects here present. Preliminary, we did, but—"

"As I recall," said Sir Alan, "Harrison there is a shorthand-writer. Aren't you, Harrison? Can't you take a record?"

The elderly detective nodded. "I can take shorthand notes," he said. "I have found it most useful in many investigations, and I—"

"We should be pleased if you would accommodate us in that respect, Harrison," said Lord William. "Have you paper?"

"I have, sir."

"Very well, then. Let us ask our questions, and each suspect may then be released. I suggest we talk to them in the chronological order of their involvement in the life of Sir Anthony Brooke-Hardinge. I believe that makes Mr. Duggs first. May we hope his second pot of coffee is ready?"

4

It would have been convenient to have conducted the examination of suspects in the library, and by now the corpse of Sir Anthony Brooke-Hardinge could have been removed; but the blood on the sofa foreclosed sitting there, and there were not enough additional chairs for the purpose.

"I like the idea of questioning the suspects in the presence of the wrapped corpse of the victim, in view of his blood," said Lord William. "But . . ." He shrugged. "The kitchen. Let us use the kitchen. Harrison can take his shorthand notes on the table there, and we shall be near the coffeepot. Agreed?"

"Agreed," said Mrs. Roosevelt.

They passed through the bath and the narrow corridor into the kitchen.

The room obviously had never been intended for cooking. To the contrary, it had been meant as a pantry from which servants could carry food that had been brought from the Palace kitchens below. Someone in the history of the apartments had insisted, apparently, that it be made possible to prepare at least a few minor meals in the rooms here, rather

67

than having them carried so far that the food was cold on arrival. The result was a hybrid room. A sink had been installed on the wall toward the bathroom—the only room with water and drainage—with pipes going through crude holes in the floor. A two-burner hot plate fueled by a cylinder of gas connected by a hose stood on a table. Duggs's second pot of coffee was perking. There was no refrigerator. An oaken chest on the north wall proved to be an ice chest. An occasional drip from the melting ice pinged musically into the pan below.

The room had an air of upstairs-downstairs, and it was emphatically downstairs. Though the walls were paneled and the wooden floor carpeted, the furniture was solid and utilitarian, nothing like the elegant furnishings of the other rooms. It brought to Mrs. Roosevelt's mind the inelegant old-fashioned kitchens on the ground floor of the White House.

The centerpiece of the room was a large table, with four chairs around it. Detective Harrison brought over another chair from the bathroom and sat down on it at a side table where he could make his shorthand record of the inquiry. Mrs. Roosevelt, Lord William Duncan, and Sir Alan Burton sat around the big table, leaving a chair for the suspect.

Sir Alan called in Duggs, and the inquiry began.

"How long have you known Sir Anthony Brooke-Hardinge?" asked Lord William.

"Since nineteen twenty-three," said Duggs.

"In what connection did you meet him?"

"I was engaged in the business of insurance brokerage," said Duggs. "I sold *Mr.* Anthony Brooke-Hardinge, as he then was, a policy of insurance on a motor car he was then driving. We became acquainted, and subsequently he suggested to me that he could send good clients my way if I would be willing to pay him a fee for each policy of insurance they purchased. It had to be understood, he insisted, that his participation must be strictly confidential. It would not do for a man in his position to gain a reputation for making money by sending his friends to a particular insurance broker.''

''And the arrangement worked to your mutual advantage, I believe,'' said Lord William.

''Oh, yes. He sent me good business.''

''Excuse me,'' said Mrs. Roosevelt. ''Could you possibly fill me in with some basic information about Sir Anthony?''

''Please do that, Duggs,'' said Lord William.

''Well, uh . . . He is—was—about fifty years old, I should think. His grandfather was Earl Hardinge of Brooke. Tony's father did not inherit the title; he was a younger son; so of course Tony had no expectancy of becoming Earl Hardinge. He—''

''I believe he served honorably in the First War,'' said Lord William. ''Was he not decorated?''

''Indeed. It was his sort of thing: the opportunity to do something spectacular and earn recognition,'' said Duggs, a note of bitterness sharpening his soft voice. ''But when the war was over, he was under the obligation to earn money. His sense of social position was a great impediment to him. He wanted to be rich, but he would not have it said of him that he was in trade.''

''He could not have been presented at Court if he had been in any form of trade,'' said Sir Alan to

Mrs. Roosevelt. "The late King George the Fifth was strict about that."

"I have interrupted your narrative, Mr. Duggs," said she. "Please do go on. You were paying Mr. Anthony Brooke-Hardinge a commission on insurance premiums—as we would put it in the States."

"Illegally, very shortly," said Duggs. "At least unethically. Tony used his family position and his war record and army friendships to obtain appointments to the boards of directors of corporations. All of those corporations—all but one, actually—brought their insurance business to my brokerage. Being appointed to a board of directors, Tony would take an early opportunity to say, 'I believe we are paying too much for our insurance. Shouldn't we take bids?' Then he would propose to me that I forgo my brokerage commissions on half a year's insurance in order to bid low. In some cases I actually bid below cost and made up the difference out of my own pocket. Tony called it an investment. Of course, as soon as we had the business, we raised our premiums back to the normal rate."

"Your business grew immensely," said Sir Alan.

"It did, of course. He had his methods. I suspect he was making unethical payments to some other people. Anyway, he brought in a large volume of business, I made a great deal of money, and paid much of it to Tony."

"How long did this go on?" asked Lord William.

"Through the nineteen twenties," said Duggs. "It was in nineteen thirty-one that he suggested he should become a partner in my brokerage. He was generating more than half the business and taking less than half the profits, he said. Which was true. I must admit that I had come to rely heavily on the business he obtained for me. I wasn't as aggressive as I should have been—I mean, about developing my own clientele, independently of Tony. So, when he implied he would take his clientele away, I agreed to make him a full partner.''

''Now he owned half your agency,'' said Sir Alan.

''Soon he owned it all,'' said Duggs. ''He employed a firm of very sharp solicitors, and they drafted a contract that provided—in effect, the matter was rather more complex than what I am about to say— that ownership of the brokerage would be proportional to the amount of income attributable to each partner. I didn't like the contract of partnership; but, still, I knew he could take his clients away from me and leave me with a very modest business indeed; so I accepted, keeping my reservations to myself.''

''A fatal error,'' said Lord William.

''No,'' said Duggs. ''My fatal error was that I trusted him. 'Surely,' I said to myself, 'dear Tony will always be fair. He is, after all, a sterling chap, from the best of families, and a war hero.' I trusted him. That was my foolish, fatal error.''

''Then what happened?'' asked Mrs. Roosevelt.

Duggs sighed. ''He proposed that we could increase the income of the brokerage very substantially by abandoning certain lines of business and concentrating on others. We ceased to handle insurance on motor cars, for example. And life insurance. Those were, of course, the lines of business attributable to me. We insured only business and industrial property. We concentrated on it. He was right about the income—it doubled. He employed slick young salesmen with public-school education to sell for us. My

administrative duties in the office became so heavy
that I had nothing to do with obtaining new business."

"And there came an accounting," said Sir Alan
gloomily.

"In nineteen thirty-seven," said Duggs. "He pointed
out that I was generating no business; he was generating all, personally and through his sales staff; and
that under the agreement my partnership interest had
diminished to nothing. I was no longer entitled to a
share of the profits. I . . . I nearly wept. It was
unbelievable! But he said he meant to be generous;
he would put me on a salary, which he did—the salary
of a chief clerk. In April 1939, he told me I was not
really earning my keep, that I was too old and slow
in my methods, and he discharged me."

Mrs. Roosevelt sighed. "What a disgusting man!
When, incidentally—and *why*—was he knighted?"

"Contributions to the Tory party, I believe," said
Duggs. "You might direct the question to Mr. Stanley Baldwin." He shrugged. "The grandson of an
earl, decorated hero of the last war, a personal friend
of the King . . . A man who concealed his peccadil-
loes most successfully. A man who generally suc-
ceeded in concealing his involvement in commerce.
His name was not on our brokerage, and he rarely
appeared at the offices."

"So," said Lord William, "you received an invitation to a supper at the Palace. Why did you come?"

"I had never been inside Buckingham Palace, and
I'll probably never have another invitation," said
Duggs simply.

"You arrived at nine-oh-seven, according to the
officer on duty at the Pimlico entry. So you were the
last guest to arrive, were you not?"

"As it turned out," said Duggs. "We expected more guests."

"Describe the scene when you arrived," said Lord William.

"The others were sitting before the fire, with drinks. Someone—Desmond, I believe it was—suggested I pour myself one, which I did. The fire was burning quite brightly, and it was very warm in the room. Uh . . . they were playing music. Everyone was mystified as to why Tony was not here and as to why he had invited us."

"Did you know the others?"

"No. I had never met any of them before. I didn't even know them by name, except Lady Letitia. I knew who she was."

"How long after you arrived was the body discovered?"

"I am not certain, exactly, but a quarter of an hour at least, and possibly a bit longer than that."

"Did you, during that time, leave the sitting room?"

"Yes. I went to the bathroom."

"From where you could have passed through the bedroom and into the library and struck Sir Anthony on the head with the poker."

Duggs nodded. "I could have done," he said simply.

Lord William glanced at Mrs. Roosevelt and at Sir Alan: a glance suggesting they might want to ask a question.

"How do you earn your living now, Mr. Duggs?" asked Mrs. Roosevelt.

"If you should have occasion to take breakfast or lunch in the Park Lane Hotel, I may have the privilege of serving you," he said. "I have been a waiter there since April of nineteen thirty-nine."

Lady Letitia Brooke-Hardinge yawned and lit a cigarette as she settled herself on the chair at the kitchen table. She had wakened reluctantly, her eyes were narrow and bleary, and she reached out gratefully for the cup of coffee Mrs. Roosevelt had poured for her.

"How long were you married to Sir Anthony?" asked Lord William.

"Seventeen years," she said. "Seventeen wretched years."

"No children?"

"He was impotent," she said.

"You mean he couldn't perform the marital act?"

"Oh, perform it, yes!" she scoffed. "With all the finesse of a buck rabbit. And as often. But to no procreational purpose. With no generative result."

"Did he know he was impotent?" asked Sir Alan.

"He knew it. It was the result of a wound he suffered on the Somme. But he didn't tell me before we married. That was his first big lie."

Sir Alan allowed himself a faint smile. "What was his second?" he asked.

"He allowed me to believe that he was well off, that he would inherit a substantial estate, either from his grandfather the Earl or from his father. In fact, he was almost penniless. He expected to live off *my* money, and in style. Which he did, while it lasted."

"And then . . .?"

"And then he borrowed, cadged, left his bills unpaid. I was constantly humiliated by tradesmen at the door, pleading for their money. Tailor. Shoe-maker. Wine seller. Greengrocer.''

"Are you saying," asked Mrs. Roosevelt, "that he spent all your money?"

She looked around for somewhere to flick the ash from the end of her cigarette and, seeing no ashtray, flicked it on the floor. "I had a modest inheritance," she said. She spoke to Lord William. "I was Letitia Wyndham. You knew my father."

"Oh God, yes," gasped Lord William. He turned to Mrs. Roosevelt. "Her father died at Gallipoli. A genuine hero in every way."

"Marrying a decorated veteran, I supposed he might be something like my father," she said caustically. "Instead, I got an impoverished impotent spendthrift, a liar, a cheat, and a thief."

"Speaking of lying and cheating—"

"And he was proud of it," she said. "Constantly. There's poor Duggs out there. Tony bragged for years about how dull Duggs was and how easy it was to take control of his business. He did the same thing to others. And he bragged about every venture where he cheated someone and stole their property."

"He became wealthy over the years," said Lord William.

"Oh, yes," she said. She drank coffee and puffed on her cigarette. "He used to say he was better off than Earl Hardinge, that he could buy and sell the Earl, and would one day buy a peerage of his own."

"After he made his fortune, you lived rather well, did you not?" asked Sir Alan.

"Rather well," she said. "He bought the house in Belgravia and the country house in Kent and made a point of living in more style than Earl Hardinge of Brooke.''

"You were divorced," said Sir Alan. "Tell us about that.''

Lady Letitia stiffened and sighed. "Very well. Our marriage was anything but successful. When he had spent my money, he thought himself entitled to scorn me, as though I had married him for *his* money and position. Because of his impotence—at least, I suppose that was the reason—he became more and more demanding about the physical side of things. I mean, he wanted bizarre things. He invented roles for me to play, invariably involving . . . Well, I suppose it is not necessary to describe what he demanded.''

"If you are charged with his murder, your jury will have to hear all of it," said Sir Alan.

"My roles, Sir Alan," she said indignantly, "involved demeaning costumes, often nudity, and sometimes chains. Is that a sufficient description?''

"Quite sufficient, Lady Letitia," said Sir Alan blandly. "But you accepted that sort of thing for a long time, did you not?''

She ground out her cigarette in her coffee cup. "I did. For a long time.''

"And then?''

"I didn't divorce Tony, Sir Alan. He divorced me.''

"On what ground?''

"Adultery.''

"I'm afraid we will have to hear some details of that," said Lord William.

She shrugged. "I became involved with another man. Lloyd Pelham, the second son of Sir Douglas Pelham, the barrister. I loved Lloyd, and he loved me. But he was, of course, married to Dorothy, and they had three children. It was quite impossible for us to think of his divorcing. Unhappily, I became pregnant. I would have loved to bear the child, but in the circumstances I had no alternative but to have the pregnancy terminated."

"An abortion," said Sir Alan. "A circumstance not likely to win you much sympathy from the divorce court."

She sighed heavily. "Yes, and it was brought before the court. Indeed, the physician who performed it was prosecuted and lost his license to practice medicine. Lloyd's name was brought before the court, and Dorothy was terribly humiliated. What I had never dreamed was that Tony had employed private investigators—despicable professional snoops —to follow me constantly. They had photographs. I was dragged through mud and slime, left without a shred of dignity."

"Except that the matter was kept out of the newspapers," said Sir Alan.

"Tony arranged that, too. The trial, before Mr. Justice Birkett, was closed to the public and the press. It would hardly have done for the wife of Sir Anthony Brooke-Hardinge to be revealed as an adulteress and a woman who had had an abortion, would it? Would he have become an equerry if my indiscretions had been splashed across the front pages of the penny press?"

"And he arranged, similarly, for you to have no money," said Lord William.

"Thank you, Lord William," she said. "For reminding me. I was set on the street without a penny, without even all of my clothes and jewelry."

"And you have—"

She glanced into the eyes of Mrs. Roosevelt, then of Lord William. "I sold my jewelry. Even some gowns—I had no need for them anymore. I moved into a tiny flat in Camden Town. I faced—I faced poverty."

"And did you evade it?" Sir Alan asked in a tone that suggested he knew the answer.

"I suppose so. Yes. I did. In time."

"Will you tell us how?"

"Why not? You know, Sir Alan. Don't you, Lord William? I live reasonably well now. I am . . ." She hesitated, drew a breath. "I am known in the magistrates' courts as one of London's most successful . . . procuresses. I am, Mrs. Roosevelt, as Lord William and Sir Alan well know, a prosperous madam. I never have fewer than five beautiful girls available for gentleman callers. Would you like the names of high-ranking American military and diplomatic officers who avail themselves frequently of my services?"

"I believe I would rather not know," said Mrs. Roosevelt.

"I promise you would recognize the names," said Lady Letitia.

"Are you suggesting that my son—"

"No," interrupted Lady Letitia firmly. "Not once."

Mrs. Roosevelt nodded. "Then may we drop the subject?"

"Of course," said Lady Letitia. "It shocks you, doesn't it? Well, understand that it shocks me. I have, Mrs. Roosevelt, in the past five years four times found myself in what in London we call the nick—in what you in the States call the common gaol. Imagine, if you will, what thoughts pass through a woman's head, what feelings constrict her heart, as she lies on a hard cot in a stinking tiny cell—she, the daughter of an honored gentleman, ex-wife of a man who *plays* at being an honored gentleman, well aware that she is there because she is in fact a common criminal.''

"So you hated Sir Anthony," said Lord William.

"That someone bludgeoned him to death is the best news I have heard in five years," she said.

"You had motive to kill him," said Lord William. "You had opportunity, too, did you not?"

"Yes. I did. If you are willing to believe I left the sitting room for five minutes, having no way to know he was in the library, dead or alive, and went in there and found him alive and beat him to death with a fireplace poker. If you are willing to believe that, charge me. Unlike the others, I have been in the nick before, and don't dread it. I don't think you can make out the charge, though. A Bailey jury will acquit me. And the trial will demolish, once and forever, the false reputation of *Sir* Anthony Brooke-Hardinge.''

"When you arrived tonight," said Sir Alan, "I was here alone. Correct."

"Yes."

"So I might have killed him, before anyone else arrived," said Sir Alan.

"Yes. You might have. I was curious about something. I had motive to kill him, so did Duggs. Since Desmond has been engaged in a business relationship with him, I assume he had a motive to kill him. And Laura Hodges—any woman who lived with him for a year or so would have ample reason to wish him dead. But *you*, Sir Alan? Why?"

"I too had my motive," said Sir Alan calmly.

*   *   *

"Suave" was the word that first came to Mrs. Roosevelt's mind when David Desmond came in the kitchen and sat down. Another was "smooth." Still another was "slippery."

She could not guess how much whisky he had consumed during the past five hours. It was enough for her to know he had drunk something, yet certainly not enough for her to regard him as inebriated in the least sense. He brought another glass with him into the kitchen, and he sat down at the heavy, rude table with a glance around the room that was meant, she guessed, to suggest that he had never before been in such a belowstairs room.

Sir Alan established his status with a quick comment. "I believe," he said, "that your real name is David Clicker. I can understand why you would prefer Desmond."

Desmond flushed, but regained his confidence instantly. "I shall be happy, Sir Alan," he said, "with any name you elect to call me—so long as it is a name and not the number of a prisoner in the nick."

"Well, you have previously been a guest in the cells under the Old Bailey, if I am not mistaken," said Sir Alan.

"Not a conviction stands against my name," said Desmond.

"Mr. Desmond," said Lord William. "Why do you suppose Sir Anthony invited you to his supper party, which seems to have been for the most part for people with reason to hate him enough to murder him?"

"Except for the fact that the party was called for his apartments in Buckingham Palace," said Desmond, "I might have thought it was to assemble us all in one room and set off a bomb."

"The others had reason to want him dead," said Lord William. "So, what of you?"

"I am an impresario," said Desmond loftily. "I produce plays and shows, and operate two night clubs. Tony wanted to produce a successful, long-running theatrical extravaganza and scoop up a hundred thousand pounds, but he had no experience in the theater. His short-term ambition was to do to me what he did to Duggs."

"You know about that?"

"In his cups," said Desmond smoothly, "Tony talked a great deal about his past triumphs—including the way he became a silent partner, then silent owner, of one of the City's most successful insurance brokerages."

"Why," asked Mrs. Roosevelt, "did he want to involve himself in the theater? Surely it's a risky business."

"But glamorous," said Desmond. "And spectacular. He had attained knighthood. A peerage seemed beyond him. To be, then, an impresario, producer of great shows, sponsor of important talents—ah, that would have been a triumph for the ego!"

"And he entered into a partnership with you," said Sir Alan. "You are a man with a mixed career, Desmond, and a mixed reputation. Seems like an odd partnership for a man with such ambitions. Unless I am in error, your productions have been mostly strip shows."

Desmond turned to Mrs. Roosevelt. "I have been harassed by Scotland Yard," he said smoothly, "and by the Lord Chamberlain. The Lord Chamberlain, as you may know, has the onerous and archaic task of censoring our country's stage plays. Since British morals must be preserved immaculate, an impulsive 'damn' spoken on a London stage may subject actor and producer to prosecution.''

"The matter is a bit more serious than that,'' said Sir Alan. "I believe there has been a question of on-stage nudity—''

"Yes,'' said Desmond, again to Mrs. Roosevelt. "Under the present law of England, a young woman may appear stark-naked on the stage—as at the Windmill Theatre—so long as she stands stock-still. If she is less than naked but moves, she may have committed a criminal offense. Thus . . . well, I need not describe further.''

"I believe,'' said Sir Alan, "your collisions with the criminal law have involved a bit more than that.''

"Gambling,'' said Desmond blandly, with brows raised. "Uh, serving some of our lords drinks after hours.''

"Pandering to prostitution,'' said Sir Alan.

"No, sir. I cannot be responsible for the misconduct of every young woman who works in my clubs.''

"I should be curious to know, Mr. Desmond,'' said Mrs. Roosevelt, "just what enterprises you and Sir Anthony were pursuing through your partnership.''

Desmond bowed to her and smiled. "At last a question that is not hostile. Thank you. Have you ever heard of a show called *Bottoms Up*? It ran for a hundred and eighty-six performances in the West End. I produced it, and my silent partner in the production was Sir Anthony Brooke-Hardinge.''

"I find that hard to credit,'' said Lord William. "I had no idea that Sir Anthony was in any way involved in that." He spoke to Mrs. Roosevelt. "The Lord Chamberlain objected to the show because the chorus girls did indeed turn their bottoms up—revealing that they were wearing very little covering on their bottoms."

"That was not the problem," said Desmond. "The difficulty was with nearsightedness. The girls' panties were flesh-colored—causing a few shortsighted, elderly lords and MPs to suppose there *were* no panties. His Lordship suggested we change to another color, which we did: white. After that, no problem."

"The show was widely regarded as vulgar," said Lord William.

"Which amused Tony no end," said Desmond. "He invested ten thousand pounds in it and banked twenty-four thousand. He liked that kind of profit."

"But why," asked Mrs. Roosevelt, "was there a twenty-thousand-pound insurance policy on the life of Sir Anthony, naming you as beneficiary?"

"That is very simple," said Desmond insouciantly. "There is an American term for the practice of insuring the life of a partner, making the other partner beneficiary. Tony and I were working on another production. In the event of his death, I should be deprived of his contribution—leaving me with my time and money invested and a show short of necessary development capital. For that reason, Tony readily agreed that we should insure his life in the amount of his anticipated contribution."

"Is your life insured in his favor, too?" asked Sir Alan.

"No. Because my contribution was to be expertise, principally, not money."

"You say you were in the process of developing a new show?"

"Yes. Something that will appeal to the soldiers who are on the streets of London—the Americans as well as the English. A musical. Tony came up with the script, but don't ask me what the show is; that's secret right now."

"You will, I suppose, go ahead and produce it, in spite of his death?"

Desmond nodded. "Unless I am convicted of his murder, in which case the life insurance wouldn't pay."

"That's a prospect that doesn't worry you much, I imagine," said Sir Alan.

"No. I had opportunity and motive, but you can't prove that I did it."

"You may be the only one here who was strong enough to have beaten a man to death with a fireplace poker," said Sir Alan.

Desmond smiled. "Except you, Sir Alan. Are you telling us you are too weak to have done it? And what of Letitia? Or Laura, for that matter? Only Duggs is possibly too weak, and I somehow imagine he could find a good deal of strength in his arms if presented with the opportunity to do in old Tony."

"You speak of 'Letitia,' " said Lord William. "Do you know Lady Letitia?"

Desmond partially suppressed a smile. "In her business capacity," he said.

"And Miss Hodges?"

"Laura Hodges is one of the thousand girls who come to London every year, thinking they have the talent to sing, dance, act—whatever—and become a star of stage or screen. Men like Tony take full

advantage of those girls. She's not his first one—
though, I must say, she lasted longer than any other.
She's very pretty, isn't she? For him to have given
her a key to his private entrance to the Palace—''

"Does she have talent?" asked Mrs. Roosevelt.

He shrugged. "She thinks she's a dancer, and
she's good enough for the chorus line, I suppose.
Tony offered her a part as a *Bottoms Up* girl, but she
wouldn't take it. She has a good deal of pride; what I
believe Americans call 'spunk.' ''

"She also had reason to be jealous, didn't she?"
asked Lord William. "I mean, didn't we hear that he
was in the process of replacing her with another girl?"

"He was never faithful to her, any more than he was
to Letitia," said Desmond. "It was a point of pride
with Tony to enjoy the favors of as many pretty girls
as possible. I don't even know who the new one is."

It was almost three o'clock when Laura Hodges
was summoned—the last suspect to be questioned.
Mrs. Roosevelt had stepped out to the sitting room to
make her summons as gentle as possible, and she
found the petite young woman poking at fresh coal
and keeping the fire blazing. The other suspects had
been allowed to leave after their questioning, and
Laura was alone with two detectives.

"We are sorry you've been kept waiting so long,"
said Mrs. Roosevelt. "It did seem we should conduct
the inquiry in an orderly way, and that of course will
ultimately be to your advantage."

The young woman rose wearily and walked toward
the kitchen.

Mrs. Roosevelt was again struck with how pretty
she was—as Desmond had said. Though tired and

distraught, she carried herself like the would-be dancer Desmond had said she was: erect and graceful on her feet. She sat down on the wooden chair at the kitchen table and crossed her legs, causing her slender gray skirt to creep back, exposing her knees and several inches of leg. She shrugged her shoulders to settle her double-breasted jacket, straightened her tie, and tossed her head to flip a bit of stray hair back from her face. The girl was poised, thought Mrs. Roosevelt, but she was not affected.

"You described yourself," said Lord William, "as Sir Anthony's 'mistress,' an old-fashioned word that can imply a variety of relationships. Would you care to be more specific?"

"I lived with him," she said with direct, unembarrassed simplicity.

"All the time?"

"No, not *all* the time. But most of the time."

"You have keys—"

"Yes," she interrupted. "But there is no need to have them any longer." She reached into the pocket of her jacket and laid before her on the table two large old keys. "That," she said, pointing to one, "opens the door between the foyer and the Palace corridor. The other one opens the confidential private entry off—well, they persist in saying the Pimlico side. Actually, of course, the entry is off Buckingham Gate. Anyway, I won't have any further use for those keys."

"You have no clothes here?" asked Sir Alan.

"A few items of underwear I can carry in my handbag," she said.

"Then you didn't live here, really."

"I also have the key to his house in Belgravia, on

Eaton Square,'' she said. "I have clothes there, and other personal things, and I would like to remove those."

"Where will you sleep tonight?" asked Mrs. Roosevelt.

"It would appear that I'm not going to," said Laura dryly. "I would probably have slept here if—" She sighed. "Or in the house on Eaton Square."

"I'm afraid we can't allow that," said Lord William. "You can enter the house and remove your things, under the supervision of a policewoman. I shall have to trouble you for that key, too."

"It's in my handbag," she said. "I'll give it to you."

"I have a large suite," said Mrs. Roosevelt. "You are very welcome to spend what's left of the night with me."

"You are kind," said Laura, "but I have telephoned a friend who is expecting me as soon as I am released."

"You have no flat or room of your own?" asked Lord William.

"No. As I said, I lived with Tony."

"Since . . .?"

"Since December nineteen forty," she said.

"But the relationship was winding down, wasn't it?" asked Sir Alan. "He had a new interest."

"He always had new interests," she said.

"You have been described as a young woman with a particularly strong interest in establishing a career," said Lord William. "Was Sir Anthony helping you with your career?"

"He had promised to help me get a role in a show," she said.

"Did you love him?" asked Mrs. Roosevelt.

"No."

"He has been described as a not-very-charming man," said Mrs. Roosevelt. "Did he treat you ill?"

Laura, who until now had maintained a sober, fatigued demeanor, abruptly smiled sardonically. "When you search his house on Eaton Square," she said, "you will find photographs of his former wife, of other women, and of me. He was a very demanding man."

"But you met his demands," said Sir Alan, "in the expectation that so doing would further your career."

She tossed her head defiantly, then tipped it and regarded Sir Alan with some amusement. "Yes," she said. "A cold-blooded, immoral trade. Hmmm?"

She faced Sir Alan down. He lowered his eyes. "Not unusual, I s'pose," he muttered.

"How did he make up the invitation list?" asked Mrs. Roosevelt.

"He wrote down a list," said Laura. "I—"

"Where is that list now?" Lord William interrupted.

"When I finished with it, I put it in the dustbin. The addresses were in his address book, on his desk. He told me to type and mail the invitations. Since he would be out, I should just type his name at the bottom. That is why there were no signatures on the invitations."

"And how did he make up the list?" asked Mrs. Roosevelt. "How had he chosen the names?"

"That's a bit obvious, isn't it? They were people he had lied to, cheated, stolen from . . . They were people he had hurt."

"How many more names were on the list?" asked Lord William.

"I believe I sent twelve invitations," she said.

"Why were you yourself included?"

Laura shrugged. "Why not? I was one of his victims."

"Uh . . . in what way?" asked Sir Alan.

She hesitated for a moment, as if regretting what she had said. "Well . . . I had, in effect, enslaved myself to him, on the understanding that he would promote my career."

"But he was keeping his part of that bargain, was he not?"

Laura nodded slowly. "I guess he was. Maybe I don't have the talent."

"It seems odd to me," said Mrs. Roosevelt, "that a man should wish to assemble for a supper party as many as possible of the people who hated him, who had reason to wish him harm. Why in the world—"

"If you had known Tony, you would understand very well," said Laura.

"Are you saying to us," asked Sir Alan, "that the man would have assembled a supper party of his enemies to *gloat* over them?"

"Yes," she said firmly. "And to sit in the library and listen to them on his microphone-and-speaker system, so he could torment them later with quotations from their own mouths. Yes. Tony was quite capable of that. Entirely capable. And enjoying it, no doubt—when one of his guests, finding him in the library and understanding all the circumstances, was furious and struck him with the nearest weapon in reach."

"A *theory*," said Lord William.

"Or maybe," she said with a sigh, "I plotted his death and killed him at the first opportune moment."

"I think," said Mrs. Roosevelt, "we need not come to that conclusion."

"How much did you know about his crimes against the others?" asked Sir Alan.

"How he cheated Duggs? How he rid himself of a wife that was no longer interesting to him? He boasted about those things. And about you, Sir Alan—" She paused to subdue a grin. "He called you a yob."

" 'Yob'?" asked Mrs. Roosevelt.

"London slang," said Sir Alan. "A not-too-bright proletarian."

"Desmond?" asked Lord William.

"He didn't talk about Desmond," she said. "I knew of the relationship, of course. I wonder if he was not a little awed by Desmond. Desmond is a real crook, a man who has been charged in the criminal courts—though I understand from him he has never been convicted. Desmond produces money-making shows—however else you may define them."

"His ex-wife has been charged in the criminal courts," said Sir Alan.

"Ah!" snorted Laura. "And he was at pains to get the charges dropped. Even if they were divorced, it would hardly have done for an equerry's ex-wife to have been convicted of operating a house of ill repute. He intervened on her behalf several times. I went with him to the gaol once—and saw her released from a cell. If you ever want to see pure, fiery hatred! She would have rather lain in that cell all night—or for two days—than be released by his doing."

"And some on the invitation list did not come," said Sir Alan.

"Could you be surprised?"

"And one was dead."

Laura shrugged.

"I believe we cannot justify detaining you any longer, Miss Hodges," said Lord William. "So thank you. And good night. One of my officers will drive you wherever you wish to go."

"And that leaves you, Sir Alan," said Lord William when Laura Hodges had left and closed the door behind her. "What can we say?"

"I don't know," said Sir Alan.

The light in the dreary kitchen was flat and dull—oppressive after an hour. By common and unspoken impulse, they rose—Mrs. Roosevelt, Lord William Duncan, Sir Alan Burton, and the detective, Harrison—and walked out to the sitting room.

The coals still blazed. The Chinese houseboy, forgotten, slept on the floor near the fireplace.

"Take him home, Dillard, will you please?" said Lord William, nodding at Wen Yung.

Sir Alan stepped to the bar and poured himself a splash of whisky. Mrs. Roosevelt accepted a small splash—"of loudmouth," as Humphrey Bogart had called it that weekend in South Carolina. She was, suddenly, very tired, very conscious that she had flown from Bristol and arrived at Paddington Station—when? A week ago? She sat down facing the fireplace and stared into the dying embers.

"The Buddha," said Lord William. "It is the key. When we find the jade Buddha, we will know who killed Sir Anthony Brooke-Hardinge."

Mrs. Roosevelt shook her head. "Not necessarily," she said. "I am not sure it is so simple."

"We are pleased you could be with us tonight," said Lord William. "Some of your questions were most insightful."

"I shall continue to be interested," said she. "Unfortunately, I have a heavy schedule tomorrow, but please keep me informed."

"We shall," said Lord William.

"I shall make a strong point of it," said Sir Alan.

5

When Tommy Thompson arrived at Mrs. Roosevelt's suite at nine-thirty, Mrs. Roosevelt had been awake for two hours, reviewing her briefing papers, studying the day's schedule, pondering what she would say during the press conference that was scheduled to begin at the United States Embassy at ten-thirty. She had accepted a breakfast tray from one of the servants, who had come knocking on her door, and had finished a small pot of coffee and a muffin with marmalade—no butter.

"Did you have a restful night?" Tommy asked solicitously.

"No, to be perfectly truthful," said Mrs. Roosevelt. "But once I did sleep, I slept well."

"I understand that Elliott left very early," said Tommy.

"Yes. Duty calls. I wish I had had more time to spend with him, but at least I will be able to report to my husband that our son is well. I will see him again, once at least, and probably several times, before we return to Washington."

"He will be flying over . . . ?"

"Tommy . . . He will be flying over the land of Gog and Magog. Over Shangri-La. Over the kingdom of Prester John."

"So," said Tommy. "You don't want to tell me."

"I *must* not tell you. It's nothing personal."

Tommy returned the little smile she had received. "Of course," she murmured. "Will there be any dictation this morning?"

"Oh, my goodness! Yes, there will be dictation. Have you any idea what has followed us all the way across the Atlantic?"

Over fifty reporters appeared for the press conference, crowding the conference room of the American Embassy. Standing at the podium, Mrs. Roosevelt calmly answered their questions.

—"Does your trip to England to visit with American troops indicate that they are about to be used to open a second front?"

—"I do not know, and if I did, I could not tell you."

—"Have you seen the destruction wrought by Nazi bombing?"

—"Only a little so far, but I expect to tour the damaged areas of London soon."

—"The valiant workers of the Soviet Union are bearing the burden of this war far more than any other people or class. Is the President aware of the anger of the working class over his failure, and the Prime Minister's failure, to launch a cross-Channel invasion *now*, to relieve the pressure on their comrades?"

—"The President is sometimes criticized for being too sensitive to the feelings of the working class. I have not yet heard him criticized for being insensitive to them.''

—''Could it not be arranged for American soldiers in England to receive the same pay as British soldiers, so they would not outbid British soldiers for every comfort and advantage?''

—''British soldiers with a weekend pass can go home. I suspect American soldiers would be happy to serve with no pay at all if they could have that same privilege.''

Twice an official tried to interrupt a question, to spare her whatever embarrassment they thought it would cause her. Each time she interrupted the interruption, and answered the question. After much practice with these exchanges, Mrs. Roosevelt had developed measured confidence in her ability to handle them—though she would never be entirely comfortable with them. They would write of her, as she knew, that she was an eminently capable woman— though some of them would be viciously critical— but none of them would ever suspect how much they troubled her.

She wore a gray knit dress, a flat hat with a feather that swept across the brim, and her fox neckpiece. No one, not even Tommy, suspected she had been up almost the entire night, listening to the inquiry into the death of Sir Anthony Brooke-Hardinge.

The subject of Sir Anthony arose at noon, when she met the King and Queen for a luncheon with the heads of British women's organizations. She felt she could not but say a word of sympathy to the King.

''I understand you lost a dear friend last night,'' she said to King George.

He seemed a bit surprised that she knew. "Yes," he said. "I shall m-miss him."

She was prepared to drop the subject then, but the King went on. "Sir Anthony was a long-time f-friend, even so I knew nothing of his p-personal life. He was divorced, I understand, and I have no idea why. He impressed me always as a fine, dutiful man, descended of one of the oldest families. I placed a g-great deal of trust in him."

The Queen had a different impression. When the King stepped away to speak to the American ambassador, she said to Mrs. Roosevelt, "I regret the death of Sir Anthony for my husband's sake. You may, however, hear some negative words about him."

"The circumstances of his death are distressing," said Mrs. Roosevelt.

"Yes, he was murdered," said the Queen.

Mrs. Roosevelt admired the way the King and Queen could discuss the murder of their friend—a circumstance that must have disturbed both of them deeply—without letting people standing three feet from them gain any impression of their distress. Their practiced self-control was, as she knew, in the best tradition of the British monarchy.

Among the luncheon guests were Colonel Hobby and her aide Lieutenant Bandel. Mrs. Roosevelt was amused to see the two women in military uniforms curtsy to the King and Queen. In all, fourteen women and the King sat down to lunch, yet he was completely at ease.

After the meal Mrs. Roosevelt joined the King and Queen in the Daimler; and, followed by a string of cars carrying reporters and photographers, they began a tour of the bombed sections of London.

As they drove out The Strand and into Fleet Street, they came to the Temple Bar, which marked the western boundary of the City of London—that is, the ancient and traditional City. There the Daimler stopped, and a wigged and gowned official—the Lord Mayor of London—stepped forward.

"My Lord, His Majesty the King requests your permission to enter the City," said an equerry.

The Lord Mayor stepped close to the open rear door of the car. He was carrying a sword, which he now reversed; and, holding it point downward, handed it to the King. "Welcome, Your Majesty, to the City of London," he said.

King George accepted the sword. "I thank you, My Lord." Gravely he returned the sword to the Lord Mayor.

The Lord Mayor bowed deeply and backed away. Still carrying the sword, he entered a car at the head of the royal procession.

"I am so pleased," said Mrs. Roosevelt to the King and Queen when the Daimler was again slowly moving. "I was afraid this might be one of the ancient ceremonies suspended for the duration of the war."

"Many ceremonies have been suspended," said the King. "But . . . this one is important to the people of the City."

Quiet crowds lined the street as they approached St. Paul's Cathedral, but Mrs. Roosevelt, stunned by the devastation all around her, hardly noticed them. The City was gutted, and the newsreels she had seen of the Blitz were here translated into reality: block after block of homes and businesses reduced to cold, ugly, dusty rubble. The few people walking or cycling through the ruined streets seemed as cold and dusty as the ruins around them.

St. Paul's was severely damaged. The Dean, who met them on the steps, took the royal party inside to see the extent to which the great cathedral had been injured. Much of the roof had been destroyed, leaving the interior open to the skies.

"During the worst of the Blitz, many of us slept below, in the crypts, in order to be available to put out fires," the Dean told them.

In a quiet moment, the King said to Mrs. Roosevelt, "I wanted to come here—to show them how very much we appreciate their dedication to saving St. Paul's."

From the cathedral they drove on into the East End, where many thousands of working-class houses, indeed slums, had been blasted, burned, and leveled.

"The government have promised the people that new housing will be built here as soon as the war ends," said the King.

Mrs. Roosevelt was appalled, too, by the ruin of the Guildhall, the London city hall which had stood since the Middle Ages.

With the King and Queen she met and interviewed a score of workers who had been decorated for their bravery during the Blitz—firemen, policemen and -women, rescue workers, air-raid wardens.

Shortly before noon Sir Alan Burton arrived at the Eaton Square home of Sir Anthony Brooke-Hardinge. With him were several policemen and detectives, Laura Hodges, and two insurance-company investigators, by name Mr. Philip Reynolds and Mr. Lawrence Muldoon. Laura Hodges carried two large and battered leather suitcases, in which she meant to remove her clothes from the house. The insurance-company investigators carried briefcases packed with files.

"You can perhaps lead us through the house," said Sir Alan to Laura.

"Yes, of course," she said quietly.

Standing inside the entrance door, Laura looked around as though awed by the silence in the handsome Georgian house. It was not very large, consisting of a living room and dining room with kitchen and pantry on the ground floor, and a library, bedroom, and bath on the first floor; but it was exquisitely kept and furnished. Since Sir Anthony had been on duty at the Palace the past two weeks, the house was cold. For the duration of the war he had no servants but Wen Yung, who customarily followed him from the Palace to Eaton Square and back.

Laura was wearing a raspberry-colored knit dress under a wrap camel coat. Sir Alan noted that Sir Anthony had apparently kept her well dressed. He was more than a little curious as to what she had upstairs in the closets.

"There is the sitting room," she said, pointing to the room to the left off the center hallway. "Dining room to the right." She glanced at the investigators. "If you are looking for objets d'art, the most likely place to find them is in the sitting room. You will find others upstairs." She turned to Sir Alan. "Damned cold," she said, "but I don't suppose we will be here long enough to justify lighting a fire."

"Let us hope not," said Sir Alan. "I had rather hoped our visit would be brief and uneventful."

"You may well find stolen property," she said calmly to the two investigators.

"I already have," said Lawrence Muldoon.

Muldoon was a sharp-faced thin man with a small gray mustache, unimaginatively dressed in gray, with a black derby hat seated squarely on his head. He had picked up a small blue-and-white porcelain vase that stood on a table beside the sitting-room door.

"What do you think?" he asked Reynolds.

"One of the Hempstead pieces," said the other investigator, a squat-faced, rotund man wearing a similar black derby. "Maybe not, but very likely it is."

"Not just likely," said Muldoon. " 'T is. Look at the inventory mark on the bottom."

"Burglary in early nineteen forty," said Reynolds to Sir Alan. "Not the first piece of the loot that's shown up in London."

"Harry Cross," said Muldoon. "I'd say Sir Anthony outbid us."

"Do you always talk in riddles?" asked Laura.

Muldoon's quick glance at her suggested clearly that he felt himself under no obligation to explain anything to her. Even so, he did. "Burglary of a fine old estate," he said. "The usual thing. Country house. Collection accumulated over the centuries. They carried off a lorryful, literally. Harry Cross is a fence, a professional dealer in stolen properties. He called and said he'd been offered part of the Hempstead loot. Wanted to know what we'd pay for it. Had a list; he did. I mean, of what he could get for us. Better for the company to recover what we can than have to pay the appraised value of the stolen items. What was on his list came to some £3,500 appraised value. We offered him £1,500. He accepted, but with a proviso that this little vase was no longer available to him. We cut to £1,200. He accepted again. Without this piece, the appraised value of the recovered items was about £3,100. So we came out £1,900 to the good. But for this vase—worth about £400—we had to pay appraised value. Apparently Harry had shown it to somebody who offered him more—and apparently that somebody was Sir Anthony Brooke-Hardinge.''

"Why don't you arrest this Harry Cross?" she asked Sir Alan. "A receiver of stolen goods—"

"He's clever," said Sir Alan. "Never has the property in his possession and says he only acts as an honest go-between, to help insurance companies recover stolen goods. We have long despaired of convicting Harry Cross."

"And we in the insurance business hope you never do," said Muldoon. "Otherwise, we'd have had to pay the full appraised value of many a lot. Better to let Harry function."

"And I suppose," said Laura scornfully, "he paid the thieves about half of what you paid him."

Reynolds shrugged. "There's not as much profit in theft as some people might think."

"You may wish to go through the rooms on this floor first," said Sir Alan. "I shall ask Miss Hodges to take me upstairs and show me what clothes she wishes to carry away with her."

"Let us not forget, Sir Alan," she said acidly, "that the clothes I wish to 'carry away' are, after all, *mine.*"

"Of course."

They climbed the graceful staircase together. The library upstairs was a gracious, cozy room, with leather-upholstered furniture and glass-front bookcases, much like the library in the flat in Buckingham Palace. The bedroom, though, was quite modern. An oversized bed with a fur bedspread dominated the room. Fur rugs covered most of the floor, and the walls were hung with erotic paintings, picturing men and women engaged in various acts of sexual intimacy.

"He had the room redecorated after he was divorced," said Laura dryly, noticing Sir Alan's astonishment at the decor.

A photo album lay on the dresser. Sir Alan picked it up and opened it.

"I suggest you impound that," she said. "I'm not the only woman who would rather the pictures in there not be seen."

The pages were filled with photographs of naked women, some of them in extraordinarily grotesque poses. He recognized Laura Hodges, and Lady Letitia; but there were photographs of at least a dozen other women, not all of them very young, but all beautiful.

"If you don't mind my asking," he said, "is one of these what we may call your successor?"

"I am not altogether certain I accept the term 'successor,' " she said. "But not to make an issue of it, yes, his latest interest is there, on the first page. He arranged the book in reverse chronological order."

Sir Alan turned to the beginning and looked at the nude photograph of an embarrassed, reluctantly posing woman he judged to be in her early forties. Her face and arms were abundantly freckled, and though the photograph was only black and white, he could guess the hair piled on top of her head was a rich red. Her face was simple, even somewhat plain. Her smile was winsomely honest, her lips compressed to keep the smile from spreading into a toothy grin. The effort flushed and distended her cheeks, lending the subdued smile an innocent, engaging charm.

"Who is she?" he asked Laura.

"You'd know her if she had her clothes on," Laura sneered.

He frowned over the picture. Unlike the others, this woman was restrained in her pose. She held one arm folded over her breasts, not quite covering them but demonstrating that she was reluctant to display them. He turned the page, but there were no more photographs of her.

"Don't make me guess," he said.

Laura Hodges let a smile spread slowly across her face. "Alexandra Dudley, Countess of Stanhope," she said. "A great-granddaughter of Queen Victoria. Royal family. A real catch for Tony. He even spoke of marrying her."

Sir Alan looked at the picture again. "So. She was indeed to be your successor," he said. "I hope it is not altogether caddish of me to have wondered why he would put you aside for this attractive but not ravishingly beautiful woman."

"What makes you think I would have been put aside entirely?" asked Laura. "He kept a girl during his marriage to Letitia."

"But not here," said Sir Alan. "Not in this style and not in Buckingham Palace. I dare say you had reason to be jealous, Miss Hodges."

"What I wanted from Tony," she said firmly, "was a boost to my career. That was understood by both of us. He promised me he would continue to promote me—Alexandra or no Alexandra, whether I continued to sleep with him or not. Besides—'' She tossed her head. ''He said I'd be seeing him anyway.''

She began to pull clothes from a closet. ''All these are mine,'' she said. ''Do you want to take inventory? Do you want to search the pockets for stolen objets d'art?''

Sir Alan shook his head, but he watched as she packed her clothes, to gain an idea of just how much she had, how much she had gotten from the relationship. It was evident from the first dress she pulled from the closet that Sir Anthony had bought all these things; a girl struggling to make her way in the theater could not have afforded them. She opened a drawer and began to pull out underthings.

He opened other drawers and searched carelessly through Sir Anthony's shirts. ''Ah,'' he said suddenly, drawing out a pair of handcuffs and pair of heavy leg irons. ''Who wore these?''

''Not I, you may be damned sure,'' said Laura. ''Ask the delightful Alexandra.''

She opened a top drawer and began to scoop out jewelry.

''You had better call up the insurance snoops,'' she said. ''I also have some bibelots. They'll want to make sure none of it is loot from some burglary.''

Sir Alan stepped to the door. ''Mr. Reynolds,'' he called. ''Mr. Muldoon, will you come up, please?''

Laura removed a half a dozen necklaces, four bracelets, a handful of small jeweled pins. She spread them on the top of the dresser. ''There, gentlemen,'' she said to the two investigators. ''See if any of that is stolen property.''

Muldoon began to scan the pieces with a magnifying glass.

"Sherlock Holmes," she muttered to Sir Alan as she continued packing her clothes.

"These pieces were his gifts to you, Miss Hodges?" asked Muldoon. "Well, there is a stolen piece here." He lifted one of the pins and handed it to her. "Since it has been long since paid for and the case is closed, I will not ask you to return it. My company paid the owner £125 for that pin. Even without a loupe, just with the magnifying glass, you can see the tiny speck of carbon that flaws the diamond. The two pearls, however, are not real—the real ones having been replaced with Majorca pearls some years before the theft. The gold is quite nicely crafted, though. I'd venture a guess that Sir Anthony paid Harry Cross too much for it."

"Not Harry," said Reynolds. "I don't think Harry Cross was the fence for that lot."

Reynolds walked across the hall and casually entered the library. "My God!" he gasped.

Laura raised her brows and told Sir Alan, "I guess he recognizes the painting."

Sir Alan hurried across the hall to the library, where Muldoon had switched on the little lamp illuminating the painting that dominated one wall—a soft, out-of-focus sort of picture of sailboats and little steamers on the Thames approaching Westminster Bridge.

"The Turner . . ." Reynolds whispered.

"It's worth a fortune," said Muldoon.

"What would you have paid a fence for that?" asked Laura. "I can tell you what Tony paid for it."

"We didn't bid on that," said Muldoon. "Not one of our companies."

"He paid £3,000 for it," she said. "Or so he told me."

"It's worth : . . five times that," said Reynolds.

"You have been living here in the presence of that and did not report it to the police?" said Sir Alan to Laura. "You're an accessory!"

"Yes," she said. "Do you want to charge me? If I had come to you day before yesterday and told you Sir Anthony Brooke-Hardinge dealt constantly with fences and had filled his Buckingham Palace flat, not to mention his house on Eaton Square, with stolen properties, would you have believed me? Would you, Sir Alan, have charged Tony—considering your experience in the child-molestation case? You'd have gotten a second rose annually, maybe a yellow one."

"He was involved in—"

"Yes," she said. "Heavily. In crime. So the number of suspects in his death may be multiplied by a major factor, may it not? Harry Cross, for example—"

"Indeed," said Sir Alan.

"So, Harry. Has the war made business difficult?"

Harry Cross nodded. He poured tea from the pot he had heated over his little stove. "Life has always been difficult," he said. "Sugar, Sir Alan? Milk? Even though you have been knighted, you were no more born to it than I. Has life not always been difficult for both of us?"

"What did you get for the jade Buddha, Harry?"

"A Buddha? A Buddha?" Harry Cross asked, turning up his eyes and affecting a mystified frown. "What in the name of all that the Archbishop of Canterbury would scorn is a Buddha?"

He lived on North End Road, not far off West

Cromwell Road and not far from the railroad yard. Sir Alan was accustomed to his pretense of near-poverty; to his three-days gray whiskers, to the ragged, stained raincoat he wore even indoors, and to his distracted air, as if he were not quite sure what day it was. Sir Alan knew this two-room flat had been searched fifty times, with never a single item of stolen property found. From time to time Harry telephoned insurance-company investigators, such as Muldoon and Reynolds, and informed those prosaic, practical gentlemen that by some odd chance he had overheard talk as to where a particular item of stolen property might be located and could possibly arrange some mutually beneficial transfer of funds and loot.

"A valuable jade statue of the Oriental god," said Sir Alan. "A jade Buddha. Stolen from a home in Warwickshire and sold to Sir Anthony Brooke-Hardinge."

"Ah . . . The late Sir Anthony," nodded Cross, turning down the corners of his mouth. "Pity . . ."

"His death has not been announced," said Sir Alan sternly. "How did you know of it?"

"Not so difficult," said Cross. He turned his spoon in his tea, stirring in sugar. "Not all the staff at Buck House are aristocrats."

"There is a very great difference, Harry," said Sir Alan, "between the jade Buddha and some of the pieces we have talked about before. The Buddha happens to be evidence in a murder. It's missing again, and I want to know where it is. It's not the kind of piece that travels in commerce without a trace. Someone knows where it is—that is, if it is on the market again."

Cross sipped tea. "Not today," he said. "If there

is such a piece on the market, no one 'as told me.''

"But they would," said Sir Alan.

"Not necessarily," said Cross. "Wot do you think I am, guv'nor? People do tell me things from time to time, 't is true; but you mustn't suppose I 'ave a catalogue of everything stolen in London. Not me. I'm an amateur, just a public-spirited citizen who from time to time has been able to 'elp the insurance companies to get their goods back.''

"As a public-spirited citizen," said Sir Alan evenly, "you are likely to know if this jade statue comes on the market. Are you not?"

"Well, I might 'ear."

"Yes. And in this instance, if you do, you will telephone Scotland Yard, not Muldoon or Reynolds.''

"Muldoon? Reynolds? Oh, yes, the insurance chaps. You want to know first, 'ey?''

"I want to know *only*," said Sir Alan.

"Ah. Yaas. Since you yourself are a suspect.''

"You know too much, Harry. But I expect to be around for years yet. Don't you?"

Harry Cross pursed his lips and ran his thumb and finger down his stubbly cheeks. "Would you like a spot of gin or whisky with your tea, guv'nor?'' he asked.

Sir Alan accepted the whisky. It was a fine single-malt: something very hard to find these days. Cross found two Havana cigars in a battered cupboard.

"A fine gentleman, Sir Tony Brooke-Hardinge," he said as he relaxed in a sagging chair. "I imagine 'Is Majesty the King would like to know who done 'im in.''

"Who did it, Harry?''

Cross lifted his whisky, drank, and wiped his mouth with the soiled sleeve of his raincoat. "The murder of a man like Sir Tony is not good for the likes of innocent subjects like me," he said.

"Loss of a good customer," muttered Sir Alan, drawing the fragrant smoke of his cigar.

"No. Puts the coppers in a bad mood. Puts you under pressure to run everyone to ground. My interest in this is not very different from yours. You got sleepless nights till you can turn this one over to King's counsel. So do others."

"So we can talk honestly to one another, can't we, Harry?"

Harry Cross smiled over his glass of whisky. "Why, guv'nor," he said. "I always speak honest to you."

"Yes. Well then, tell me about the jade Buddha."

"It was lifted from an old 'ouse in Warwickshire by a couple of fellows as was named Rose and Gresham. Not part of a lot, the Buddha. Single piece. They went in for it alone, knew it was there. The old man of the house had bought it of a Methodist missionary who brought it back from China. Probably stole it there, or bought it from a Chinese fence, fact be known. Rose was the family driver. Gresham was a professional. They lifted the Buddha one night and brought it into London to sell, but nobody would dare look at it. It was the only one of its kind, and the first investigator wot looked at it was going to know it. I 'eard about it, and wouldn't even let them bring it to me for a look."

"Well, how did it get into the hands of Sir Anthony?"

"I never knew it did. I swear. I never saw it."

"What about some of the other stuff?" asked Sir Alan. "The Turner? The painting."

Cross shook his head. He paused while he touched the flame of a wooden match to the tip of his big Havana cigar. "Can we talk confidential, guv'nor?"

"Yes. Absolutely. You have my word."

"The Turner was lifted from the 'ome of the Duke of Westminster, as you probably know. By Moran. Who else? It passed by me—at a distance, as you might say. The insurance chaps wanted it back, but they didn't want it as much as Sir Tony. I tried to get it for the insurance company, but Sir T outbid me. Outbid *them*, actually."

"He was a regular customer," said Sir Alan.

"Not reg'lar. Dishonest, 'e was. You couldn't ever make a deal with 'im and be sure it would be carried through the way 'e'd agreed. He welshed, did Sir T. Often. Some honest burglar may have done 'im in— for good reason."

"What do you know of Clicker, also known as Desmond?"

Cross shrugged and scoffed. "Makes 'is livin' showin' off little girls' bare titties." He shook his head. "Not got the courage to kill a man, either, if you want my judgment."

"How about the girl? Laura Hodges? Do you know anything about her?"

"No. Never 'eard the name before this morning."

"You will let me know, Harry, if you hear anything."

"Of course, guv'nor. Of course."

As darkness fell, Sir Alan reached Piccadilly Circus and plunged into the milling crowds.

London theaters, which had remained open even during the Blitz, were now filled with people, affording weary Londoners and thousands of British and American servicemen and -women evenings of light entertainment. Clubs, legal and illegal, had opened everywhere, in cellars, in lofts, in space that had previously been occupied by shops and offices. Soldiers, sailors, and airmen, enlisted men and officers, jostled each other and civilians in their anxiety to find the entertainment of their choice. Prostitutes mingled with the crowds, hawking their services to likely customers. Anyone with money to spend could find someone to take it.

Turning up Shaftesbury Avenue, Sir Alan pushed his way into the heart of Soho, much of it in ruins now, but much of it still standing, catering to its old trade. On Wardour Street he found the address he wanted and knocked on the door.

Though the brick building stood just across the street from a pile of dusty rubble, its windows had been reglazed, the frames repainted, the dark-green door freshly repainted, and the brass knocker polished only today.

"I wish to speak to Mr. Mallory," said Sir Alan to the small old man who opened the door.

"There's no one 'ere by that name, sir."

"Tell Archie Mallory that Sir Alan Burton of Scotland Yard is here," said Sir Alan, stepping inside the foyer and beginning to shrug out of his overcoat.

In a moment an inner door opened and Archie Mallory came out of a warmly lighted room behind the foyer. "Official or unofficial?" he asked.

"Entirely official," said Sir Alan. "I require a bit of your time and the answers to some questions."

"About *my* business?"

"Let's hope not," said Sir Alan. "Indeed, I doubt it."

"Then come in, Sir Alan," said Mallory, gesturing toward the door that opened into his office behind the foyer.

Mallory led the way, limping on the artificial leg that had exempted him from national service in this war and enabled him to remain in London, produce musical shows, operate a gaming club, and generally prosper. Except for the artificial leg—the knee joint of which squeaked as he walked—he was a well-put-together, handsome man—black hair, heavy black eyebrows, blue eyes, a cleft chin. He wore a well-cut single-breasted tuxedo.

"Have a chair, Sir Alan," said Mallory when they were inside his office. Despite his urbanity, he spoke in a thin, nasal voice, and strove to overcome an East London accent. "Whisky?"

"Yes, thank you," said Sir Alan.

Mallory swung his way to his bar and poured two drinks. "You say you would like to ask me some questions?"

"Are you aware of the death of Sir Anthony Brooke-Hardinge?" Sir Alan asked.

"My Lord, no! Tony? My God! How!"

"He was murdered. Please regard the matter as confidential."

"Murdered! By—Oh, no! If you're here to ask me if I know anything about it, the answer is no."

"I didn't think you did, Archie. I just want some information about a few people."

Mallory walked behind his desk, stopping for a moment to hand Sir Alan his drink. He sat down.

"Sure," he said. "David Clicker, now known as Desmond. What would you like to know about him?"

"First I'd like to know why you mention him so quickly."

"Oh, not to accuse him," said Mallory. "But it's no secret in the West End that Tony was backing some of Desmond's shows. I guess they called themselves partners."

"I know that," said Sir Alan. "What do you know about Laura Hodges?"

"What do you want to know about her?"

"Anything you can tell me."

"London girl, she is," said Mallory, raising his glass and taking a sip of whisky. "Wanted to be a singer, she hadn't got the voice. Wanted to be an actress, she hadn't got the talent. She had small parts in two plays. Pretty, of course, but wooden on stage. Then she decided she would be a dancer, and I don't know if she has any talent for that. She took some training and performed in one of the revues at the Prince of Wales—you know, in a couple of scraps of rayon, nothing more. Tony spotted her somehow—I don't know how—and she caught his fancy. He took her out of the show and told her he'd find her a part in something better. That was almost two years ago."

"Did he really try to find her a part?" asked Sir Alan.

"I don't know, but I doubt it. Why should he? He had what he wanted of her. If he promoted her into a stage star, he'd only lose her."

"He bought her a lot of expensive clothes."

"Of course he did. That was Tony's style. It was known in some quarters that she was his girl, and he wouldn't have her looking shabby."

"Who are her friends?" asked Sir Alan.

"She has two special friends that I know of," said Mallory. "A brother, to start with. Stanley Hodges. Then I think she's also a special friend of Ken Kane."

"Who are they? What do they do?"

"The brother hangs around the theaters. He'll do anything, so long as it has to do with theater. Wounded in the navy in 'thirty-nine, so he's exempt from further duty. Ken Kane is a dancer. He's dancing at the Prince of Wales tonight. You know the sort—top hat, white tie, tails, lots of bouncing around the stage with a glued-on smile. Stanley Hodges and Ken Kane have written a show, that they've carried to every producer in London—to most of us half a dozen times. They keep changing it, working it up. I keep saying no, but they refuse to give it up."

"And Laura . . . ?"

"I'd guess Ken Kane is what she has in reserve, when Sir Anthony Brooke-Hardinge tires of her. Now, of course—"

"Yes," said Sir Alan. "Now, of course, she has him to fall back on. Tell me something, Archie. Would you engage her to dance in a show of yours?"

Mallory pursed his lips and considered. "Without she slept with me, you mean . . . Well, maybe. Not in a featured part, I'll tell you that, but in a chorus line . . . Actually, she's too short for that; we need taller girls. As a nude maybe. You know—near nude." He shook his head. "The problem is that I have my choice of a thousand girls."

"Rather tragic, isn't it?" said Sir Alan glumly.

"Is she suspected of killing him?"

"Yes, she's that," said Sir Alan, "but I was thinking of how she could arrange her life now. Girls who elect to do what she's done become shopworn very soon. The next man who takes her in is not likely to offer her the lavish style of living she had with Sir Anthony.''

"Young people with little talent have a difficult life in the theater," said Mallory. "As Ken Kane ages, he's going to have a hard time finding work, and he's more talented than either Laura or her brother.''

Sir Alan finished his whisky and put the glass aside. "I can't help but feel sorry for her," he said.

6

A reporter for the *Telegraph* took Tommy Thompson aside just before Mrs. Roosevelt returned to the car for the drive back to Buckingham Palace.

"Remarkable woman," he said. He shook his head. "A day like today—"

"What about today?" Tommy asked.

"Why, she shook every hand extended toward her," he said. "Answered a thousand questions. *Asked* a thousand, and seemed to be interested in *everything*. She must be exhausted. Is tomorrow a day of rest for her?"

"Tomorrow is a day like today," said Tommy.

"Well, anyway, she'll get a nap now," the reporter persisted.

Tommy shook her head. "She hasn't written her column, and she has letters to write as well. And of course this evening she is guest at another state dinner."

That dinner was for the Labour Party members of the wartime coalition government. Mrs. Roosevelt found them easier to talk to than Winston Churchill.

She particularly enjoyed big, gruff Ernest Bevin

and confided in him that Elliott, who had been something of an American Anglophobe when he arrived in England, had come to respect the English people and to admire English ways. "When this war is over, our two peoples will know each other better than ever before," she said. "Because so many young Americans have spent so much time here. We will be a great English-speaking family."

"Some of your young men have been so friendly," said Bevin with a smile, "that we will be a family in more ways than we anticipated."

After dinner, Mrs. Roosevelt found Sir Alan Burton waiting in her suite for her. He stood with his back to her weak, cheerless fire, trying vainly to find some warmth.

"I should have been with you all day," he said. "Instead, I have been pursuing some leads in the matter of the death of Sir Anthony Brooke-Hardinge. I suppose the other chaps guarded you competently."

"Quite competently," she said. "Actually, I see no reason why I should be guarded. I saw no one today but friendly people."

"Somehow," he said, "you have avoided all our German spies. Unfriendly of them not to come out to greet you. Unfriendly, but to your good fortune."

She sat down. Having brought only one evening dress to England, she was wearing again the pale-green silk she had worn last night.

"I've been given a code name," she said. "Do you realize that?"

"Yes," he said. "In all radio and telephonic communication you are to be called 'Rover.' Actually, I think the word was suggested for you by the President. I assume, therefore, it is complimentary.''

"Possibly it is," she said. "Have you learned anything new?"

"One or two things," he said. "The autopsy turned up nothing surprising. Sir Anthony had drunk a considerable amount of whisky shortly before he died. And there is something curious about that. His fingerprints were not found on the whisky bottle in the sitting room."

"Perhaps Wen Yung had served him," she suggested.

"No. That's something else odd. Wen Yung's prints were not on the bottle either. Mine were on it. Desmond's were on it. Lady Letitia's. And Duggs's. And that's all."

"Miss Hodges?"

"No. Her fingerprints were on the gin bottle, on the seltzer bottle, and on some of the glasses. Her fingerprints are to be found all over the apartment, indeed—which is consistent with her having lived there. But her fingerprints were not on the whisky bottle."

"Meaning that someone wiped the prints off the whisky bottle and the vodka bottle," said Mrs. Roosevelt. "Then the guests arrived and poured whisky, putting their prints on that bottle. No one drank vodka, leaving that bottle clean."

"Exactly," said Sir Alan.

She frowned. "Now . . . Let's see. When the first guest arrived—"

"Which was I," he interrupted.

"When the first guest arrived," she went on, "two of the bottles on the bar were clean of all finger-prints. Why? The only reason that occurs to me is to suppose that someone other than last night's guests came to the apartment before the guests arrived, touched those two bottles and thus put fingerprints on them, and then wiped them off. That suggests someone whose presence in the apartment could not be satisfactorily explained—someone who had no invitation to be there last night.''

''My own thoughts are along the same line,'' said Sir Alan. ''And I have taken a great liberty. I hope you will forgive me.''

''What's that, Sir Alan?''

''I invited someone to come here tonight and meet you, and I communicated the invitation in your name. She will be here presently, I think.''

''Who?''

''Alexandra Dudley, Countess of Stanhope. I realize the name means nothing to you, so let me explain. Searching Sir Anthony's London house this morning, I came across an album containing nude photographs of a substantial number of women with whom he seems to have had amorous relationships. One of them is Alexandra, Countess of Stanhope. Miss Hodges, who was with me at the time, identified her as the woman who may well have replaced Miss Hodges in Sir Anthony's affections.''

''But why have her come here?''

''She is a great-granddaughter of Queen Victoria,'' said Sir Alan. ''A member of the royal family. It would be rather awkward for me to summon her for interrogation. But—''

''So you deceived her,'' said Mrs. Roosevelt.

''As I said, I have taken a great liberty.''

''Is this lady a suspect?''

''Allow me to give you some facts. The apartment

contained a hotch-potch of fingerprints. Sir Anthony's of course, everywhere. Laura Hodges's and Wen Yung's, similarly everywhere. Then, of course, those of last night's guests. But in addition, there were a few unidentified prints. One of the unidentified sets turned out to be the fingerprints of Countess Alexandra.''

"If you found her nude picture in his album, obviously he was intimate with her, and obviously she visited him in the Palace.''

"A satisfactory explanation except for one thing," said Sir Alan. "The Countess's fingerprints were found on a Chinese bronze figurine standing in the cabinet—indeed, on the very shelf—where the jade Buddha had been kept.''

"Oh, dear!''

"Her prints were also found on a bottle of Napoleon brandy, which is not so significant. What is more, she was in the Palace yesterday evening. The officer on duty let her in and out.''

"You must question her, I suppose,'' said Mrs. Roosevelt.

"I feel obligated to question her.''

"Well,'' said Mrs. Roosevelt, "if I am receiving one of the King's cousins—''

"Uh, second or third cousin, ma'am.''

"—then I am entitled to burn a few lumps of coal. And a pot of coffee might not be inappropriate.''

"I shall order them,'' said Sir Alan as he picked up a telephone.

The Countess Alexandra was a surprise to Mrs. Roosevelt, though of course not to Sir Alan, who had seen her picture. She was not the tall, gray, bosomy, diamond-bedecked woman of Mrs. Roosevelt's image but a young, smiling woman with bright red hair. Her pale blue eyes were full of mirth, her skin was almost white, though sprinkled liberally with orangish freckles. She wore an emerald-green wool coat with a fur collar, a matching hat with a wisp of fur as a band. When she put her coat and hat aside, she revealed a form-fitting knit dress of the same color and seemed well aware that the green afforded a flattering contrast to her skin and hair. Her only jewelry were small emerald earrings and a gold necklace set with a single larger emerald.

The sitting room was not yet comfortably warm, but the fire was burning and promised relief from the chill. The servants had also brought coffee in a silver service. After introductions and pleasantries, Mrs. Roosevelt poured coffee, and they sat down as close to the fire as possible.

"It is an awkward hour to have invited you here," said Mrs. Roosevelt to Countess Alexandra. "I hope you don't mind."

"I should have gladly come at three in the morning for the opportunity to meet you," said the Countess in high, Oxford-accented tones. She sat in one of the two wing chairs facing the fire, glancing curiously from time to time at Sir Alan, obviously wondering why Mrs. Roosevelt's bodyguard remained hovering behind her chair. "Still, I *am* curious about the invitation."

"I owe you an abject apology," said Mrs. Roosevelt. "I am playing the role of officious intermeddler in the investigation of the death of Sir Anthony Brooke-Hardinge. Sir Alan Burton is officially involved. We hope you will not object to hearing a few questions about Sir Anthony—that is, about your relationship with him.''

''I know he is dead,'' said the Countess. ''In mysterious circumstances. What happened is being kept secret.''

''May we trust you with the secret, My Lady?'' asked Sir Alan.

''You want my pledge that I will not reveal what's not been officially revealed? You have it.''

''I am sorry to have to tell you this,'' said Mrs. Roosevelt gently, ''but Sir Anthony was murdered.''

The laughter had disappeared from the Countess's eyes, but it was not replaced by any sign of shock or grief. ''I am hardly surprised,'' she said quietly.

''Why do you say that?''

''Sir Anthony lived a life very different from what His Majesty supposed when he made him an equerry— very different from what I had supposed before I came to know him well.''

''It has been said by one of the persons we have interrogated that you were perhaps engaged to be married to Sir Anthony,'' said Sir Alan. ''Is that true?''

''That is not true,'' said the Countess.

''I must tell you,'' said Sir Alan, ''that in the course of searching Sir Anthony's house in Belgravia this morning I came upon a photograph album containing a photograph of yourself, My Lady. Allow me to assure you that I have placed the album in a sealed packet in my office at Scotland Yard, from which it will not be removed unless it becomes important evidence.''

Countess Alexandra blushed and lowered her eyes. ''What can I say?'' She shrugged.

"Have you any idea where the negatives are?" he asked.

She shook her head. "I hope you find them—and seal them up, too."

"He made the photographs himself?" asked Sir Alan.

"Yes."

"It requires no explanation," he said.

Her eyes were expressive, and now they hardened with annoyance. "What does require explanation," she said, "is why I am interrogated. Am I a suspect?"

"Not really, I suppose," said Sir Alan. "You will perhaps understand that when a nude photograph of a lady of your rank is found in a murdered man's album of nude photographs of actresses, shop girls, and the like, a question does arise as to the nature of the relationship."

She sighed. "Did you know Sir Anthony?"

"No, I didn't," said Sir Alan. "And, of course, Mrs. Roosevelt did not know him."

Countess Alexandra nodded. "He was a man of great charm. I am sure he worked hard at developing it. He was a sportsman, a race-car driver, a yachtsman. He was a connoisseur of foods, wines, art, theater. To be escorted by him to an evening at the theater or to a shooting weekend or a regatta . . . well, it was always a memorable experience—one which of course remained quite impossible so long as he was married to Letitia. But once she was guilty of so grotesque an indiscretion as to lead to the divorce . . . well, you see. Six months after the divorce he invited me to go out with him. I could not. I explained to him that my father would make my life miserable if I kept company with a divorced man. He laughed, and four months after my father died and I inherited the title—which was a year ago—Sir Anthony telephoned and asked me if the impediment to our seeing each other had been removed. I said it had. I enjoyed my evening with him, and when he invited me again I accepted.''

"Did it become a romance? Did you ever think of marrying him?" asked Mrs. Roosevelt.

"I did, yes. After a few months of seeing him occasionally, I . . . I agreed to that which can only be described indelicately. You know what I mean. And I was glad I did. He was a marvelous man, I thought. Among the things I consented to do was pose for the photographs. When later I discovered that my photograph had gone into an album, in company with many other such photographs . . . well, you can imagine. It was the first defect I discovered in his character.''

"Then you discovered others?" asked Mrs. Roosevelt.

"Yes, I did. When I upbraided him about keeping my picture in such an album, he laughed; and then he proceeded to leaf through the album and to name and describe every young woman pictured there. As you can testify, Sir Alan, my own photograph might be described as . . . artistic. Many of the others were vulgar.''

"That is true," said Sir Alan gravely.

"I found myself part of a *collection!*" she said indignantly, her voice rising.

"And then you broke off the relationship?"

Countess Alexandra blushed and frowned. "Well, no. Not entirely, but I ceased to think of any possibility of marriage with him. On the other hand, he was such a . . . such a *companionable* man. I

continued to see him from time to time. And to do
. . . what we did.''

"Did you find other faults in his character?'' asked
Mrs. Roosevelt.

"Well, he was a great braggart.''

"About his exploits with other young women?''

"Yes. And about the way he rid himself of Letitia.
He came to have cause to regret his great victory
over her, of course.''

"What of stolen goods?'' asked Sir Alan.

The Countess shook her head. "What stolen goods?
I've no idea what you mean.''

"Well, how did you suppose he acquired the Turner
that hangs in the library in the house on Eaton
Square?'' asked Sir Alan.

"Turner?''

"The large painting in the library.''

"Oh. Of the Thames, of the sailboats. Is that
valuable?'' Countess Alexandra asked innocently.

"It's by Turner,'' said Sir Alan. "It's worth twenty
thousand pounds, maybe more. It was stolen some
time ago. Sir Anthony paid three thousand pounds
for it, we are told—another fact about which he
enjoyed boasting. He never told you?''

She shook her head firmly, pursing her lips
tightly.

"The house has many stolen items in it, as does
the apartment here in the Palace. You didn't know?''

The Countess shook her head again. "I swear I did
not,'' she muttered.

Sir Alan, who during most of this conversation had
stood behind the chairs occupied by Mrs. Roosevelt
and the Countess, now stepped around, nearer the

fire. "Tell me, My Lady," he said. "Did you ever visit Sir Anthony in his apartment here?"

"Never," she said. "I could not imagine doing what we did under the King's roof!"

"I see. So you have never been in his rooms in Buckingham Palace?"

"No," she insisted. "Never."

"I am afraid then that I am compelled to ask you a somewhat unfriendly question," said Sir Alan. "If you have never been in those rooms, how do you explain our investigators having found your fingerprints in two places in those rooms?"

"I have never been there," she persisted flatly.

"Then you can offer no explanation for your fingerprints?"

"I might be able to, if you would tell me where you found them."

"Very well," said Sir Alan. "On an Oriental figurine of bronze, also stolen property, which sat on a shelf beside an extremely valuable jade Buddha that was also stolen and is now missing. Besides that, on a bottle of Napoleon brandy."

Countess Alexandra spoke to Mrs. Roosevelt. "He moved items from Eaton Square to the Palace and back. He was much absorbed in his collections."

"The brandy, then?" asked Sir Alan.

She shook her head sadly. "I don't know."

"When were you last in the Palace?"

"Yesterday," she said. "Late afternoon. Early evening."

"Yes. Your name appears on the record at the Pimlico entry. You arrived at six, left at half past eight."

"In other words," she said, "I was here when Sir Anthony was murdered. Do I guess right?"

"He was not seen alive after eight o'clock," said Sir Alan. "His body was found about half past nine."

"You can check my whereabouts very easily," said Countess Alexandra. "I spent the time with the princesses. They and other children will play in a Christmas drama to be staged at Windsor. We have begun to choose children for the roles, to design costumes and scenery, and Princess Elizabeth has already begun learning her part. I spend two hours with them each Friday afternoon."

"I hope," said Mrs. Roosevelt, "it will not be necessary to inquire of the princesses. I assume—"

"There were others present," said Countess Alexandra.

"Then one final question, if I may," said Sir Alan. "The negatives of the photographs have in fact been found— except for yours, My Lady. Can you explain that?"

"I wish I could. It chills me to think the negatives of those pictures might be—"

"Might be in the hands of someone who would misuse them."

"Yes."

"Do you know Miss Laura Hodges?" asked Mrs. Roosevelt.

The Countess shook her head. "I know who she is. I've seen *her* pictures. I've seen her clothes hanging in the house on Eaton Square. And her jewelry. Sir Anthony insisted he only let her wear the more valuable pieces, that they were not gifts to her. I imagine he had to pry them out of her hands to get them back."

"What valuable pieces?" Sir Alan asked. "The most valuable piece I saw this morning was valued by an insurance investigator at one hundred twenty-five pounds."

"There were pieces worth five hundred pounds," said Lady Alexandra.

Sir Alan sighed. "I see. The case takes on still another complexity."

"I dislike leaving London with this mystery unsolved," said Sir Alan when Countess Alexandra had gone.

"You should stay here and solve it," said Mrs. Roosevelt.

"My assignment is to accompany you," said Sir Alan. "I asked for that assignment, I was given it; I asked to be reinstated in it even though I was suspected in the Brooke-Hardinge murder, and I *was* reinstated as a concession by Lord William Duncan. I can hardly ask to be relieved now."

"In any event," she said, "we still have a little time. I am remaining in London a few more days, although I will be moving from Buckingham Palace tomorrow, as you know. Our ambassador, Mr. Winant, has kindly made his flat available to Tommy and me, and we shall stay there until I go down to Chequers to visit Mr. and Mrs. Churchill. And after the Chequers visit I shall begin my round of visits to American soldiers and airmen in Britain."

"I have reviewed your schedule," he said, amusing her by pronouncing "schedule" in the English way, "shedyool." He shook his head. "Clubs, factories, hospitals, orphanages—before you leave London —then more of the same, plus camps and aerodromes, throughout the United Kingdom. I despair being able to keep up with you.''

He was aware that her attention was not focused on his statement.

"Sir Alan," she said. "Do you ever experience what might be called nagging insights? I mean, does some fact ever nag at your subconscious, as though it were urging you to recognize it and assign to it its appropriate significance.''

"If we may believe Sir Arthur Conan Doyle,'' said Sir Alan, "that is one of the chief props of criminal investigation.''

"Yes. Well, I am troubled with the idea that I overlooked a fact of some considerable consequence when we were looking around Sir Anthony's rooms yesterday. Is it possible that we could have another look, tonight?''

"There is no reason why we shouldn't,'' said Sir Alan, "but may I suggest you change into something more suitable for night prowling?''

She grinned and laughed. "Of course, Sir Alan.''

Warmly dressed in a black wool suit with a gray sweater, Mrs. Roosevelt stood with Sir Alan as he turned the key in the door to the Brooke-Hardinge suite. Stepping inside ahead of her, he switched on the lights, then rushed across the sitting room to close the blackout curtains. As she looked around he closed all the curtains.

Without coal fires blazing, the apartment was not only cold; it was barely lit. The flickering yellow glow of the flames had lent the rooms a welcoming air—now it was eerily silent.

"Who has been in these rooms since last night?" she asked.

"I was here this afternoon," he said. "After I saw the photograph album this morning, I returned to look for the negatives. Uh . . . Since I remain a suspect, I was accompanied by a junior-grade detective. Other than that, no one has been here. You saw the notice on the door. The Palace staff would not think of entering in violation of that notice, and they have the only keys other than the ones I am carrying."

"The ones Miss Hodges gave you last night."

"Yes."

"Except for the negatives, what has been removed?" she asked.

"Nothing."

"Everything should be in place as it was last night."

"Yes."

"It isn't," said Mrs. Roosevelt.

"No?"

"Look. The fire screen has been moved. Someone has been poking in the ashes. Look at the ash scattered over the hearth."

"It wasn't that way when I was here looking for the negatives."

"And you found them in . . . ?"

"They were in a box in a locked drawer of his desk. I forced the lock with a tool fetched along by my junior detective. You can see."

"You are certain the ashes hadn't been disturbed and scattered," she said.

"No, no. I'd have noticed that. Someone has been here since."

"We should look in the library," she said.

They entered the library. The bloodstains remained on the couch, rug, and floor. They carefully compared the present position of everything as they had seen it the previous night. The fire screen had not been moved, nor the ashes disturbed. Nothing, so far as they could see, was changed.

"The bedroom—*Sir Alan!*"

Someone had flushed the toilet. The rush of water echoed through the rooms. Sir Alan ran through the bedroom door toward the door between the bedroom and bathroom. Mrs. Roosevelt stepped into the door between the library and sitting room just in time to see a black-clad figure—heavy coat, trousers, hat, gloves—run from the bathroom across the foyer into the kitchen.

"In the kitchen!" she screamed.

They had left the door open between the foyer and sitting room, and she saw the black figure throw open the kitchen door and run across the foyer. For an instant he was stopped by the closed door between the foyer and the long corridor outside, but he wrenched it open and ran through, kicking it shut behind him.

Sir Alan ran from the bathroom and through the kitchen—the same route the black-clad figure had taken.

"Damn!" he grunted as he twisted the knob of the outer door. "Damn!" He fumbled in his pocket for the key. "He stopped long enough to lock it from outside. *Damn!*"

He turned the key in the lock and kicked the door open. Mrs. Roosevelt followed him into the corridor, but the figure was nowhere in sight.

"Telephone!" cried Sir Alan as he ran back into

the rooms. In a moment he was on the telephone alerting the Palace security forces to the presence of a burglar in Buckingham Palace.

They did not find him. Within two minutes the apartment was swarming with Palace security officers— until Sir Alan had to order most of them out, lest they destroy evidence.

"The odd thing is that the bathroom floor is wet," said Sir Alan to Mrs. Roosevelt.

"What is odd to me is that our burglar flushed the toilet," she said. "Surely he heard us."

She stood looking at the old-fashioned toilet, with tank high on the wall, flushed by pulling on a chain. What Sir Alan had said was true: several large puddles of water stood on the tile floor.

"He was in here when we arrived," said Sir Alan. "In the dark. He must have entered with a key. Obviously, he knew the Palace well; he did not leave the Palace through the private door that could be opened by Sir Anthony's other key—because when I telephoned the security station, I told them to block that exit. I suspect he came in that way, but knew there are other ways to get *out*."

"Our questions," she said, "are what he was looking for in the ashes in the fireplace and what he was doing in the bathroom."

"Precisely," said Sir Alan.

She looked up at the tank on the wall, then down at the toilet seat, The old toilet had only a seat, with no lid. "The Buddha," she said suddenly, pointing up at the tank. "It was hidden in the toilet tank! In the water—which he splashed out as he recovered it. Look at the scuff marks on the seat! He was standing on the seat, fishing the Buddha out of the tank. He must have lost his balance and instinctively grabbed the chain to stop himself from falling.''

"Did he get it, then?" asked Sir Alan. "Is the Buddha still there?"

He dragged in a kitchen chair and ordered a tall officer to climb and look down in the tank. The jade Buddha was not there.

Mrs. Roosevelt and Sir Alan sat down on the couch in the sitting room. It was now well past midnight—Sunday, October 25, 1942. During the day and evening she had heard reports of the battle raging at El Alamein. Within two weeks, she knew, many of the American troops she was about to visit would be landed on the northwest coast of Africa, in Algeria and Morocco; and the first major American commitment of men to battle against Hitler would begin.

She could give little more time to this murder mystery—and only hours like this. It was a diversion for her, she had to admit: an odd diversion, and maybe one it was wrong for her to take. Yet, it was stimulating to give some measure of thought to it.

"If Sir Anthony was killed for the Buddha," said Sir Alan, "then why was it not simply taken away by the killer, immediately? Why did he hide it and return for it tonight?"

"We may assume, I think," she said, "that the murderer took from his body the keys to the private entry to the Palace and to this apartment."

"Whilst you are touring the city tomorrow," he

said, "I shall with your consent pursue some further
lines of inquiry."

"Do so, Sir Alan," she said. "By all means. But I
am convinced we are in possession now of all the
facts we need to solve the mystery."

7

Mrs. Roosevelt said farewell to King George, Queen Elizabeth, and the princesses on Sunday morning and moved into Ambassador Winant's apartment—as he had insisted she do, arguing it would be no inconvenience for him and his family to move into smaller quarters for a few days.

She began her scheduled round of visits in the London area.

"I am surrounded by faithful security people and am more than adequately protected," she told Sir Alan Burton. "Please continue your investigation of the Brooke-Hardinge murder as long as you can, before we leave London. My curiosity is nothing short of painful."

They talked in the back seat of a big car as she and Tommy Thompson were driven to the USO club on Piccadilly to meet scores of American servicemen and -women.

"You said we are in possession of enough facts to solve the mystery," said Sir Alan. "I am inclined to believe you are right. Yet, to solve it we must understand the facts correctly. And for now, I must confess, I do not."

"It is much like working a crossword puzzle," she suggested. "To make sense from one clue, you must study others, and in turn you cannot understand those clues until you have found the meaning of still more."

"The difference," said Sir Alan dryly, "is that a crossword puzzle has boundaries, whilst a mystery has none."

"I beg to differ," said Mrs. Roosevelt. "The mystery has its boundaries. It is, in the final analysis, self-contained."

After the car dropped Mrs. Roosevelt and Tommy Thompson on Piccadilly, the driver took Sir Alan on to Scotland Yard. He sat down at his desk, with his back to a view of the Thames, and picked up his telephone to inquire who was on duty that Sunday. In a few minutes Inspector Reginald Harrison, the white-haired man who had taken shorthand notes in Sir Anthony's kitchen, came into the office.

"Ah, Harrison. On duty into the small hours of Saturday morning and here again today?"

Harrison shrugged. "I'm a widower, sir. Son's in the army. Nobody at home. I volunteer for extra duty."

Sir Alan looked into the man's lined, pale face. "Well . . . Sorry, Harrison. I, uh—I left word that someone should check into the whereabouts of the several suspects in the Brooke-Hardinge murder. I mean, their whereabouts at the time last night when someone apparently lifted the jade Buddha out of the flush tank in Sir Anthony's loo."

"I heard about that," said Harrison. "Fortunate that Mrs. Roosevelt wasn't injured."

"So Lord William commented this morning," said

Sir Alan. "I should like to see how he would discourage her from being a part of this investigation." He sighed. "Anyway, has anyone reported on the several—"

"Yes, sir," said Harrison. "We have several reports. I'm afraid the substance of them is that none of the chief suspects can be accounted for during the hours after midnight last night. Mr. Duggs, for example, insists he was at home in bed; but since he lives alone and has no servants, he could have been out—who knows? Mr. Desmond says he was checking into his clubs and theaters. And maybe he was, but who can tell? He was about the streets, on the move. He could have—"

"Yes, yes. What of Letitia Brooke-Hardinge?"

Harrison allowed himself a weak smile. "I'm afraid it's in the nature of her business to move about rather secretly. She was away from her place of business for quite some time—delivering a young woman to a gentleman's hotel room, she says. Left about half past eleven."

"Did she name the gentleman? Has it been checked?"

"Yes. An American wire-service correspondent. He acknowledged—once he was promised the inquiry had nothing to do with him—that a young woman was brought to him last evening. The hotel is in Kensington. Lady Letitia had plenty of time to pop by the Palace on her way back to Mayfair, and who's the wiser?"

"And Countess Alexandra?"

"At home in bed. But—servants in bed, too, all fast asleep. She could have slipped out. No. I'm afraid none of them has a tight alibi. Except perhaps Laura Hodges. She says she was with her brother

Stanley and the stage dancer Ken Kane. They confirm it. Each of them would lie for her, though. Obviously.''

"Damn," grunted Sir Alan. "I would like to be relieved of *one* suspect at least.''

"The Yard is relieved of one, sir," said Harrison. "You are off the list, since you were with Mrs. Roosevelt when the tank chain was pulled.''

"Unless I was working in concert with one of the others," said Sir Alan.

"Anyway, sir, that's how it is. I've got some other—''

"Well, let's enter this on the chart," said Sir Alan. He flipped the cotton cover off a white board standing on an easel and wrote another line across it.

Sir Alan stepped back and stared thoughtfully at his chart. For now, he knew, it meant nothing. But if he kept building on it . . . If there could be just one big black NO on that final line, the number of suspects would be one fewer. But—

	Laura	Desmond	Duggs	Letitia	Alexandra
Invited?	?	Yes	Yes	Yes	No
Arrived:	?	9:04	9:07	8:57	?
Know Palace?	Yes	No	No	No	Yes
Opportunity?	Yes	Yes	Yes	Yes	?
Sat. night	?	?	?	?	?

"Two bits of information," said Harrison. "First, it seems that person or persons unknown entered Sir Anthony Brooke-Hardinge's house in Belgravia last night. Nothing stolen, apparently—at least nothing valuable enough to have been on the inventory. But the men charged with watching out for the house had left some indicators on the doors and windows. Someone entered through the front door, apparently with a key.''

"To steal nothing much, hmm? Except evidence. Have the house sealed, Harrison. We can't have this going on.''

"No, sir. I'll see to it. Now, the other bit of information is that the boys scooped all the ash out of the two fireplaces in Sir Anthony's suite in the Palace and brought it into the laboratory, as you ordered. Some interesting results.'' He handed over a type-written sheet:

Analysis of Fireplace Ash
Apartments, Sir Anthony Brooke-Hardinge
25/10/42

The contents of the fireplace in the library of the subject apartments contain nothing that appears out of the ordinary: the ash and cinders of bituminous coal, a small quantity of wood ash, a small quantity of paper ash.

The ash taken from the fireplace in the living room is of the same sort—with, however, the addition of a considerable quantity of paper ash and some bits of melted glass.

The paper ash is not that of newsprint but of paper of a somewhat higher quality. All of it is so thoroughly burned that it is not possible to say whether it bore writing or printing. It seems not to have been bound, however, since no traces of a book binding, for example, have been found.

It is not possible to estimate the quantity of

paper burned, except to say that it was more than a few sheets. Fifty or more sheets appear to have been burned. Substantial quantities of ash may have risen up the flue on the draught of hot combustion gases, so the whole quantity may have been hundreds of sheets.

The glass was found on the bricks of the hearth, beneath the grate. It consists of four small globules.

Two of these globules have been sent to the Maddox Glass Manufactory in Hempstead, together with a request for an estimate from them as to what sort of glass it is and how it may have been used.

"You were the first of the guests to arrive," said Harrison. "No one could have put fifty or more sheets of paper in the fire after you came in. Correct?"

"Correct," said Sir Alan.

"And the apartments were uncomfortably warm, with quantities of coal blazing in the fireplaces."

"Incinerating evidence, you think," said Sir Alan.

Harrison shrugged. "Why not?"

Sir Alan turned and looked out over the Thames, gray and choppy under a sky covered by low, wind-running clouds. The barrage balloons tugged at their tethers. "We had two possible motives: revenge and theft of the jade Buddha. Now we may have another: destruction of some sort of document. An incriminating document, do you suppose?"

"It would seem likely."

"Maybe it was not the Buddha that was hidden in the toilet tank," said Sir Alan. "Maybe it was something entirely different."

"Possibly," said Harrison. "Anyway, how did

our burglar of last night enter and leave Buckingham Palace? It had to be someone with knowledge of the Palace.''

"I am thinking in those terms, Harrison," said Sir Alan. "But let's look at something— In the first place, Sir Anthony Brooke-Hardinge could have given any number of people keys to his own private entrance to Buckingham Palace. In the second place, do we deceive ourselves with the innocent supposition that a clever man or woman, with motive and a bit of daring, cannot enter the Palace without authorization? I wish I could be that confident of Palace security.''

"You have just extended our list of suspects to the whole world, Sir Alan," said Harrison.

"No, Harrison. No. We must distinguish possibilities from probabilities. We must remind ourselves constantly that the improbable is not impossible. Our list of suspects remains intact. Probably one of them killed Sir Anthony. But let us not suppose it is impossible that someone else did it.''

Sir Alan meant to attend services at St. Margaret's Church at eleven, but just as he was leaving his office he had a call from the post office at Buckingham Palace—where, too, people were at work on Sunday morning. Instead of going to church, he had himself driven to the Palace.

"We thought Scotland Yard would be interested in this, Sir Alan," said a senior clerk, a bald man with little round eyeglasses. He handed to Sir Alan a letter addressed to Sir Anthony Brooke-Hardinge. "The name is one of those on your list.''

Sir Alan had earlier given the Palace post office a

list of the people to whom Laura Hodges said she had addressed Sir Anthony's invitations to the Friday-night supper party. He was to be notified if any more invitations were returned undelivered or if mail arrived from any of those addressees.

The envelope had been addressed in a typewriter and had been mailed from Aberdeen, Scotland, by Captain Gerald Exeter.

"Knife, if you please," said Sir Alan.

The clerk handed over a paper knife, and Sir Alan slit the envelope and pulled out the typed letter. It read:

> Tony, you are impossible! Join you and a few friends for supper, indeed! From Aberdeen? Would that I could.
>
> Seriously said, old boy, I know I can trust you not to have extended the invitation also to Cecilie. I should be distressed if you were to do that, in the circumstances. But I hope you and your friends have a jolly time and will lift a glass or two to me.
>
> Best and kindest regards,
> Jerry

The letterhead and address showed that the captain was stationed in Aberdeen with his regiment.

Sir Alan thanked the clerk. He went to the Palace security office and used a telephone there to put through a call to Captain Gerald Exeter. In a quarter of an hour the operators managed to reach the captain.

"Exeter? Senior Inspector Sir Alan Burton here. Scotland Yard."

"Scotland Yard?" asked the distant, metallic voice

that reached London over the wire. "Burton, you say?"

"Yes. I've a question or two to ask you, Captain Exeter. I assume you are personally acquainted with Sir Anthony Brooke-Hardinge."

"I am indeed. I count him among my best friends."

"Captain Exeter, I am going to give you a bit of information that is confidential. What I am about to tell you is not to be revealed. Sir Anthony Brooke-Hardinge is dead. He has been murdered."

"Tony? *Dead!* My God! What happened to him? Scotland Yard? My God, man! What happened to Tony?"

"He was murdered in his suite in Buckingham Palace, just before the supper party you were invited to attend and likely by one of the invited guests. For reasons of national security and morale, we are holding the information confidential, at least for the time being. I must ask you not to reveal anything I'm telling you."

"Does my wife know?"

"I suppose not, actually."

"Then I will ask you to do me a favor," said Captain Exeter. "I should not want Cecilie to learn of Tony's death from a stranger. The news will be most distressing to her, and I should prefer to tell her myself. I should like your consent to tell her, by telephone. I assume you know why."

Sir Alan did not, of course, know why. A suspicion dawned, and he determined to let the captain talk—to see if he would tell why without being asked. "She will understand the necessity of confidentiality?"

"I can assure you she will," said Captain Exeter.

"Then you have my consent. But please do emphasize—"

"I shall do so, Sir Alan, you may be sure."

"Very well. Can you give me a brief description of your wife, Captain Exeter? I mean, her personal appearance."

"You've found photographs of her among Tony's effects," said Captain Exeter ominously.

"Uh, yes," said Sir Alan. "You know about the photographs, then?"

"Yes. She told me. And Tony admitted he photographed her. I should have preferred he destroy those pictures, but I suppose I can understand why he didn't. You have seen the photographs?"

"I have impounded an album, Captain. It contains the photographs of several women."

"Ah, yes. Tony . . . well. You wish to know which of the photographs are those of Cecilie?"

"Yes."

"Very well," said Captain Exeter, though a new tone of reluctance came through the telephone line. "She is a quite attractive woman, actually—some years younger than myself. I am forty-two years old. Cecilie has dark hair and brown eyes. Regular features, I suppose one would say. A good figure. Tony Brooke-Hardinge found her attractive, obviously."

"And there was, I suppose, an affair between them?"

"Yes. She confessed it all to me, and when I confronted Tony with the matter, he was a gentleman about it. He apologized effusively and promised never to see her again. I accepted his apology and his word. I could, after all, understand; and I continued to count him a friend. I do wish he'd destroyed the photographs, as he promised to do.''

"I assure you, Captain, they will remain in a sealed file at Scotland Yard and will be destroyed by us as soon as we are certain they need not become evidence in the case.''

"Who killed him? And why? Do you have any idea?''

"We've several suspects,'' said Sir Alan. "I believe I can assure you the matter has not the remotest relationship to your wife's affair with him, and I think you'll not be embarrassed in any way.''

"Thank you,'' said the captain crisply. "But . . . Tony. Tony Brooke-Hardinge, of all people! Cecilie will be devastated.''

When he put down the telephone, Sir Alan went to his locked cabinet and retrieved the packet in which he had sealed Sir Anthony's photo album. He hadn't far to look. Reverse chronological order, Miss Hodges had said. Mrs. Exeter should be near the front of the book, if she were there at all. And she was, immediately after the photograph of Alexandra Dudley, Countess of Stanhope—who may have been Sir Anthony's most recent model or who was first as a matter of honor, since she was a countess.

In any event, the second photograph in the album—and the third and fourth—were pictures of the woman Captain Exeter had described: handsome, dark-haired, dark eyes, a pretty face, and trim, full-busted figure. She had enjoyed posing, from the look of her pictures. Sir Alan made a note that this album and the negatives must be destroyed as soon as the mystery was solved.

*   *   *

Because it entertained servicemen, chiefly, the Prince of Wales Theatre was one of those that had received special permission to open on Sundays during the war. Men and women with twelve-hour passes flocked into Piccadilly Circus on Sunday afternoons and evenings, filling the seats of the Prince of Wales and other theaters, to enjoy fast, rhythmic revues featuring lots of bare skin.

Sir Alan arrived a little after noon. A good-sized crowd of servicemen was already queued before the box office, laughing and jostling each other in a friendly way. Sir Alan drew a few catcalls when he showed his Yard identification, but he turned and waved good-naturedly at the queue as he passed through the doors.

"There is a dancer performing here named Kane," he said to the wispy old man who led him inside the still empty theater. "Is that not correct?"

"Yes, Sir. Ken Kane. Our featured dancer."

"Backstage, is he?"

Sir Alan looked around. He had never been inside the Prince of Wales before, and was surprised at how small it was. The curtain was open, and he could see a group of women fussing about the stage, adjusting the set, sweeping the floor, shrieking at someone called Fred to direct some lights differently.

The old man led Sir Alan backstage. The Prince of Wales billed itself as "London's Folies Bergère," and he wondered if the chorines at the real Folies were as plain-looking before they were costumed and made up. Coming in the stage door, they were anything but glamorous: girls who might have been working in shops or waiting tables in restaurants.

Ken Kane sat at his dressing table, applying the stage makeup that looked effeminate and grotesque here but would make his face more expressive under the brilliant stage lights.

"Scotland Yard," he said. "Twice in one day. Laura was with me last night for a late supper after the show—as I told your man this morning."

"Yes, I've looked at the report," said Sir Alan. "My interest is in a different matter."

Ken Kane turned away from his mirror and regarded Sir Alan with skepticism verging on hostility. He was a trim young man, the sort that made you wonder how he had avoided military service. His blond hair was smoothly plastered to his scalp, so firmly that the teeth of his comb had left visible parallel lines. He put a cigarette in one corner of his mouth, and the other corner turned up in a faint smile that was closer to a sneer.

"I'll continue dressing," he said. "The show must go on, as they say."

"So it must, Mr. Kane. So it must. Tell me, though—putting aside your friendship with Miss Hodges—didn't you have a personal relationship with Sir Anthony Brooke-Hardinge?"

"I knew him," said Kane. "Is that a relationship?"

"Knew him in what context?"

Kane sighed. "I think you already know," he said wearily. "Stan Hodges and I have written a play, a musical show—a damn good one, too, if you don't mind my saying so. We've carried it to every theatrical producer in London, including David Clicker, recently known as Desmond, and Tony Brooke-Hardinge."

"Did he take an interest in your show?"

Kane shrugged. "More than some others. But he did not agree to fund it."

Ken Kane left his dressing table and stepped to a rack where his costume was hanging: white tie, tails, a top hat. He put aside a robe and began to dress.

"If it were produced, Miss Hodges would dance the leading role, would she not?" asked Sir Alan.

"Yes. I would hope so. And I would have the leading male role."

"Was that a sticking point? I mean, were producers less willing to produce the show because you wanted Miss Hodges for the female lead?"

Kane paused and cast an inquiring look at Sir Alan. "That was not the reason producers were hesitant," he said. "She is a talented girl."

"On the other hand," said Sir Alan, "your chances of seeing the show produced would have been better if you had not insisted that Miss Hodges—"

"Yes," Kane interrupted irritably. "Yes, I suppose so. But the show is to be a career-maker for all three of us. That has always been our understanding. We agreed to it."

"Are you in love with Miss Hodges?"

"When Sir Anthony Brooke-Hardinge was murdered," said Kane, "I was onstage here at the Prince of Wales, before a packed house. If you come for the evening show, you will see that there is no time between seven-thirty and ten-thirty when I could leave this theater. If you want to know if I was jealous of Tony Brooke-Hardinge's relationship with Laura, the answer is yes, damned right I was. But I was *here* when he was murdered."

"I am well aware of that, Mr. Kane," said Sir Alan. "We checked that point very early in the investigation. But tell me, Mr. Kane—was Miss Hodges's prospective role a sticky point with Sir Anthony?''

"Sir Anthony didn't believe she was a dancer," said Kane. "He did not appreciate her talent. But let me tell you something more, Sir Alan. He insisted to Laura that he *did*. He led her to believe that if our show—which, incidentally, is to be called *Star Blitz*—is staged, she would not only dance the lead but would be featured in every newspaper, every magazine, every radio show in the country. I never believed him on that point.''

"But the best he ever really offered her was a role in *Bottoms Up,* right?"

"Right. A chance to bare her bums in public."

"Last night? I know you've been questioned about this before, but . . .''

Kane was buttoning his waistcoat. "The show ends at about ten-thirty, say ten forty-five after curtain calls. I came backstage and found Laura waiting in my dressing room. Stan was here, too. By the time I changed, it was probably eleven. We walked to Ricardo's and ordered a late supper. I imagine it was almost quarter to one when we left. We separated on the street, and Laura went with me to my place. She is living with me, Sir Alan, since she has no digs in Buck House anymore."

Kane stood, shrugged into his black tailcoat, settled a high silk hat on his head, and grabbed an ebony walking stick from a shelf.

"P'raps I'll stand in the wings and watch you perform, Mr. Kane. Unless I am mistaken, the house is sold out."

* * *

The girls, who only a little while ago had come in off the street in gray coats and hats, danced all but naked onto the stage, singing a shrill tune, their faces dramatized by heavy makeup. They were visions they had not been when they came in.

Shortly they were followed by Ken Kane, tapping and pirouetting, banging his stick on the stage floor to emphasize his rhythm, grinning, leering, rolling his eyes.

"Sir Alan Burton."

Sir Alan turned and found himself facing David Desmond.

"Mr. Desmond. Do you own a part of this show, too?"

Desmond glanced toward the stage. "No. Just popped by to say hello to friends. I'm surprised to see you here."

"Maintaining His Majesty's peace and justice draws a man to peculiar places, Mr. Desmond," said Sir Alan.

"I can think of less pleasant places," said Desmond, glancing significantly at the chorus line dancing behind Ken Kane. "And more pleasant. Have you had lunch? May I invite you to have it at a club of mine?"

Sir Alan glanced at his watch. "I accept," he said.

The club had no name. It was above a restaurant on St. Martin's Lane. Walking through an inconspicuous door, guests emerged in a quiet, softly lighted clubroom, furnished with deep leather chairs and couches. Except that it was smaller and lacked the elegance of antique furniture and old paneling, drapery, and rugs, it might have been the quarters of one of London's traditional gentlemen's clubs.

It might have been, but plainly it wasn't. The bar ran along one wall of the room, and a dozen uniformed men sat on stools there, engaged in conversation with a comely barmaid who was naked above the waist. Other girls in corselets, showing their long legs and their ample bosoms pressed tightly upward, carried trays to the chairs and couches. Music and applause from an adjoining room intruded on the quiet one would have expected in a gentlemen's clubroom.

"I trust you won't call for me to be closed," said Desmond as he led Sir Alan to a pair of chairs facing a round table.

"Let us say I am here only unofficially," said Sir Alan.

"Whisky, Sir Alan?"

"If you please."

Desmond snapped his fingers at the bare-breasted girl behind the bar. "Whiskies, Sheila," he said. He smiled at Sir Alan. "Do you recognize any of the gentlemen at the bar?"

Sir Alan shook his head. "Can't say that I do."

"You don't, or you are being circumspect. The gentleman without much hair is General Eisenhower. He pops in occasionally, usually on Sundays, for a drink or two. I don't know the other officers with him, the Americans; but if I read the pips on their shoulders right, they are generals, too. Nice sort of fellow, Eisenhower. Bearing a heavy load, I imagine. Comes in here to get away from it all. Buys a round for his chaps. Quiet sort. A word or two with Sheila. Leaves her a nice tip each time."

"Americans . . ." murmured Sir Alan.

"Decent fellows, most of them. Away from home. Looking for a place to relax. Not always accepted in London clubs. I'm glad I can provide—"

"I dare say they pay well," Sir Alan interrupted.

"Why, no, Sir Alan. I operate this place as a patriotic duty." Desmond chuckled.

"Did Sir Anthony Brooke-Hardinge own a share?"

Desmond shook his head. "Not of this. No. Not his sort of thing. Wouldn't do, you know—a man with apartments in the Palace."

The barmaid had come from behind the bar to bring their drinks. As she leaned over them to place the glasses on the table, Sir Alan could not refrain from staring fleetingly at her naked breasts.

"A round on the house for General Eisenhower and his friends," said Desmond. "And give him my compliments—and those of my friend Sir Alan Burton of Scotland Yard."

The girl's eyes, which had moved on, returned to Sir Alan's face as she heard him identified as an inspector from Scotland Yard. She snapped her eyes away, though, after a moment and returned to the bar.

"You know what happened last night?" asked Sir Alan.

"Only as much as the officer who woke me this morning cared to tell me. Some new event, I gather— past midnight last night."

"Let me change the subject," said Sir Alan. "Did you know Lionel Foster?"

Desmond shook his head.

"Sir Anthony never mentioned him?"

"No, never."

"He was invited to Friday night's party."

"And didn't appear," said Desmond. "How fortunate for him. He avoided becoming a suspect."

"Foster has been dead for some months," said Sir Alan.

"Also murdered?"

"No. He was once a business associate of Sir Anthony's, years ago. Never mentioned him, hmm?"

"Not to me."

"Dead for six or eight months," said Sir Alan. "And still invited to Friday night's supper party. Odd, don't you think?"

Desmond shrugged. "I suppose so. You understand, the extent of my interest is any fact that diverts suspicion from me."

"Another point," said Sir Alan. "What do you know about Sir Anthony's relationship with the handsome Alexandra?"

"The Countess? Everything," said Desmond. "Sir Tony was proud of getting his hands on her. Spoke of marrying her, actually."

"Did he, by any chance, give you her photos?"

"No, but I've seen them. Jolly girl, the Countess Alexandra. Quite jolly."

"Was he blackmailing her?"

Desmond laughed. "No. No, Sir Alan. You're off on the wrong track. In the first place, he wanted to marry her. He wanted to marry a countess. He wanted a peerage of his own, but if he couldn't get it, he would marry into one. Anyway, I don't think Alexandra Dudley is the sort of woman who'd be blackmailed. Descended from the Elizabethan Dudleys, you know. Don't overlook her as a suspect, Sir Alan. Tony abused her, and she is—in my humble estimation

—quite capable, either of doing Tony in herself or of employing someone to do it.''

''He showed you her photos?''

''He showed them to me and others. He was immensely proud of them—not of the photos, you understand, but of having been able to undress Alexandra, Countess of Stanhope, and pose her naked before his camera. It wasn't in Tony's nature to have been pleased by his artistic achievement with the camera, but it was like him to gloat over his conquest of the woman.''

''I am becoming a little weary, to be altogether frank,'' said Sir Alan, ''of hearing animadversions on the character of Sir Anthony Brooke-Hardinge. I wonder what he might have had to say in his own defense.''

''Something plausible and convincing, you may be certain,'' said Desmond.

Sir Alan sipped whisky. ''Was there ever any chance,'' he asked, ''that you and Sir Anthony would have produced the show written by Ken Kane and Stanley Hodges?''

Desmond shrugged. *''Star Blitz,''* he said. ''It is not impossible. The two boys have kept working at it, revising it, improving it, so that it's not a bad property. Not at all.''

''Was there ever any chance you would have starred Laura Hodges?''

''That is one of the difficulties with *Star Blitz*,'' said Desmond. ''The boys insist the show must co-star Ken Kane and Laura Hodges. That discourages most producers.''

''A problem, hmm?''

''Yes, quite. Ken Kane is a second-rate dancer.''

"And Laura Hodges is no dancer at all, I suppose," said Sir Alan. "I mean, she seems to have auditioned a great deal—and never got a role."

"She never got a role because Tony had put the word around that she was *not* to get any," said Desmond, turning down the corners of his mouth. "He wanted her for himself."

"Is this a fact?" asked Sir Alan. "Is it a fact, or just a supposition?"

"It's a fact," said Desmond. He rose, extended his hand, and beckoned General Eisenhower to stop at their table as he passed on his way out of the club. "General," he said. "Let me introduce Sir Alan Burton of Scotland Yard."

General Eisenhower shook Desmond's hand, then Sir Alan's. His smile failed to conceal that he was mystified as to why he should be introduced to this detective.

"It's a pleasure to meet you, General," said Sir Alan. "We may be seeing each other again. I have been assigned as bodyguard for Mrs. Roosevelt during her stay in England."

"Ah," said Eisenhower. "Well, guard her carefully, Sir Alan. She's a national treasure."

When the Americans were gone, Sir Alan returned to the subject of Laura Hodges as a dancer. "Are you telling me that Sir Anthony deliberately destroyed the young woman's career, after making her believe he was promoting it?"

"Ah, well, I wouldn't want to make animadversions on the character of Sir Anthony Brooke-Hardinge," said Desmond wryly.

"What prospects did she have?" asked Sir Alan, letting the sarcasm slide past him without notice. "I mean, what would her career prospects have been if Sir Anthony had not discouraged producers from hiring her?''

"Who knows? She's pretty. She has a nice personality. Careers have been built on that and nothing more. Particularly if a girl has a sponsor. Sir Alan—*I* could have made her a star. I could yet, maybe. Tony could have, but chose not to.''

"Built up her hopes—only to cast them down,'' Sir Alan mused, shaking his head.

Desmond turned up the palms of his hands. "Yet another aspersion cast on the character of the deceased,'' he said. "But, yes, I am telling you that. He loved to use power that way—enjoyed being able to manipulate other people's lives.''

"Everyone seems to agree on that,'' said Sir Alan. "So allow me to change the subject once more. How much did Sir Anthony tell you about Cecilie Exeter?''

Desmond shook his head. "I don't recall ever having heard the name.''

"Captain Gerald Exeter?''

"No. The name means nothing to me.''

Sir Alan raised his brows. "A recent conquest,'' he said. "The wife of one of his friends, apparently. Surely he boasted to you of—''

"Sir Alan,'' Desmond interrupted. "Tony and I were associated in business; we were not close personal friends. You must not suppose we were constantly together. He did his boasting over drinks. It has been some time, several months, since we spent an evening together. In fact, it was the last time when we spent such an evening that he showed me the photographs of the charming Countess of Stanhope. That was in April or May, I imagine. You say his conquest of this Cecilie was recent." He shrugged. "I'd have heard about it sooner or later, probably, but I hadn't heard of it yet."

Sir Alan rubbed his hands together. "So. Curious. Uh . . . I say, did you or did you not offer lunch?"

Mrs. Roosevelt returned to Ambassador Winant's flat late in the afternoon. She had spent an interesting day, during which she had spoken with dozens of American servicemen and had filled a small spiral-bound pad with notes—requests, complaints, the addresses of families to whom she would send notes. As they sat in the ambassador's living room, Tommy Thompson began copying those notes into a larger notebook, expanding on them so they would remember, when they were back in the White House, just what each serviceman had asked of the First Lady.

Several had complained that they had to go marching in cold, wet weather in thin cotton socks. Mrs. Roosevelt wrote a note to General Eisenhower, asking why the soldiers were not provided with wool socks. Only after she had written that note and handed it to Tommy to dispatch did she pick up the telephone to return Sir Alan Burton's call.

"A few minor things to report when you have time," he said when she reached him at Scotland Yard.

"Well . . . I am attending another dinner this evening," she said. "Perhaps afterward. I am sure we will be back here by ten."

"Unfortunately," said Sir Alan, "I have an appointment to interview Miss Hodges at ten-thirty. After-show-supper sort of thing, with her brother."

"I should like to be there when you talk with her."

"Would you like to join me?"

"Where is this supper?"

"Little restaurant in Mayfair. Allow me to come by with a car. We can readily keep a ten-thirty appointment if you return to the ambassador's apartment by, say, ten-fifteen."

"I shall have dined," said Mrs. Roosevelt, "but I look forward to spending an hour with you and Miss Hodges."

8

The restaurant to which a uniformed policeman drove Mrs. Roosevelt and Sir Alan Burton at ten-thirty that evening was called The New Kentish. It was a modest place, of only about a dozen tables, served by a late-middle-aged couple who were apparently the owners. A child who couldn't have been more than thirteen, perhaps their grandchild, helped them. The plate-glass windows in front had been blown in during the Blitz and had not been replaced, only covered with boards and isinglass. Each small round table was neatly set for four, with serviceable heavy ware spread on darned but clean cloths. Clear glass bulbs with glowing filaments cast a cheerful yellowish light.

"One has always been able to find a good meal here," Sir Alan said to Mrs. Roosevelt when they were seated. " 'T is not grand, as you can see, but—"

"It is delightful, Sir Alan," she said. "Like the restaurants I remember from my years in school here."

Fortunately no one recognized her. She had worn her black coat with the fox draped around her shoulders, a flat black hat with a bit of a veil, and a skirt and sweater. She kept her coat on at the table, as all

159

the women in the restaurant were doing. The dozen or so people eating at the other tables saw no reason to take any particular notice of her.

"If you will forgive my telling you so, you look tired," said Sir Alan.

"Not physically," she said with a wan smile. "What I've done today was emotionally exhausting."

"Visit hospitals, did you?"

"One, yes. And an orphanage where they are caring for children whose homes were bombed. I guess what impressed me most was my talks with some workingmen in shops in Wapping. Some of them told me they'd had to keep working nights when raids were in progress."

"Yes," Sir Alan interjected. "If production had stopped every time the bombers came over, the Nazis would have beaten us. For the factory workers it was like being soldiers at the front—they had to stay at their posts even if shells were flying."

"They could hear bombs falling into neighborhoods nearby," she went on solemnly. "And knew those bombs were falling amidst their own homes. They had no way to be certain their families had reached shelters and couldn't be sure they would find their homes standing or their families alive when they left work."

"Yes," sighed Sir Alan. "And many of them found their worst fears realized. They went home and—" He stopped and shook his head. "Their courage—" Again he stopped and shook his head.

"And pride, too," she said quietly. "They know they won."

"Yes. We won."

"In a sense I wish I could have been here during

the Blitz," she said. "In another sense, I'm glad I wasn't, of course."

"Except for the nights when the bombers actually came over," he said, "it wasn't much different from what you see. We didn't go underground and stay there. Pubs were open. Theaters. Restaurants. Until the sirens sounded."

Mrs. Roosevelt glanced at her watch. "Is it possible that Miss Hodges will not come?"

"I don't know," he said. "But I'm going to order dinner. I've not had any yet, nothing since a sandwich I ate early this afternoon in an illegal club run by David Desmond. You, uh—"

"I'll have tea."

His food was on the table by the time Laura Hodges arrived, accompanied by her brother Stanley. She entered the restaurant with a haughty air, as if she were not accustomed to eating in such undistinguished places—dressed in a gray fur jacket and a deep-red knit woolen dress. She drew attention immediately.

"Ah, Mrs. Rose-vult," she said when she saw who was with Sir Alan. "How nice. May I present my brother, Stanley Hodges? Stanley, this is Mrs. Rose-vult, the wife of the President of the United States."

Stanley Hodges was a short, plump, pink-faced young man, walking with a cane. Mrs. Roosevelt remembered that he had been wounded very early in the war, while serving in the Royal Navy. He was dressed rather shabbily, in marked contrast to his sister. Chairs were drawn back, and he lowered himself stiffly.

"Rutabagas," said Sir Alan, noticing Stanley Hodges peering curiously at his plate. "Before the war they were grown to feed pigs. Now we eat them ourselves.''

"Actually," said Mrs. Roosevelt, "with butter, they are quite tasty."

"Sautéed in butter, pencil erasers are tasty," said Sir Alan. "If I had butter, I should assault the chef who melted it to cook rutabagas."

Laura Hodges looked up and saw the old proprietor coming with menus, but before he could reach them she smiled and asked, "A successful day of detective work, Sir Alan?"

"An interesting one. When you have ordered, I shall tell you."

The menu was limited, and both ordered the mutton that Sir Alan was having, and both asked for whiskies.

"A few curious developments in the case," said Sir Alan. "I haven't reported them to Mrs. Roosevelt, so she will be hearing them for the first time, too."

"I hope you are making progress," remarked Laura.

"Our laboratory analyzed the ashes from Sir Anthony's fireplaces," said Sir Alan. "Oddly, they found in the sitting-room fireplace an extraordinarily large quantity of paper ash, as though perhaps a hundred sheets of paper had been burned there. Do you have any idea what that was, Miss Hodges?"

She shook her head. "I have no idea. He did use the fireplaces as incinerators for his trash. Sometimes he burned his newspapers there, sometimes letters, and so on."

"An extraordinary amount of paper," said Sir Alan. "Can you think of anything he would have wished to destroy?"

She shook her head again.

"Or anything his murderer might have wished to destroy?"

"No, Sir Alan. In fact, I am not even aware of any large amount of paper in the apartments. Of course, he had many books—"

"It doesn't seem to have been books," Sir Alan interrupted. "Or newspapers. Some sort of document or documents."

"I can't imagine what it could have been," she repeated.

"Also, in the same fireplace were found four small globules of melted glass. What, if anything, does that suggest."

"Phials perhaps," she suggested. "Pill bottles."

Sir Alan nodded. "Perhaps. You are aware, are you not, that someone entered Sir Anthony's rooms last night and was interrupted there by Mrs. Roosevelt and myself?"

"We were questioned about it this morning."

"It is our theory," said Mrs. Roosevelt, "that the jade Buddha was hidden in the toilet tank, that the murderer returned to retrieve it, and that we surprised him—or her—in the act."

Laura nodded. "Sounds reasonable," she said.

Sir Alan frowned at the whiskies now put on the table and told the proprietor he would have one, too. Mrs. Roosevelt declined to join him.

"Tell us about your play, Mr. Hodges," said Mrs. Roosevelt to Stanley.

Stanley Hodges shrugged. "It has been rejected by every producer in the West End," he said sullenly.

"Including Sir Anthony Brooke-Hardinge?"

"Including Sir Anthony Brooke-Hardinge."

"Surely," said Sir Alan to Laura, "you could have exerted some influence."

"Not enough to get him to invest thousands of pounds," she said. "Anyway, I think the problem was Desmond. He didn't like it, and Tony relied on his judgment."

"I spoke with Mr. Kane this afternoon," said Sir Alan. "He describes *Star Blitz* as the key to all your careers."

Stanley spoke. "When I came out of the navy"—he pronounced it nye-vee—"with a game leg and nothing much ahead of me but hobbling around with a cane for the rest of my life, I decided I didn't want to spend my days as a wounded veteran: maybe a museum guard, maybe a traffic warden where children cross the streets. I know I've got *talent*, Sir Alan; many have acknowledged it; and the theater is my life. It's Laura's, too. Fortunately, we knew Ken Kane—"

"*I* knew Ken Kane," said Laura.

"Laura knew Ken Kane. He has marvelous experience in the theater, and agreed to work with us. Together we'd create a musical show that would establish us as top-rate theater people. Is it a dream? Of course it is, but—"

"But we all have our dreams," interrupted Mrs. Roosevelt. "And what good would our lives be without them—if you don't mind the cliché?"

"We wrote the show together, Ken and I, with the understanding that all three of us would benefit from it: Ken and Laura as the lead dancers, I as the writer and maybe the director. It's a damned fine show— funny, bright, with good songs. . . ." He shook his head. "Some people don't want to give new young talent a chance."

Sir Alan had listened to this talk about *Star Blitz* with an air of mild impatience, and he took Stanley's bitter little statement for an opportunity to change the subject. "I want to ask you about a couple of people, Miss Hodges," he said. "First, tell me what you can about Lionel Foster."

"Lionel Foster is dead."

"For how long?"

"I don't know. I only know he is dead because the invitation Tony had me address to him was returned by the post office."

"Why was he invited?" asked Sir Alan.

"For the same reason as everyone else," said Laura. "Tony knew Foster hated him. Foster served time in prison for his part in some kind of land-fraud scheme; but of course actually it was Tony who was behind it. Tony was scornful of Foster, called him a stupid man."

"Very well," said Sir Alan. "Then tell me about Cecilie Exeter."

Laura laughed. "You should ask *her*, actually."

"I'd rather not."

Laura shrugged. "She's an unhappy woman. Her husband is in the army, stationed in Scotland. He's a bit old for combat service, so he's with a unit that guards a part of the coastline, waiting for the German invasion that never came. He was a friend of Tony's, a yachtsman, before the war. He left Cecilie—and she's a quite good-looking woman, as you might expect—at home to look after her invalid father and two small boys. Tony had always admired her, and . . . Well, you can imagine what happened. For about three weeks, until she confessed to Captain Exeter . . . She's in the photo album, incidentally. You should take a look at her."

"I have," said Sir Alan.

"Can you imagine a woman submitting to that? During a three weeks' affair, particularly?"

"When did this affair occur?"

"August. September."

"And Sir Anthony told you all about it?"

"Yes. And he showed me her pictures. He was almost as proud of them as he was of the ones of Countess Alexandra."

"Have you finished for the night, Sir Alan?" Mrs. Roosevelt asked as they were driven back to the residence of the United States Ambassador.

"Not quite, I think," said Sir Alan. "I think I shall pay a call on Letitia Brooke-Hardinge. She keeps rather late hours, you know."

"May I accompany you?"

"Oh, Mrs. Roosevelt! She—I mean, you know what business she is in! I—"

"Sir Alan," Mrs. Roosevelt interrupted with a sly smile. "Surely she has a private parlor where one can meet with her discreetly."

"With a private entry," he said.

Mrs. Roosevelt waited in the car on Hertford Street while Sir Alan went inside the solid brick house to see if she could enter privately. After a moment he returned, and Letitia Brooke-Hardinge appeared in the door. Mrs. Roosevelt was guided into a handsomely furnished small parlor to the right of the entrance door, just as she had expected.

Letitia wore a lavender-and-white wool dress, with an unpretentious string of pearls around her neck. She invited Mrs. Roosevelt to take one of two Victorian chairs, upholstered in wine-colored plush, then said,

"I hardly expected ever to see the like of you here, Mrs. Roosevelt." Then she shrugged and smiled wryly. "No more, actually, than I expected ever to see the like of myself."

"Surely," said Mrs. Roosevelt, "there must have been other ways for you to earn a living."

"None so likely to subject Tony to painful embarrassment. My business is going to have to prosper as never before now that he is dead. As you will discover when you review his bank account—if you haven't already—Tony paid me a subsidy. That is, he paid me not to circulate the word that Letitia of Hertford Street was Letitia Brooke-Hardinge. Also, he used his influence a few times to get me out of the nick. His death complicates things for me."

"Then he was not so ungenerous as you described him Friday night," said Mrs. Roosevelt.

"He was totally ungenerous," said Letitia coldly. "If I'd taken employment in a shop, for example, he wouldn't have sent me a penny. He would not have paid me alimony or made a decent property settlement, but I found a way to get a monthly check from him. I couldn't get justice from an English court, so I had to get it for myself."

"Was he also subsidizing Lionel Foster to keep him quiet?" asked Sir Alan.

"A monthly check." Letitia nodded. "Sent to Mary Foster while Lionel was in prison, then to Lionel himself. At least, he was paying while I was still married to him; I can't say if his payments continued until Foster's death."

"It would seem," said Mrs. Roosevelt with a little smile, "that Sir Anthony was not invariably the victimizer—he was the victim sometimes, too."

"God has his ways of balancing the accounts," said Letitia. "Especially if one can find a way to help Him a little."

"What of Cecilie Exeter?" asked Sir Alan.

"What of her?" asked Letitia with a shrug.

"Her husband was invited to Friday night's party. Apparently she was not, but he was."

Letitia frowned. "I don't understand that. The rest of us—Are you telling me that Tony . . . God!"

"Do you think he did?" asked Sir Alan.

"Jerry Exeter was one of his best friends. Cecilie . . . My God!"

"Let's regard the matter as confidential," said Sir Alan. "Captain Exeter was on duty in Aberdeen on Friday night. He is not a suspect."

"Of course, I *am*," said Letitia. "One of your polite young men called on me at a very un-Christian hour this morning."

"I would like to talk to the young woman you escorted to the hotel in Kensington on Saturday night," said Sir Alan.

"She's here," said Letitia. "I'll see if she's free."

Letitia Brooke-Hardinge left the room and in a few minutes returned with a small, mousy girl, surely no more than nineteen years old and—as Mrs. Roosevelt judged—a most unlikely prostitute. She was dressed in a gaily flowered red-orange-yellow wrapper and high-heeled black shoes. Letitia introduced her as Barbara Ryan, and the girl sat down and regarded Mrs. Roosevelt with a look of surprised curiosity.

"A few questions, Barbara," said Sir Alan. "Did you leave this house on Saturday night?"

Barbara nodded. "Yes. Letitia took me to a hotel in Kensington, and I was there the balance of the night.'' She spoke softly, with an Oxonian accent that surprised both Sir Alan and Mrs. Roosevelt.

"What time did you leave here?"

"About ten-thirty, as I recall."

"And how did you travel to the hotel?"

"By taxi."

"Did Letitia drop you off or go into the hotel with you?"

"She went in. That was the idea, to see if the gentleman was sober and proper—and to collect payment."

"How long did she remain?"

"Only a minute or so. The gentleman was waiting in the hotel bar. She'd had the taxi wait, and she went on."

"Are you sure about the time?"

Barbara shrugged. "It could have been fifteen minutes earlier or later."

"Thank you. That's all."

Mrs. Roosevelt watched with sympathetic curiosity as the small, quiet girl left the room. Odd. She had found it difficult to believe that Moira Lasky—the pretty young woman who had helped solve the Hannah murder back in 1935—could be a call girl, either. She had offered to help Moira find a different life, and the girl had declined to be helped. And this one seemed unashamed. Obviously this was a milieu of which she had distressingly inadequate knowledge.

"So?" asked Letitia Brooke-Hardinge.

"So," said Sir Alan to Mrs. Roosevelt when they were again in the car, "Barbara Ryan says they left Hertford street at half past ten, give or take a quarter of an hour. Letitia told the detective this morning that she left at half past eleven. The little prostitute does not seem stupid.''

"No," said Mrs. Roosevelt. "Not at all. And if in fact Letitia left Hertford Street in a taxi when Barbara Ryan says she did, then she could easily have reached Constitution Hill and Buckingham Palace in time to have been the figure in Sir Anthony's bathroom."

"Exactly," said Sir Alan. "What is more interesting, why did she tell my detective she left Hertford Street an hour later?"

"Of course, the girl *could* be wrong. . . ."

"I must find out," said Sir Alan. "I am going to ask the American at the Pembroke Hotel—an errand which I think it best for me to pursue alone."

The night clerk at the small Kensington Hotel was hostile and all but refused to ring Mr. Barker's room. Sir Alan was firm. He picked up the desk telephone and ordered the clerk to ring.

"Barker."

"Mr. Barker. Sir Alan Burton, senior inspector, Scotland Yard, here. Sorry to ring you so late, but I have a few questions and need answers immediately."

"You can go to hell, Mr. Inspector Whoever-you-are."

"Then you can go to gaol, Mr. Barker. I shall have you picked up within the quarter hour and put in a cell until it is convenient for me to see you tomorrow."

"Do you know who you're talking to, mister? Have you ever heard of International News Service?"

"Yes, of course I've heard of INS, Mr. Barker. Your superiors there will be interested in learning that you refused cooperation with Scotland Yard—

especially when our investigation involves your having had intimate relations last night with an underage girl brought to you by a procuress, whom you paid for the girl's services.''

"Hey, your man this morning said the investigation had nothing to do with—''

"I can protect your name, Mr. Barker—for what it's worth—if I have your cooperation. Will you come down, or shall I come to your room?''

"I'll be right down.''

Barker arrived in three minutes, still tucking his shirttail into his pants. Sir Alan led him to the chairs farthest from the desk and the ear of the clerk, and they sat down.

"Hey, you understand that it's a late hour and all. I—''

"Describe for me, Mr. Barker, the girl who was with you last night.''

Barker was an overweight, flush-faced man, his uncombed hair falling over his forehead. He gleamed with nervous sweat. "Uh . . . brown hair, light brown; uh, blue eyes. I mean, she looked *twenty-five* if she looked a day! I swear!''

"Appearance can be deceiving," said Sir Alan calmly. "What did she call herself?''

"Bobby. Just that. That's all. She didn't give me any other name. And, anyway, she was *experienced*. I mean, hey, look, that girl was no—''

"Describe her voice, her way of speaking.''

"Very cultured. Very English. Hey, this girl's not *dead*, is she?''

Sir Alan smiled. "She wasn't when I spoke with her half an hour ago. And she was brought here by . . .?''

"Uh, the madam from the place on Hertford Street.

Letitia. I go there sometimes, and I called her and asked her—''

"At what time did they arrive here, Mr. Barker?"

"Quarter of eleven. Before eleven."

"And how long did Letitia stay?"

"Oh, just a minute. She collected the money and left."

Sir Alan rose. "Thank you, Mr. Barker. You have been most helpful."

"Am I in trouble?"

Sir Alan shook his head. "I believe on fuller investigation we will probably find your Bobby is not underage after all."

"I think I've been had," said Barker glumly.

"If I understand the American expression, I judge you have at that. Good night."

When he left the hotel he was not far from home, so Sir Alan walked, through blacked-out streets sufficiently lighted by a full moon sailing behind broken clouds. He arrived at his flat and let himself in with his key.

"Well. I was about to give you up and go to bed. Where have you been, a bawdy house?"

"In fact, I have been," said Sir Alan as he bent over her chair and kissed Peggy on the forehead. "In the line of duty, of course."

"Did you do your duty or did some bawd do hers? Or did both of you?"

Peggy Arbuthnot flipped her cigarette into the fireplace, where a few coals glowed under a teapot. She got up and laid out cups and saucers on the fireside table, while Sir Alan put aside his coat and hat and sat down wearily to share tea with her.

"It's good of you to stay up," he said.

She shrugged. Peggy was a woman of Sir Alan's age, that is, about fifty. She was the widow of one of his longtime colleagues at Scotland Yard, and when she was bombed out of her flat in 1941, he had invited her to come live with him. She was a full-figured woman, a blonde, with what he and others called an honest English face. Her carefully plucked eyebrows formed perfect arcs, which characteristically she lifted in an expression of detached skepticism. She wore a gray wool dress, with a sweater over it.

"You had dinner, I suppose?" she asked.

"With Mrs. Roosevelt."

"Ah. You do move in exalted company. Uh . . . You had a caller early this evening. A ragged old bum, from the look of him; but I knew his name when he told it. Harry Cross. The fence."

"Harry . . . Did he say what he wanted?"

"Wants to talk to you. Says you'll be interested to know that an item of property has appeared on the market. A jade Buddha."

"Aha!"

"Yes, of course. Very enlightening, 'Aha!' Would you care to explain?"

"Perhaps a break in the Brooke-Hardinge murder," he said. "Mrs. Roosevelt . . ." He glanced at his watch. "Well, I couldn't ring her now. But it may be a break."

9

A cold rain was falling on London the next morning, Monday, October 26. Londoners going about their business did not know that before dawn great convoys of troopships had left ports on the western coast of Great Britain and were steaming south. Other convoys were moving east from the United States, across the Atlantic toward the western coast of North Africa. Operation Torch was underway.

Mrs. Roosevelt knew. As she began her round of appointments in London and its vicinity, she knew the ships were at sea, that tens of thousands of young Americans were on their way to landings in Algiers.

Sir Alan Burton did not know. His late hours of the past few days had begun to take a toll on his vitality, and it was with reluctance that he left the warm bed he shared with Peggy Arbuthnot and shaved and dressed in the cold. By nine, just the same, he was in a police car, on his way out West Cromwell Road, driving to the digs occupied by Harry Cross.

He was lucky to find him at home, since it was the nature of his business for Harry to prowl about the city constantly. Throwing open his door, Harry ad-

mitted Sir Alan to his rooms, complaining that it was
an early hour to waken an old man. He yawned, but
he was fully dressed, including the stained and tattered raincoat he seemed never to take off. He wore
two or three days' beard, of course—and his voice,
normally hoarse, was gravelly.

"Do you take whisky at this hour?" he asked Sir
Alan.

"No, not so early, thank you."

"Nor do I," growled Cross. "But"—he smiled
slyly—"a spot of gin is something else again. Tea?"

Sir Alan nodded.

The old fence lifted a teapot from an electric heater,
where it was already steaming, and poured two mugs
of tea. Then he splashed gin into a glass and put it
beside his mug. "Well," he said. "Your 'ealth,
guv'nor." He snatched up the glass and tossed back
the gin. "Ah. Charmin' lady, that one wot lives with
you. Widow of old Inspector Arbuthnot, hey?"

"How do you know that?"

" 'Cause she told me. We 'ad a bit of talk, she and
I. Didn't offer me anythin' to drink, but—knew my
name, she did."

Sir Alan sipped his tea. It was good. Harry Cross
knew good tea and how to brew it—also how to
obtain it when it was scarce. He didn't eat rutabagas
for his dinner, Sir Alan would wager.

"You asked me about the jade Buddha," said
Harry.

"Yes."

"Well, there's a jade Buddha on the market, as of
yesterday morning. Can't say it's *your* jade Buddha.
On th' other 'and, 'ow many jade Buddhas *is* there?
Not many, 'ey?"

"Who has it, Harry?"

"You remember I told you I wouldn't even look at it when it was pinched from that 'ouse in Warwickshire. And that's a fact. I wouldn't—and didn't. Neither would any other honest man. But . . . well, you know 'ow business is. Not every man is honest. So there was a man who took a chance on it. 'E didn't pay much for it and made a big profit when 'e sold it to Sir Tony Brooke-Hardinge, and—"

"I thought you didn't even know Sir Anthony got it. Isn't that what you told me?"

"I didn't know, until yesterday. But it's back on the market, and there are some as know about it. It's worth a lot more now."

"Why?"

Harry shrugged. "It's been a while since it was pinched. Dealers figure there's not so much risk in 'andling it now. O' course, they don't know what you told me—that it's wanted as evidence in a murder. Oh, it's being offered. The word's out."

"You still haven't said who has it," said Sir Alan.

"Suppose I 'ad it. Which I don't. But suppose. Might there be a bit of a reward in it? I mean, if I 'ad it and turned it over?"

"Indeed," said Sir Alan. "Your reward would be that Scotland Yard would be confirmed in its long-time judgment that Harry Cross is an honest citizen who only wants to help the police now and again when he can—and therefore he is to be allowed to go on in his line of work."

Harry grabbed his bottle and poured himself another splash of gin. "I don't 'ave it, like I said. I'd 'ave to buy it. 'Ow am I going to recover my investment?"

"You needn't make an investment, Harry. All you have to do is tell me who has the Buddha—and you will have earned the gratitude and good opinion of Scotland Yard."

"At the risk of my life, Sir Alan," Harry protested. "If certain parties was to discover that 'Arry Cross told an inspector from the Yard—" He stopped and shrugged. "Well. They'd find poor 'Arry floating on the tide some morning, you can be sure of that."

"I'll protect your identity," said Sir Alan.

"Sure ye will. Parked a police car in front of my digs this morning. You've got to take me in, guv'nor. You've got to lock me in the nick a couple of days. Couple of days, mind you, no more. That gives me a kind of story. I can say you was looking for some silver."

"Harry—"

"It's got to be, guv'nor. You've got to 'andcuff me. Make it look right. Let me pour down my last swallows of gin for a couple of days. Then we can go. I want out on Wednesday. You put the cuffs on me now. Put 'em on me."

"I don't even carry handcuffs," said Sir Alan indignantly.

"That's a police car you've got outside. There are some in there. I should know. You bring the cuffs in, guv'nor, while I pour down me last swallows."

Annoyed, Sir Alan hurried out through the rain to the car, where in fact he found a pair of handcuffs, as Harry had said he would. He found no keys. They would have keys at the station where he dropped Harry, and someone there would have to unlock the manacles. Back in the house, he handed them to

Harry, who snapped them on himself and then went about the flat, locking cabinets, checking the latches on all the windows, humming to himself, quite undisturbed to have his wrists chained together. Outside he made a display of being in handcuffs, miming an angry complaint until he was inside the car and Sir Alan had pulled away. Then he grinned and lit a cigarette.

"Best 'Arry's safe in the nick when what's going to 'appen 'appens," he said. "But mind, I've got your word. Wednesday."

"Wednesday, Harry. You have my word."

"Ah, the glories of British law," laughed Harry. "When a copper's give you 'is word, you can depend on it."

"Now your word," said Sir Alan. "Who's got the Buddha?"

Harry drew deeply on his cigarette. "Gresham and Rose was the lads what pinched the Buddha. You remember, I told you. Rose was the inside man. Gresham was the professional. But there was no market for the Buddha, remember, as I told you."

"It was too hot, as the Americans say."

"A good way to put it. 'Im as touched it would have got 'is 'ands burned. No honest man would touch it. Until you came to see me Saturday, I never heard what happened to it. Then you said Sir Tony got it, and I couldn't understand how it passed from Rose and Gresham to Sir Tony Brooke-Hardinge. Well, yesterday I found out. Sir T wasn't careful about who 'e dealt with."

"Who, Harry, for God's sake?"

Harry bobbed his head and raised his hands to take his cigarette from the corner of his mouth. "It was worth ten thousand. An honest man would have give three, maybe four—that is, if an honest man would have touched it. Gresham took one thousand for it, finally. 'E was paid one thousand—*by Narberth Crowley*. That's who it was, Narberth Crowley; and he sold it to Sir Tony Brooke-Hardinge for *six thousand pounds*.''

"Who has it *now*, Harry?" Sir Alan persisted.

"Narberth Crowley. 'E's got it back. That's the word, sent out to the honest men, and 'e wants six thousand for it *again!* What's more, 'e thinks 'e'll get every shilling of it. It's still worth ten. 'E thinks an American will buy it. Some of them as is over 'ere has ten thousand easy—''

"Ten thousand pounds . . ." Sir Alan mused.

"It's an antique, it is," said Harry. "Fourteenth century. They don't do that kind of work no more. I judge it is worth that much. Good enough motive for a murder, what?"

"Particularly if Narberth Crowley is involved," said Sir Alan.

"Yes. You see why I insist on going to the nick. I wouldn't want 'im to think I gave you 'is name.''

Sir Alan dropped Harry at a police station in Earl's Court, leaving word that he was to be held until noon on Wednesday and not an hour longer. He could understand Harry's aversion to being suspected by Narberth Crowley. Indeed, before he would venture into the presence of Crowley he wanted backup for himself, and he used a call box to alert the Yard to have two men standing by to accompany him as he went looking for Crowley.

He expected to find him in Southwark. Turning the

car over to one of his juniors to drive, he settled in the back seat and recalled what he knew of Narberth Crowley—

Born about 1900, the son of an Anglican clergyman with a parish in Whitechapel, Narberth Crowley had been too young for service in World War I and was too old to be drafted for World War II. It would have been wholly out of character for him to volunteer. When his father died in 1910, the young Narberth dropped out of school and might have been expected to work. But, so far as the record showed, Narberth Crowley never worked a day in his life—never worked, that is, at any trade or occupation; but he had demonstrated remarkable industry and ambition, fighting his way to the leadership of a street gang by the time he was twelve, establishing a reputation for ruthlessness and cruelty by the time he was fifteen, earning a sentence to a borstal when he was seventeen. Far from reformed by his borstal experience, he returned to the streets of the East End after a year and regained the leadership he had surrendered when he was sent away. And from there—

He never served another sentence. Not because he was innocent—far from it—but because he was shrewd and totally amoral and unrestrained. He was in his forties now, and owned a labor union. Owned it. He had had its member-leaders beaten into submission—though no one could prove it. In fact, few of the members wanted to, since his tactics won them concessions from their employers that their honest leaders had never been able to obtain. He lent money at rates of interest rumored to be 100 percent per month. He managed—through middlemen, never touching the business himself—a string of fifty prostitutes;

some said it was a hundred. Since the war began, he had made a fortune in black-market goods.

And yet he had never been convicted of any crimes. At Scotland Yard, it was suspected he also owned a few police officers. But that was only *suspected*, as it was only suspected that bodies found downriver in the Thames had got there by challenging Narberth Crowley. He was not a man to be crossed, even if you were a senior inspector from the Yard.

Blackfriars Bridge brought the car bearing the three men from the Yard into Southwark. Narberth Crowley kept offices above a large garage, where he could be reached only by walking through a vast expanse where a dozen lorries might be parked, then climbing steel stairs to a platform off which his office doors opened. It was a daunting walk, under the eyes, one always suspected, of three or four toughs who would be watching out for the privacy of their boss.

This morning the wide garage doors were open. "Drive in," said Sir Alan.

" 'Ey! You can't—Ow, Scotland Yard. Mr. Crowley's upstairs. Oi s'pose 'at's 'oo y' want t' see."

By the time they reached the top of the steel stairs, Crowley had emerged from his office and stood beaming just outside the door. "Sir Alan Burton!" he said with a grin. "I am honored."

Sir Alan accepted Crowley's outstretched hand, shook it, and allowed himself to be escorted into the office.

Narberth Crowley was a short, stocky man, with a broad, flat face. His eyes were dark and narrow beneath bushy black brows, and they peered out on the world with hostility and suspicion the man seemed unable to suppress even when he was feigning cordiality. His mouth was wide, with thin lips that curled when he spoke and at rest settled into a sneer. His voice was flat, and he spoke slowly, dragging out his words. He wore a black, pin-striped, double-breasted suit, with a white shirt and a shiny red necktie.

His office had something of the aspect of Harry Cross's parlor—furnished with a scarred old desk and old chairs sitting on cracked linoleum. He had two telephones. A big glass dish on his desk was filled with cigar ash and butts, and a lit cigar sat there now.

"Cigar?" he asked Sir Alan.

"No, thank you."

Crowley sat down behind his desk facing Sir Alan, who sat on one of the battered wooden chairs. The two officers who had accompanied him remained standing. Crowley picked up his cigar but did not offer cigars to them.

"I suppose you've come on official business. Senior inspectors from Scotland Yard rarely visit me for social reasons."

"Yes," said Sir Alan. "I'm looking for an object—an objet d'art, as we say."

Crowley smiled and pinched one of his brows—a characteristic gesture for him. "Well, I am not an art dealer, Sir Alan. I'm afraid I can't assist you in locating any objet d'art."

"This particular object is a carving," Sir Alan went on. "A jade carving of a Buddha, some six hundred years old. It is worth ten thousand pounds."

"Ten thousand pounds!" said Crowley, shaking his head. "Imagine that!"

"And well worth stealing," said Sir Alan. "It was probably stolen in China, late in the last century. It was brought to this country by a missionary who may not have been aware of its value, and it wound up in a home in Warwickshire. From there it was stolen by two men named Rose and Gresham. Gresham was a thief by trade, and he brought it to London to fence it. The usual fences wouldn't take it, but somebody did, and it was sold finally to Sir Anthony Brooke-Hardinge.''

"I've heard of him."

"Did you know he is dead?"

Unless Crowley was a skilled actor, the news surprised and troubled him. "Dead? No, I didn't. Since when?"

"Since Friday night. He was murdered, and the Buddha was stolen again."

"Murdered . . . Brooke-Hardinge? The news . . . hasn't . . ."

"No. His death has been kept confidential as a matter of national interest. But he was beaten to death with a fireplace poker, and the Buddha was stolen."

Crowley's narrow little eyes dropped to the cigar in his hand, and he pondered the information. "Well . . ." he said after a moment. "That's bad news. Sir Anthony was a fine man. Or so I'm told by those who knew him. Never met him myself."

"Mr. Crowley," said Sir Alan. "We know Sir Anthony bought the Buddha from you."

"Oh, no. I wouldn't touch the thing. I don't deal in stolen property."

"I don't care if you did or didn't, Mr. Crowley. The point is, the jade Buddha is worth ten thousand pounds, and whoever stole it must sell it. There are relatively few men in London who could handle a transaction of that size; and if you aren't one of them, you will at least hear about it. I came to see you to solicit your cooperation. If you hear about the Buddha, I'd appreciate a call from you."

Crowley nodded gravely. "I will be happy to do that, Sir Alan. If I hear anything, I'll phone immediately."

In the car on the way back to Scotland Yard, Sir Alan settled a smug little smile on the detective beside him in the back seat. "I believe," he said, "I have just created a serious problem for whoever stole the jade Buddha."

"Uh, meaning . . .?"

"Whoever it is didn't tell Narberth Crowley he—or maybe she—killed Sir Anthony Brooke-Hardinge. Until just now, Crowley didn't know the thief is also wanted for murder. Oh, he's going to resent that!"

Sir Alan had himself driven to the Park Lane Hotel, where Jennings Duggs worked as a breakfast and lunch waiter. He planned to lunch there, and interview Duggs when his shift was over. He was moved by a sense that he had overlooked Duggs for two days and that maybe the old fellow had more to say than had so far been heard.

"Mr. Duggs? Mr. Duggs? Oh, no, sir, he did not appear for work this morning. Strange, too. He's always been a very reliable man. On the rare occasion when he's been ill or otherwise could not come in, he has always telephoned. Scotland Yard? I hope you're not suggesting there's anything wrong about Mr. Duggs."

"Not at all," said Sir Alan. "He may have a bit of

information we could use. Not involved in anything wrong. Not at all.''

Odd, though. Sir Alan went then to Duggs's flat. He wasn't there. His neighbors were away, at work. The pubkeeper down the street knew him but hadn't seen him. Sir Alan telephoned the Yard and reported Jennings Duggs as missing.

A telephone message waited for him. Mrs. Roosevelt asked that he call her, and she had left a list of her afternoon appointments, with telephone numbers.

"Mrs. Roosevelt? I hope I am not interrupting—"

"If you are, Sir Alan, you are doing so at my request. It is a fascinating day for me, but my mind does keep coming back to the puzzle we are trying to solve. What new developments?"

He filled her in briefly on his visit to Narberth Crowley.

"I keep thinking about Alexandra, Countess of Stanhope," said Mrs. Roosevelt. "Why would Sir Anthony's files have included negatives for all the pictures in his album except ones for the picture of her?"

"I have been wondering about that myself," said Sir Alan.

"I wonder if we should not regard two things missing from Sir Anthony's apartment—the jade Buddha and those negatives."

"I agree."

"Is the Countess short of funds, do you suppose?" asked Mrs. Roosevelt. "Can you look into the bank records of the several suspects?"

"That requires an order," said Sir Alan. "I've asked for it. It will probably be tomorrow before I can obtain the banking records for Sir Anthony and the suspects."

Alexandra Dudley, Countess of Stanhope, occupied a Regency house on York Terrace, bordering Regent's Park. Sir Alan telephoned, found her at home, and told her he would like to stop by for an interview. She said he would be in time for tea.

The house was elegant. The Countess led him into a small sitting room at the top of the broad staircase, saying it was the one room in the house she kept warm. A coal fire did burn there, and the room was warm, though not so warm as Sir Anthony had kept his rooms in the Palace. He noticed that the furnishings of the room included several handsome Chinese vases.

Countess Alexandra was wearing a tartan skirt, a white silk blouse, and an emerald-green sweater. The heavy silver tea service was already laid out, with some scones and marmalade also on the tray. As she poured tea into porcelain cups, she asked, "Have you found out who killed Tony?"

"I regret that I haven't," he said. "I haven't even eliminated a suspect."

"Which leaves me on the list, I suppose."

"I'm afraid it does, My Lady."

She smiled, the same puckish little smile he had seen in the photograph in Sir Anthony's album; it spread from her mouth up over her freckled face until her eyes were smiling, too: an amused and amusing smile.

"I hope you won't object to answering a question or two," he said.

"Of course not," she said. "Indeed, have I any

choice?'' Her smile broadened. ''I've a right to be tried before the House of Lords, you know. I shall insist on it.''

''I sincerely hope no trial will be necessary.''

''Ah. That's graceful of you.''

''Actually, what I had in mind,'' he said, ''was a hope that you will plead guilty—if the evidence warrants it.''

She laughed. ''Ever the policeman, hey, Sir Alan? I hope you haven't come to arrest me. If I thought you had, I'd have poisoned your tea.''

''Not at all. Just a few questions. What does the name Lionel Foster mean to you?''

She shook her head. ''Not a thing. I don't believe I've ever heard it.''

''Cecilie Exeter?''

Countess Alexandra shook her head again, then lifted a finger. ''Oh. Exeter. Yes. Cecilie Exeter would be the wife of Captain Jerry Exeter. Oh, yes.''

''What was the relationship between Cecilie Exeter and Sir Anthony Brooke-Hardinge?''

The Countess lifted an eyebrow. ''Relationship? What are you suggesting? Something scandalous?''

''What can you tell me?''

''Nothing at all. Tony spoke of Jerry Exeter as his friend. I never met him. He has been away with his regiment for some time, you know.''

''When Sir Anthony showed you his album, did he identify the young women in the photographs?''

''Laura Hodges. He identified her. I guess . . .'' She frowned. ''I believe he mentioned the names of one or two others. They were none of them girls whose names meant anything to me. They were all pretty. They had that in common. I . . . in one sense, I must confess, I was flattered to be among them.''

"You are a beautiful woman, My Lady. Distinctive—''

She laughed. "Ah. The qualifier. 'Distinctive.' I should like your compliment more if you had stopped one word short.''

"The word 'distinctive' does not diminish the compliment, My Lady,'' said Sir Alan. "It enlarges it.''

"You are a gallant man, Sir Alan. But . . . More tea? Have you further questions?''

"Yes," he said soberly. "I am afraid so. So far as our investigation has determined, only two things were missing from Sir Anthony's apartments after his death: the jade Buddha and the negatives of your photographs. It is a most curious circumstance—don't you agree?—that his file contained negatives for all the photographs in his album except yours.''

"Also, you found my fingerprints on a bronze figurine and a brandy bottle,'' said the Countess.

Sir Alan nodded. "Yes.''

She sighed. "Yes. The conversation takes on a more ominous tone. Would you care for something a bit stronger to drink, Sir Alan? A whisky?''

"If you are having something, I will join you, My Lady.''

She rose, opened a cabinet, and took out two bottles and glasses. She poured generous drinks— whisky for him, vodka for herself.

"I lied to you, Sir Alan," she said somberly. "To you and Mrs. Roosevelt. I admit it. I told you I had never been in Tony's apartment in the Palace. That is not true. I have been there often. When you asked me about it Saturday night, I was in the first place deeply upset by the news of Tony's death, which I had heard only late that afternoon. Then to learn that you were in possession of a nude photograph of me . . ." She sighed. "And to have to confess, in front of you and Mrs. Roosevelt, that I had been involved in a meretricious relationship with Tony Brooke-Hardinge . . . Well . . . I was not at my best, Sir Alan."

"P'raps I did you a disservice by interviewing you in the presence of Mrs. Roosevelt."

"Well, one would prefer that one's indiscretions not be aired in the presence of the wife of the President of the United States."

"My apologies, My Lady."

"Anyway, I lied to you," said Countess Alexandra. She lifted her glass and swallowed vodka. "I have been in Tony's suite in the Palace. I must confess I have slept there many nights—though not lately, I might say, since we argued bitterly about the pictures. About two weeks before he was killed, I went there to demand of him that he give me the photographs he had taken of me—and the negatives. I told him I regretted ever having posed, and I asked him to give me the pictures and negatives or destroy them."

"And . . .?"

She drank the rest of her vodka and went to the cabinet to pour another drink. "He gave them to me. I have them. The pictures and the negatives—except for the one which he insisted he would keep. Since it was the most modest of the lot, what could I do? If I had refused to let him keep that one, he might have kept them all."

"So you *were* in his apartment . . . And—"

"And examined the bronze figurine," she said. "I

have some interest in Oriental objects, since I inherited a few vases and figurines and one particularly fine screen that is in my bedroom. I left my fingerprints on the bronze—and on the bottle because I took a drink of brandy while I was there.''

"I see. Did you notice the jade Buddha?"

"Of course. He took it out and showed it to me, said it was worth a fortune. My fingerprints may be on that, too, if it's ever found."

"It's *been* found, in a sense," said Sir Alan. "That is, I know where it is—I think."

"And it is . . . *where?*"

"In the hands of a man who buys and sells stolen property," said Sir Alan.

"And if you recover it and find my fingerprints on it—"

"That will not prove you guilty of murder, My Lady."

10

"It is absolutely essential," said Ambassador Winant.
"It is absolutely essential, too, that the conversation
be limited to pleasantries, the glory of French cul-
ture, and the like."

"I am well aware," said Mrs. Roosevelt, "that
my husband holds the man in a degree of contempt."

"You are aware of what the Prime Minister has
said." Winant chuckled. "Have you heard? 'The
heaviest cross I bear is the Cross of Lorraine.' Still
. . . The man represents France as no one else quite
manages to do. I feel you really must pay a call on
General DeGaulle. He is always alert for slights, and
it would be a slight if you meet with King Haakon,
Queen Wilhelmina, and so forth, and do not meet
with him. France, after all—"

"You need not persuade me, Mr. Winant. I have
agreed to pay a call on General Charles DeGaulle,
but I do it with a degree of apprehension."

Her apprehension was well placed. So far as Charles
DeGaulle was concerned, he *was* France; he believed
he was the sole representative of what he grandly
called "Free France," and he took any slight to him

as a slight to France. The flag of France flew on his headquarters, and he received visitors as though they had come to call on a head of state.

Besides, he was an extraordinarily tall man, a memorable figure with a memorable face: great Gallic nose, bristly dark mustache, and roundish lips forming an expressive mouth. He spoke English but preferred not to and kept an interpreter at his side.

"Nous pouvons parler français, Monsieur Général," she said to him immediately.

He could not conceal his surprise. He smiled, and they spoke French.

"At Allenswood School, all our classes were conducted in French," she explained. "And Mademoiselle Souvestre was my favorite teacher and my friend as long as she lived."

General DeGaulle escorted her into a graceful parlor, where silent, efficient waiters served dry vintage champagne to Mrs. Roosevelt and Ambassador Winant.

DeGaulle sat rigidly erect even while sipping champagne and chatting about inconsequential matters. He dragged deeply on one cigarette after another, and his eyes flitted around the room as though he were afraid an assassin might be hidden behind one of the curtains. She had never seen such intensity in a man—the result, she felt sure, of his country's defeat in 1940 and of the necessity imposed on him of living in a not-altogether sympathetic city and dealing with not-altogether sympathetic allies.

Indeed, he said as much. "I know that President Roosevelt hopes to ally the United States with another French leader. I am a bristly fellow. But none of the others are as dedicated to the cause as I am. *We will destroy Hitler, Madame! I say destroy!* Nothing less. Is General Giraud committed to that? Is Admiral Darlan? Is the President willing to settle for something less?"

"I will be happy," Mrs. Roosevelt said with a smile but with firmness in her voice, "to convey any message you wish to the President. Please, General DeGaulle, take this opportunity to do so."

The tall, saturnine Frenchman regarded her with appraising eyes. He sucked smoke deep into his lungs. "Within two weeks," he said, "an American force will land in North Africa. The President hopes to deal with Admiral Darlan, perhaps even with General Pétain, and has kept the campaign a secret from me. Tell him I know about it. Tell him I understand why he has felt compelled to treat me as though I were not his most steadfast friend. Tell him I forgive him. Tell him he and I will work together in the end. He and I. He and I alone. No one else. No one else for France."

Mrs. Roosevelt nodded and smiled. "I will give the President that word, General," she said.

When Sir Alan Burton left the York Terrace home of the Countess of Stanhope, he stopped for a moment at the apartment of Ambassador Winant, on the chance he might find Mrs. Roosevelt there. She was not. He determined then to have an early dinner and try to reach his home and Peggy and bed before midnight. A hundred thoughts ran through his mind, but he decided to dine early at The Beefsteak Club, then call on Mrs. Roosevelt before going home.

His intentions had no chance of being realized.

David Desmond, aka Clicker, had somewhat similar plans. He spent the late afternoon in the club where he had given Sir Alan lunch yesterday. Sitting in a leather chair facing a round low table, he reread the script of a play, pondering its possibilities. The topless barmaid brought him whiskies until he told her to bring him beer instead.

He was, as the young woman decided as she watched him from her station at the bar, a formidable man—physically large, with a powerful personality. From the day she came to work at his bar she had wished he would invite her to a personal relationship, but he never had.

He sat there, absorbed in whatever that document was—smoking, sipping whisky, then beer. She wondered what he was pondering and wished she could help him.

Desmond rose. He walked toward the checkroom, and she rushed out to get his coat for him. She held his coat as he shrugged into it, then watched as he settled his hat squarely on his head. With a brief nod of appreciation to the girl, he left the club and strode down the stairs toward the street door, the script under his arm.

He passed the door to the ground-floor restaurant and opened the street door. It was dark on St. Martin's Lane. His destination was The Savoy, where he meant to dine with Lucinda Bancroft, and he walked south on St. Martin's Lane as he always did, and turned into William IV Street as a shortcut to The Strand.

"Clicker."

Desmond turned in the direction from which the voice in the darkness had spoken to him. He had no forewarning, then, of the man who darted out of a doorway behind him and struck at him with something heavy. But he was moving yet, and in the darkness the blow glanced off the side of his head. Bellowing in pain and anger, he staggered toward the obscure figure who had spoken. Still he did not react to the man behind him, poised to strike him a second blow.

" '*Ere! 'Ere!* What's 'is?''

Desmond, confused and terrified, lurched to the side to avoid this new threat—and in so doing avoided the second blow toward his head. The bludgeon caught him on the ear, a painful blow but not staggering.

"*Police! Police!*"

In the distant gloom, somewhere near the end of William IV Street, a police whistle sounded. Desmond's assailants ran. He fell to his knees, then twisted and dropped to his side on the cold, wet pavement.

"I am told by your doctor that your injuries are more painful than serious," said Sir Alan to Desmond.

Desmond lay in a bed in Middlesex Hospital. A thick turban of white cotton was wound around his head. "I suppose I should be glad for that," he muttered.

"You were attacked by two men, we believe," said Sir Alan. "Fortunately, a porter, on his way to the bus stop from his pub, came through William IV Street just as you were being beaten. He raised a cry, and a policeman heard him. I rather think they would have killed you, Desmond, if the porter hadn't happened along."

"They wanted to steal my money and watch, likely."

"Well, maybe. They were driven off before they

accomplished their purpose, whatever it was. Did you get any kind of look at them? Can you give me any description?''

''None,'' said Desmond.

''I'm told you'll be released from hospital in the morning. Where will you be tomorrow?''

''At home, I suppose. You have the address.''

The policeman who had run to Desmond's aid was waiting outside his room. Sir Alan took him aside for conversation.

''Did you get a look at the men who attacked him?''

''No, sir. They'd run out of the street by the time I found Mr. Desmond. I thought it more important to stay with him and get help for him than to run after them.''

''Have there been other incidents of the like in the neighborhood?''

''No, sir. An unlikely place for that sort of thing. It's my guess that they were not just common robbers, rather that they were waiting for Mr. Desmond specifically—either to steal something from him that they expected to find on his person or just to do him harm.''

''Yes,'' said Sir Alan. ''My thought, as well.''

''Anyway, they didn't rob him. I have his effects here. Is there any reason they shouldn't be handed to him?''

''No, but let's see what he was carrying.''

''More than a hundred pounds in cash,'' said the policeman as he opened an official valise and began to lay out Desmond's effects. ''A rather nice watch. And this . . .''

The officer handed to Sir Alan a loosely bound

manuscript of a hundred pages or so. It was a typed
script, a carbon copy on onionskin paper. Sir Alan
opened it and looked at the title page—

STAR BLITZ

A New Musical Play by

STANLEY HODGES

and

KEN KANE

"We'll not return this to him for the moment,"
said Sir Alan. "I want to know whose fingerprints
are on it. Also, I will want photocopies of a few
pages. So I'll take this. You can return the rest of his
things to him."

At Scotland Yard he found a telephone message
from Mrs. Roosevelt. He reached her at the ambassador's home. She wanted to discuss the mystery with
him, she said, and hoped it would not be inconve-
nient for him to call.

"In fact, ma'am, I was going to lift a friend out of
the nick."

"I beg your pardon?"

"To secure the release of Harry Cross."

"Oh, I should like to meet him."

"I am reluctant to have you do so, dear lady. He is
an uncouth character."

"You have just increased my curiosity. Please, Sir
Alan."

"Very well. I shall stop for you in twenty minutes."

"McDougal," he said to a subordinate on duty.
"Put three plainclothesmen on guard around David
Desmond's room at Middlesex Hospital. They are to

stay with him when he goes home. I'd rather he
didn't know they were there, but even if he catches
on, don't diminish the security."

He stopped by to pick up Mrs. Roosevelt in his
car, and they drove to the police station in Earl's
Court, where he had left Harry Cross only that morning. He asked Mrs. Roosevelt to wait in the car while
he retrieved the old fence.

Harry yawned as he emerged from his cell. He still
wore his raincoat, and jammed his stained old brown
hat on his head. "Should I be grateful for the re-
prieve, guv'nor—or apprehensive like?"

"I want to talk to you," said Sir Alan brusquely.
"There is no reason for you to stay in gaol, I think.
But in a moment I am going to introduce you to an
elegant lady. I want you to be on your very best
behavior, Harry. And I want you to promise me that
you will tell no one that you met her or repeat
anything we say."

"Umm. I *got* no behavior, guv'nor. 'Arry is 'Arry,
as you might say. On t' other hand, I've done business with swells in my day. None of them seemed to
object. So far as secrets is concerned, 'Arry's liveli-
hood is keeping 'is trap shut. It's a special talent o'
mine."

Two policemen stared in amused curiosity as the
shabby figure swept off his hat and bowed low to the
woman with a fur neckpiece who peered out from the
rear seat of the Scotland Yard car. He climbed into
the front seat and turned to speak to her as the senior
inspector went 'round and took his place behind the
wheel.

"We owe you dinner, Harry," said Sir Alan.
"Someplace where they'll let a fellow like you in—

and where Mrs. Roosevelt won't be offended. You have a suggestion?''

"Yas. Down my way, guv'nor. Fulham. They'll welcome 'Arry, and Mrs. R. won't be offended.''

He directed Sir Alan to a narrow street in an industrial neighborhood, then to a small brick building overshadowed by the bulk of a huge noisy factory. Leaving Mrs. Roosevelt and Sir Alan to wait, he went inside.

"Harry is reliable," Sir Alan said to Mrs. Roosevelt, as if he detected her apprehension about this street.

She looked up at the factory. It was dark, in accordance with blackout rules, but that it was busy was attested by the banging and clanging that were clearly audible on the street. Once, during one of the campaigns, she had been driven at night through industrial neighborhoods in Pittsburgh and Wheeling, which was a vivid memory; but one essential was missing here—the yellow-red glow from factory windows.

Harry returned, beckoning them to follow. They left the car and went around the side of the little brick building, stepping carefully to avoid puddles of rainwater, to a side entrance. Harry opened the door, and they peered into a small, warmly lighted dining room, where a table for four was set with a red-and-white-checkered cloth, serviceable white dinnerware, two candles in bottles, and wine already opened.

"Friends of 'Arry's," said Harry. He put his hat aside but left his raincoat on as he sat down.

Sir Alan helped Mrs. Roosevelt with her chair.

"They can serve veal or chicken," said Harry.

"I'm sorry," said Mrs. Roosevelt, "but I have dined."

"We'll order you a plate anyway," said Harry. "You should taste it. And I imagine Sir Alan and I can finish up what you don't eat, 'ey, Sir Alan?"

She said she would taste the veal. So did Sir Alan. Harry called through the door behind his chair, and someone outside grunted a response. Harry poured wine—full water glasses.

Sir Alan had not yet told Mrs. Roosevelt what had happened to David Desmond. "An interesting development this evening," he said. "David Desmond was attacked on the street just after he left his club. Bludgeoned by two men. They might have killed him except that they were interrupted. And that, Harry, is why it's safe for you to be out of the nick."

"Why?" asked Harry. "Wot connection 'as it got?"

"I went to see Narberth Crowley this morning," said Sir Alan. "He didn't know about the murder of Sir Anthony Brooke-Hardinge. He didn't know that whoever stole the jade Buddha probably killed Sir Anthony."

"So why am I not still safe in my cold little cell?" asked Harry.

"You said he'd be furious at someone. And he was—at the man who brought him the Buddha and didn't tell him he had killed Sir Anthony to get it."

"Are you saying the mystery is solved?" asked Mrs. Roosevelt.

Sir Alan sighed. "I wish I could. To my mind, David Desmond is now the number-one suspect. Within a matter of hours after Narberth Crowley learns the jade Buddha is so hot he can probably never recover his investment in it, Desmond is attacked and nearly killed. That cannot be a coincidence, Mrs. Roosevelt."

"But the party, the invitations . . . Oh, Sir Alan, this theory leaves too many things unexplained."

"He didn't work alone," said Sir Alan. "He could have been allied with any one of them."

Harry Cross had listened to this conversation with growing curiosity. His eyes shifted back and forth between Mrs. Roosevelt and Sir Alan, and he pursed his lips and frowned, as if pondering deeply. "That's how Crowley works," he mumbled. "Yas. Have a man knocked on the head in the dark. Hmm. Crowley."

Sir Alan turned to Harry. "You're afraid of him, aren't you?"

"Every man of sense is afraid of 'im," Harry growled. " 'Is Majesty the King would be afraid of 'im if 'e knew 'im."

"Do you know him, Harry? Or just heard about him?"

"I know 'im. 'E knows me, too."

"Would you go talk to him?"

"Me? Talk to 'im? Wot about?"

Sir Alan glanced at Mrs. Roosevelt. "Suppose," he said to Harry, "I provided you with, say, a thousand pounds—government money. Suppose you went to Narberth Crowley and told him you'd heard it around town that he had the Buddha. You pretend you have no idea what it's worth. You tell him you think you can get fifteen hundred pounds for it, and you offer him a thousand."

"Wot good would that do anybody? Particularly 'Arry?"

"Suppose he sells it to you," said Sir Alan. "We've recovered the Buddha, which is worth many times

the thousand pounds. I expect we can find some way
to pay you a reward."

"Somefin' besides another measure of the gratitude of 'Is Majesty's government?"

Sir Alan nodded. "Something besides that. Now.
Suppose he says he won't sell it for a thousand. And
suppose you say you'll try to get a higher offer. Then
we'll know he has it."

"So? So you know that. 'Arry's worked for the
coppers and—"

"I've got something more in mind, Harry," said
Sir Alan. "It may be possible to worm out of Narberth
Crowley where he got the Buddha."

" 'Ow?"

"I am curious to know, myself," said Mrs.
Roosevelt.

"Try to get him to bargain with you as to how
much the Buddha is worth," said Sir Alan. "Tell
him you have a gentleman who wants to buy the
Buddha and has offered fifteen hundred. Tell
him you might be able to get the gentleman to make a
better bid. Then say, 'I know he can pay more. He's
in the theater and makes a lot of money.' "

"Meanin' Clicker," said Harry.

"Exactly," agreed Sir Alan. "I suspect Crowley
has paid somebody handsomely, as much as five
thousand, for the Buddha, expecting to sell it for a
price approaching its true value. Now he has learned
from me that the Buddha figures in a murder investigation. Suddenly what was marketable for ten thousand will be difficult to market for two—if he can
sell it for that. So, he may accept your one thousand
for it."

"But—" said Mrs. Roosevelt.

Sir Alan smiled at her but continued. "If he paid Desmond five for it and has to take one for it, he will be angry enough with Desmond to want to kill him—which, unless I'm wrong, he tried to do tonight. But suppose he then comes to believe that Desmond is now dealing with Harry, trying to get the Buddha back for fifteen hundred or two thousand. He'll believe Desmond has a much better sale and is scheming to increase his profit—at Crowley's expense."

"You are putting David Desmond's life at stake, Sir Alan," Mrs. Roosevelt protested.

"Not really," said Sir Alan. "I've put a special guard around him. Plainclothesmen. Night and day."

"You propose to put *mine* at styke," grumbled Harry.

"Would you like plainclothesmen to follow you when you go to see Crowley?" asked Sir Alan.

Harry smiled slyly. "I'd like you to put them on me to see if they could follow me," he said. "What would you wager I could be shed of them in a quarter hour?"

"A bet I wouldn't want," said Sir Alan. "Except that in this case they would know where you're going."

"Still, there is risk," said Mrs. Roosevelt. "I—"

She stopped while two silent men brought plates heaped with generous servings of veal and pasta, accompanied by green salads. Although she had dined, the savory odor of the food tempted her, and she tasted it. It was as good as it smelled, the best meal she had been served since she arrived in England. Elaborate cuisine had never interested her much, but this simple, wholesome food, expertly seasoned, was appealing. She sipped sparingly of the red wine and ate a little more of the veal.

"The risk," said Sir Alan, who had not lost the thread of the conversation, "is minimal, both to Harry and to Desmond. And it may well solve the murder. What is more, there is a side advantage—putting an end to the sordid career of Narberth Crowley."

Harry Cross was harvesting veal and pasta with noisy enthusiasm. "It'd put an end to 'Arry, too, if 'e got mixed up in that."

"I can protect you," said Sir Alan. "I won't use you as a witness."

"I won't *be* one," said Harry. "I'll disappear."

"I'll help you," said Sir Alan.

"Suppose Crowley tells Harry he doesn't have the Buddha," said Mrs. Roosevelt.

Sir Alan shrugged. "Then the ploy will have failed. But I am beginning to wonder, Mrs. Roosevelt, if we have not been pursuing the wrong line in the case from the beginning. We've concentrated on the suspects' personal motives, instead of on the fact that a jade Buddha worth ten thousand pounds is missing. Crowley may be the key. Perhaps one of the suspects may have been working with—or for him. The Buddha would have been motive enough for some people to have killed Sir Anthony."

"The money," said Mrs. Roosevelt. "That might eliminate some suspects. The Countess . . . Perhaps Letitia. If you think of it, Sir Alan, David Desmond hardly seems desperate for money."

"We'll know more when we've looked into their bank records tomorrow," said Sir Alan.

"Yes," she said quietly. She shook her head. "This is not coming out as I'd thought. Too many questions remain, and too many new ones have been raised."

"Anyway, old fellow," Sir Alan said to Harry Cross. "Will you go to Crowley in the morning and offer him a thousand for the Buddha?"

"If you want to trust 'Arry with a thousand quid, I s'pose 'Arry can trust you a little."

"We've trusted each other before, Harry."

Harry looked up from his half-empty plate. "Never been any profit in it," he said.

"There is another fact about Desmond," Sir Alan said to Mrs. Roosevelt when they had dropped off Harry Cross and were alone in the car. "When he was attacked, he was carrying a copy of the play written by Stanley Hodges and Ken Kane. *Star Blitz*. Is that an odd coincidence? Or does it mean something?"

"I could only guess."

"One other fact," said Sir Alan. "On his way to hospital in the ambulance, Desmond asked someone to telephone The Savoy and tell Miss Lucinda Bancroft he could not have dinner with her. Ever the gentleman—as a man is apt to be who only plays the gentleman and was not born to the role. Anyway . . . do you know who Lucinda Bancroft is?"

"I'm afraid not."

"She is a musical-comedy actress, very well known in this country. I wonder if Desmond was not considering producing *Star Blitz* with Lucinda Bancroft in the role Laura Hodges so fervently wants to play."

"Suggesting that Laura Hodges attacked Desmond?" asked Mrs. Roosevelt. "Really, Sir Alan, do you consider that possible? Anyway, if that were true, what of your Narberth Crowley theory?"

"I didn't want Harry to know he might be pursuing a will-o'-the-wisp. Actually, of course, I think it wholly unrealistic to think Miss Hodges could have attacked Desmond on the street. David Desmond is a big, powerful man.''

"Of course, there were two of them. . . .''

"Yes, and he was struck from behind—while the other distracted him.''

"You discount the possibility it was ordinary street crime—what in the States is called 'rolling drunks'?''

"Yes, I do, essentially. Anyway, I have ordered the script examined for fingerprints. After I drop you, I am going to find out what prints were on it.''

"Tonight?''

"Yes.''

"I should like to go with you. I've never seen the inside at Scotland Yard—and what better time to see it than the middle of the night!''

"Mrs. Roosevelt,'' said Sir Alan. "When do you sleep?''

"When do you, Sir Alan?''

Although the number of staff on duty between midnight and dawn was sharply diminished from what was on duty during the day, Scotland Yard was still a busy place at half past one. Men and women hurried through the corridors, and pots of tea steamed on electric heaters. Here and there someone slept at a desk.

The report was probably on Sir Alan's desk, but Mrs. Roosevelt asked to see the fingerprint laboratory, so they went there. She found the room surprisingly small, the equipment extremely spare. The fingerprint lab at FBI headquarters in Washington, which she had once seen, was far more extensive.

An aged, bald man was on duty. "Oh, yes," he said. "That work was done." His artificial teeth clicked and whistled as he spoke. "I have a copy . . . Here are the names. Uh . . . Mr. David Desmond." He looked up from under his eyeglasses. "Fingerprints from the criminal records. David Desmond is also known as David Clicker. Uh . . . Mr. Stanley Hodges. Fingerprints from Royal Navy files. He served in the navy. And, uh . . . Sir Anthony Brooke-Hardinge." Again he looked up from under his glasses. "Fingerprints from the morgue. He's recently deceased, you know."

"Yes. Any others?"

"Yes. Two other sets—badly smudged. Not sure who they are."

"Thank you. The script is in my office?"

"Yes, sir."

Sir Alan led Mrs. Roosevelt to his office, picking up tea for them on the way. They sat down, both of them unable to conceal their fatigue.

"In daytime I have a nice view of the Thames," he said. He began to shuffle through a few papers left on his desk since he was last in. "Here's something. Hmm. Odd."

"And what is that, Sir Alan?"

"I asked officers to inquire into the whereabouts of our several suspects tonight when Mr. Desmond was attacked. Uh, I have made a chart. Perhaps I should amend it. Look."

He took the cover off his chart and with a pen began to add another line.

"Dancing, Sir Alan? Miss Hodges was dancing? Where?"

	Laura	Desmond	Duggs	Letitia	Alexandra
Invited?	?	Yes	Yes	Yes	No
Arrived:	?	9:04	9:07	8:57	?
Know Palace?	Yes	No	No	No	Yes
Opportunity?	Yes	Yes	Yes	Yes	?
Sat. night	?	?	?	?	?
Motive	£+	£	Hate	Hate	?
Whereabouts	Kane	Usual	Missing	Usual	Usual
Mon. 26/10	Dancing	XXX	Missing	Usual	?

"In the chorus line at the Prince of Wales Theatre. In the show starring Ken Kane."

"And was so doing at the hour when Mr. Desmond was attacked?"

"Well . . . probably. If not, she would have been backstage dressing. Undressing, actually. Curtain time . . . I'm not sure how closely curtain time coincides with the time when Desmond was attacked."

Mrs. Roosevelt smiled. "Apparently, anyway, she did not bludgeon Mr. Desmond."

"I guess not. Even so, I find her dancing in that chorus line a rather peculiar circumstance."

"How so, Sir Alan?"

"She has made a point of being unwilling to dance nearly nude, as those girls do. Yet—"

"She lost her benefactor, Sir Alan," said Mrs. Roosevelt. "The poor girl has to support herself now."

Sir Alan nodded. "Probably that's right. I made that point with Archie Mallory just the other night— that girls like her are quickly shopworn and descend lower and lower on the scale. You have to feel sorry for them all."

"I feel sorry for Miss Hodges," said Mrs. Roosevelt. "Is this the script?" she asked then.

"Yes." He handed it to her. *"Star Blitz.* I'll have to return it to Desmond now that we've taken the prints."

"It's quite thoroughly marked up," she said. "With pencil. Do we know whose handwriting all this is?"

"I've not had a chance to look through it."

"It's quite thoroughly edited," she said. "Quite thoroughly. And here in the back is a little label, from a typing service. I wonder if the other fingerprints are the typists'?"

"I suspect I shall have to find out," said Sir Alan. He glanced at the calendar. "Tuesday. When do we leave for Chequers, Mrs. Roosevelt?"

"Friday," she said. "It would be good to know the solution to this puzzle before we leave."

Sir Alan smiled wanly. "If you weren't keeping hours at least as late as mine, plus a busy schedule all day long, I should complain that your anxiety to solve this mystery has kept me up too many nights beyond my bedtime."

11

With her breakfast on Tuesday morning, Mrs. Roosevelt was handed a message from the President. It had arrived at the United States Embassy, been decoded, then carried to her by messenger. She read—

Dearest Babs—

I shall be most interested in hearing from you what the English think of our "Torch" prospects.

We face every sort of uncertainty, including especially the attitude of the French. I am, incidentally, glad you met with DeGaulle. (Winant reported immediately by cable that you set just the right tone during the meeting.) What was your impression of the man?

Confidentially, I expect we are going to suffer a substantial loss in the Congressional elections next month. The "old campaigner" simply cannot take the time to go on the hustings this year, and we are being sniped at from all sides. Do not be surprised if it looks bad and we get editorial chortling from Bertie McCormack and his ilk.

Has Penhaligon survived the Blitz? If so, and if you have time, pick me up a couple of boxes of that marvelous talcum I favor. I can't think of anything else that smells so good.

I hope you have seen Elliott by now. When you see him again, be sure and give him a kiss for me.

With Love,
Frank

She refolded the letter, stuffed it back in its envelope, and handed it to Tommy Thompson. "Put that in the grate and be sure it burns," she said. She was accustomed to the occasional necessity of destroying a confidential communication from her husband.

Harry Cross had walked from the underground station, and as he stood before the garage where Narberth Crowley kept his office he realized his shoe had become untied. He stood for a moment in the light rain, staring down at the errant lace. It wouldn't trip him, he decided, so he would not take the trouble to bend down and tie it. Shuffling his way to the door, he opened it and stepped inside the big garage.

" 'Ey, you! 'Is is proivate propitty."

Harry squinted at the menacing tough who strode across the garage toward him. He slapped water off his raincoat and hat.

"You—"

"Tell Mr. Crowley that 'Arry Cross is 'ere to see 'im."

" 'Oo says there's any Mr. Crowley 'ere? 'Oo says 'e'd want to see any 'Arry Cross if 'e wuz?"

Harry tipped his head back, as if he could get a

better view of this well-greased hoodlum by looking down his nose at him. He pursed his lips. "Do *you* decide who Mr. Crowley wants to see?" he asked. "Better be careful. If 'e learns you turned away 'Arry Cross, 'e might break your arm, sonny."

The hoodlum rose on the balls of his feet, as if considering punching Harry in the nose. Then, thinking better of it, he turned and strode to the back of the garage and the stairs to the office.

" 'Ere, you. Come up."

Harry shuffled to the rear of the garage and climbed to the office. As he walked in, Crowley did not rise from behind his desk. Looking up, Crowley smiled faintly. Then his mouth curled into a contemptuous sneer.

"Man of your resources, Harry, could dress better," he said out of the corner of his mouth, raising one eyebrow.

Harry nodded. "Then too many people would know wot resources I might 'ave."

"You don't fool many people anymore, Harry. Cigar?"

"Thank you," said Harry, reaching to take the offered cigar.

They paused while they lit their cigars, then Crowley asked, "Why are you here?"

"Maybe for nuffin'," said Harry, savoring his cigar. "Story that's around. May be wrong. Rumor. You know?"

"What rumor?"

"Walking around, talking to people," said Harry, "I 'ear you might 'ave a nice piece of merchandise I might be able to sell—if I can buy it from you."

"What piece of merchandise?"

"Objet-d'art sort of thing. Antique. They say it's six 'undred years old. Jade. A little statue, like. Some Chinamen's god."

Crowley shook his head. "No. I wouldn't know about it."

"Umm. Got any idea who might? I got a gentleman who'd like to have it. Cash money."

"How much?"

Harry smiled. "Well . . . I'd 'ave to make a little on the deal. I could give a thousand quid for it."

"A thousand! Why— A thing like that is probably worth five thousand, Harry. Maybe more."

"I wouldn't know," said Harry.

"What have you been offered for it?" Crowley demanded to know.

"I wouldn't try to fool you," said Harry. "A certain gentleman has offered fifteen hundred for it."

"Could that certain gentleman come up with more?"

Harry shrugged. "I don't know. Why not? In 'is ..e of business, 'e must make a tidy sum."

"What line of business is he in?"

"Wot you call show business, as I understand. Theaters and clubs."

"How does he come to know about this piece of jade?"

Harry smiled to himself. He had been wondering how he was going to open this subject, and now Crowley had done it for him. " 'E wasn't wot you'd call specific on that point," he said. "Said 'e knew the gentleman wot owned it last. Said 'e'd seen it at 'is 'ouse. Said 'e understood it was missing and 'e'd like to 'ave it if 'e could get it for a price."

"If he offered, say, five thousand pounds," said Crowley, "I might be able to locate the object."

"Five thousand! I don't think he'll do that."

"I would guess your gentleman is no fool," said Crowley. "His fifteen-hundred-pound offer is a ploy."

"Five thousand . . ." Harry marveled.

"Does he know who you're talking to?"

Harry shook his head emphatically. "Course not," he said indignantly. "You know 'Arry better than that."

"Well, don't tell him," said Crowley. "Tell him you've located someone who might be able to get the jade Buddha for him for five thousand."

"And 'ow much does 'Arry get if the gentleman offers five?"

Crowley tipped his head to one side, contemplated his cigar for a moment, then shrugged and asked, "What should I give you, Harry?"

"Way I see it," said Harry, "you've got the merchandise and no buyer, 'Arry's got the buyer but not the merchandise, so 'Arry needs you, and you need 'Arry. Fifty-fifty split, seems to me."

"Fifty-fifty split of what?"

"The five thousand—or wotever we gets."

"You think I can get the Buddha for nothing, Harry? Somebody has paid for it. It may *cost* five thousand. I might be losing money at five thousand."

Harry frowned. "Then why bother with the deal?" he asked innocently.

Crowley pushed back his chair and stood. "Harry," he said. "I'll tell you what. You hoped to make five hundred on the deal. All right. Five hundred it is. I'll see if I can get the Buddha for four thousand."

"Wot if my gentleman only offers four? Or three?"

"Talk to me again," said Crowley. He put out his hand for a handshake, and Harry stood. "The deal may be a little delicate, Harry. Third party and so on. Be careful. Keep my name out of it.''

"Goes wi'out saying, guv'nor.''

"How'd you come here?''

"Underground.''

"I'll have one of my boys drive you. Keep in touch, Harry.''

When Sir Alan called at Ken Kane's flat in Bloomsbury, a little after nine, Laura Hodges answered the door.

"I am looking for your brother, actually," he explained to her. "Or Mr. Kane. I'd like to ask a quick question or two.''

"Ken's still in bed,'' she said. "I'll wake him. Have a chair.''

The scene in the little flat was entirely domestic. Through the door between the living room and the kitchen Sir Alan could see a teapot steaming on a hot plate. Laura was wearing a wool robe and slippers, and had not yet combed her hair or applied any makeup. She was a pretty girl just the same, he judged appreciatively.

"Ken will be with you in a minute,'' she said when she returned. "Would you care for a cup of tea?''

"Thank you, yes,'' said Sir Alan.

As she put cups and a teapot on a tray, he glanced around the living room. It was decorated with theatrical posters featuring Ken Kane. One—just one—listed Laura Hodges in small type as a dancer in a show.

"I have something to show you,'' Sir Alan said to her as she carried the tray to a small table in the living room. He opened a black valise from which he pulled out the script of *Star Blitz*. "Have you ever seen this before?"

She glanced toward it as she poured. "Yes, of course. That's my brother's play—and Ken's."

"Can you guess where I got this copy?" he asked.

"I have no idea. *Should* I know?"

He accepted the cup she handed him. "Probably not. Look at this particular copy. Have you ever seen it before?"

She took the script in her hands and riffled through the pages. "No, I've never seen it before," she said. "All these marks—"

"Do you recognize the handwriting?"

She shook her head.

Kane came in, similarly dressed in a wool robe and slippers. He had not yet shaved, but had taken the time to wet his hair with dressing and flatten it with a comb. Smoking a cigarette, he went to the tray and poured himself a cup of tea, adding both milk and sugar.

"I'll ask you to take a look at this, too," said Sir Alan, handing Kane the script.

Kane put down his cup and took the script. He, too, flipped through it and frowned over the pencil-marked pages. "Where did this come from?" he asked.

"Last evening, about half past seven," said Sir Alan, "David Desmond was attacked on the street—bludgeoned from behind and knocked down. Except for the timely intervention of a workman who happened to be walking through King William the Fourth Street, he might well have been killed. He was carrying this script."

"Desmond," said Kane. "I don't even know where

he got this." He frowned over it. "In fact, I don't know where this came from at all. I've never seen it before."

"It *is* your play? Yours and Stanley Hodges'?"

"Yes . . . But who typed it like this? I mean . . . this was typed by a typing service." He shook his head. "Stan typed our scripts himself. Actually, we couldn't afford a typing service."

"Do you recognize the handwriting on that script?"

Kane shook his head. "Desmond's, I suppose."

"No, it isn't. We've checked that. How many copies of *Star Blitz* are there, Mr. Kane?"

Kane tipped his head and scratched his ear. "I'm not sure. A great many, because Stan and I have revised it several times, as different producers have suggested. Each time, Stan has typed several copies."

"Have you had any word from David Desmond that he was thinking of producing it?"

"No."

"When he was attacked last night, he was on his way to a dinner engagement with Miss Lucinda Bancroft."

Kane's face flushed. "He . . . he was carrying our *play* to a meeting with Lucinda Bancroft?" He glanced at Laura. "That—I can't believe it! And where'd he get it?"

"That's what I'm trying to find out," said Sir Alan.

"Well, I am sorry," said Laura firmly, "but we don't know anything about it. Does it have anything to do with Tony's murder?"

Sir Alan shook his head. "I'm trying to find out."

"I'm afraid we can't help you," she said. "We never saw this script—or those marks."

"Very well. Thank you for the tea. I shall continue my inquiry. Oh . . . I understand you were onstage at the Prince of Wales last night, Miss Hodges. Shall I come this evening and see you?"

"No," she said. "I was only filling in last night for a girl who was ill. I won't be appearing again."

"Not a new job for you, then."

"No," she said.

Script Services, Ltd., was a small shop above a men's clothing store in Oxford Street. There, in the light from a window that overlooked buildings ruined in the Blitz, half a dozen gray-haired ladies sat grimly pounding at typewriters.

The manager said her name was Mrs. Rose, and, peering at the *Star Blitz* script through her bifocals, she said yes, it had been typed here.

"For whom, Mrs. Rose?" Sir Alan asked.

"That's confidential information," she said. "We never disclose the identities of our clients."

"Not even for Scotland Yard?"

She shook her head. "Not even for Scotland Yard."

"Mrs. Rose," Sir Alan sighed. "The client was either Mr. David Desmond or Sir Anthony Brooke-Hardinge. Sir Anthony is dead, and Mr. Desmond is suspected of murdering him."

"Oh!"

"Yes. So which one was your client?"

Mrs. Rose seemed staggered. Anyway, she gripped the counter as if to steady herself. "It was Sir Anthony," she said. "He made quite a point of the confidentiality of his work."

"Do you know who did all this marking in the script?"

"Oh, yes. Sir Anthony. You see, sir, he came in about . . . oh, I should judge about two months ago. He had a script and wanted us to type copies for him. We made two. This is the carbon. He came back about a month later with this one, marked as you see it, and gave us the job of typing the script again, as he had revised it."

"How many copies did you make of the revised script?"

"Only one."

"And when did you deliver it to Sir Anthony?"

"He came in for it. Two weeks ago."

Sir Alan knocked on the door of David Desmond's flat in Portugal Street. Before entering the building he had spoken to the plainclothes officers, who had reported a quiet morning. He told them to be especially watchful for the rest of the day; the danger to Desmond might increase as the day went on.

Having admired the brick Regency building from the sidewalk, he had concluded that Desmond lived well. Now the door was opened by a six-foot-tall blonde, who, looking down on him, raised her eyebrows and waited for him to say who he was and what he wanted.

"Sir Alan Burton. Scotland Yard," he said. "To see Mr. Desmond."

She nodded and stepped back from the door. "I'll tell him you're here," she said.

He was somewhat startled by the flat. It was the kind of thing one saw in films—quite modern, with furniture that was all straight lines, almost everything black and white. The carpeting was white and thick and covered the entire floor, all the way to the walls. The lamps, on chrome stems, seemed designed to cast their light on the ceiling, and the wall above the fireplace was covered to the ceiling with mirror glass.

"Sir Alan," said Desmond. "I rather anticipated I would see you again soon." Desmond wore a black silk dressing gown over white silk pajamas. His head was still bound in a cotton turban. "Please have a seat and let me offer you a whisky, though it's not yet noon. Maureen. A whisky for Sir Alan. One for me, too."

The tall blonde went to a cabinet and took out a bottle. She, too, was wearing white silk pajamas, with a long white silk negligee that swept away behind her as she walked.

"You said you saw *Bottoms Up,* I believe," said Desmond. "If so, you saw Maureen—the star."

Sir Alan had indeed seen *Bottoms Up,* and he did remember the "statuesque beauty" who played the lead role.

"Feeling better this morning?" Sir Alan asked.

"More angry than anything else," said Desmond.

"Still can't imagine who it was?"

"No. Believe me, I'd tell you if I did."

Sir Alan opened his black valise. "I'll return this to you now," he said, handing Desmond the script.

"Ah. Thank you. Though I have another copy, I should have disliked losing this one."

"Why?"

Desmond flipped through the pages. "Sir Tony's revisions are marked on it. They're extensive, as you can see. I'd not want to lose those—though I may not use them."

"You are going to produce *Star Blitz*, then?"

"That's not settled, actually," said Desmond. "I am seriously thinking of it."

"When Mrs. Roosevelt and I talked with you Friday night, you said you and Sir Anthony had been planning to produce a show. You declined to say what show, said it was a secret. Was it, then, *Star Blitz?*"

"Yes. Tony was putting up twenty thousand pounds. That's the origin of the twenty-thousand-pound insurance policy on his life. We hadn't finally decided. I remain unconvinced Tony's revisions improve the show, and I've been looking for opinions on that."

"Why is it a secret?" asked Sir Alan.

Desmond glanced at Maureen. She had brought their whiskies, plus one for herself, and was listening curiously to the conversation. "The problem," said Desmond, "is Laura. Her brother wrote this show. She and Ken Kane are lovers and insist they are partners in it, as you might say, and she must be starred as the lead dancer. That would practically guarantee the failure of the show. She is just not good enough. Tony was anxious that she not find out what we were planning—in fact, that Stan and Ken not find out, either—until we could announce we were definitely going to produce *Star Blitz*."

"With, of course, another actress," said Sir Alan.

"Yes. Once the three of them were faced with the fact their show was really going to be staged, they would have changed their minds. Or so we hoped."

"Is that the purpose of the revisions—to write Miss Hodges out of the show?"

"No," said Desmond. He flipped through the pages

again, frowning over the extensive revisions. "I don't know exactly what Tony had in mind."

"He gave you this copy?"

"Yes, and another copy—the original. He had the typing service make two copies from the script Laura brought him. He made his revisions on the carbon copy. There are no marks on the original."

"And you say this is the only copy of his revisions?"

"Yes."

"All right, Mr. Desmond. Thank you for the whisky. I shall be speaking with you again."

"I am afraid you will at that, Sir Alan. I hope someday we may become acquainted in another context."

Sir Alan telephoned the embassy and asked where Mrs. Roosevelt might be found. She was touring the Fighter Command base at Uxbridge, he was told, and would not be back in London before evening. He took his lunch at his desk, scanning the reports that had been delivered there since last night. Bank messengers would arrive during the afternoon, bringing the records he had asked for. Harry Cross had not yet telephoned.

Studying the loose ends of the case, he decided to telephone the Park Lane Hotel and ask if Duggs had reported for work this morning.

"Reported, yes, sir. For work, no," said the indignant headwaiter. "He phoned early this morning to say he was quitting his employment here."

"Indeed? And did he say why?"

"He said he was returning to his former line of employment—in the insurance business, I believe."

Sir Alan checked through his file. The insurance

brokerage Sir Anthony Brooke-Hardinge had taken away from Duggs . . . He telephoned. Yes, Mr. Duggs had returned to work there. At the moment he was out to lunch.

An hour later he sat across from Duggs at his desk in the insurance brokerage in the City.

"I've many friends here," Duggs explained. "They remember that I founded the business, that I know a great deal about it. But Tony had given strict orders I was not to be allowed on the premises. When I came here yesterday morning, they didn't even know he was dead. I told them, and they welcomed me. I'm not a partner here anymore, or even a manager, but—"

"Sir Anthony's death was of great advantage to you, apparently, Mr. Duggs."

"I can't deny that. I won't deny it. In fact, Sir Alan, I won't deny that I'm glad he's dead. He was a cruel man."

"Where were you last evening about seven-thirty, Mr. Duggs?"

"At my pub, celebrating my good fortune, if you don't mind."

Back at Scotland Yard, Sir Alan found the bank records waiting for him. There was also a telephone message from Harry Cross. "See me at Rose & Thistle, Ongar Road, before closing."

Weary of driving all over the City, Sir Alan let himself be driven to Fulham and the pub on Ongar Road, where he found Harry contentedly drinking beer and chatting with the landlady.

" 'E bought it," said Harry. "I'm sure 'e did. 'E

wants five thousand quid for the Buddha. 'E's got it, that's for sure.''

"Desmond?"

"I dropped the 'int that the gentleman wot wants to buy it is in the show business. If 'e and Clicker 'ave been doing business, 'e'll know who that is."

"Could you telephone him?"

"Wot for?"

"Tell him your gentleman offers three thousand—that's his final offer. I'd like to keep the contact open, but I don't want him to think he can get his five."

Harry smiled. "Make 'im mad, that will."

Sir Alan nodded. "That's the idea."

He went home, bathed, and had dinner with Peggy—as he had promised her he would, if he possibly could.

"I realize," he said to her, "that it seems I spend all my nights with Mrs. Roosevelt; but count it up, Peggy, and you will realize that it is only the past four nights that I have kept late hours, working with her on this confounded business."

"Well, I'm not jealous of her," said Peggy Arbuthnot.

"If our circumstances were very different—very, *very* different—you might have reason to be," he said.

"She's no raving beauty," said Peggy.

"Neither are you, my dear," he said. "Which proves my ability to discern and appreciate the finer qualities in a woman. And Mrs. Roosevelt, let me assure you, is possessed of *all* the finer qualities."

"You mean you're infatuated with her?"

"Not at all. Not at *all*. That would be presumption. But—" He sighed and shrugged. "I do admire her in a detached sort of way. I will simply leave it this way, Peggy: the man who is married to that woman is most fortunate indeed."

Peggy Arbuthnot smiled. "They say men in their fifties, particularly coppers, lack romance. But you haven't, you old dear. And you've not lost your ability to be a good bed companion, either—which advantage I suppose I shall not enjoy before the small hours of the morning."

Sir Alan sat down with Mrs. Roosevelt in the comfortable living room of Ambassador Winant's apartment at about ten, when she had returned from dining in the enlisted men's mess at the base she had visited during the afternoon.

"Diplomatic privilege, I suppose," she said as she poked at the warm fire in the grate.

"Americans," he said. "You make no distinction between warm and too hot."

He spent some time reporting to her all he had learned during the day.

"The bank records," she said. "What do they show?"

"A variety of things," he said. "I've only given them a quick review, so let's look at them again. Countess Alexandra. Nothing specific in these, I should think. But I can't help think she keeps a rather small bank balance for a woman in her circumstances."

"She's short of funds?"

"Well . . . Wouldn't you think a countess with a home on York Terrace would have more money in her account than this?"

Mrs. Roosevelt looked through the record of Countess Alexandra's checks for the past several months. "She spends rather freely," she observed.

"Anyway . . ." said Sir Alan. "I am chiefly interested in Sir Anthony's account. Look at the summary. Interesting . . ."

"Indeed," said Mrs. Roosevelt.

"A monthly check to Lionel Foster," said Sir Alan. "Then no more. And after that a monthly check for half the amount to Mary Foster. He was paying for the Fosters' silence, clearly enough."

"Letitia . . ." said Mrs. Roosevelt.

"Yes. Checks to her. Very interesting. The victimizer was himself a victim, after all."

"I find these entries most significant, Sir Alan," said Mrs. Roosevelt. "I would suggest to you that there is a key to the mystery in—"

"But look at this," Sir Alan interrupted. "Two checks to Script Services, Limited. The first for eight pounds, the second for five. Script typing."

"Why the difference in amounts?" she asked.

"Exactly what the woman told me. He had a carbon made when he had the script typed the first time. But when he had his revisions typed, he had only one copy made."

"I find the checks to Lionel Foster, then to his wife, a good deal more significant," said Mrs. Roosevelt. "Don't you see? If they—"

She looked up. Tommy Thompson had come in.

"Sorry to interrupt," said Tommy, "but there is a telephone call for Sir Alan."

He went to the telephone. In a moment he returned. "Mrs. Roosevelt," he said. His voice was strained. "Laura Hodges has been attacked. Very much the same way David Desmond was last night. She has refused to go to hospital and is being treated in her flat. I must of course go there.''

''I will go with you.''

''It may be a public appearance,'' he warned.

''Even so, Sir Alan,'' she said grimly.

They arrived at Ken Kane's Bloomsbury flat a little after eleven o'clock. An emergency-services vehicle and a police car were parked in front. They had been there for some time, and the crowd had diminished to three curious women who stood on the sidewalk, none of whom recognized Mrs. Roosevelt. Sir Alan showed his identification to the officer who guarded the door, and they proceeded up the steps and to the door of the flat where Sir Alan had visited some twelve hours ago.

''Oh, my dear!'' cried Mrs. Roosevelt when she saw Laura Hodges.

Laura lay on the couch in the living room, still submitting to the attention of a doctor. Unlike Desmond, she had not been struck on the head. Instead, she had been beaten about the face and slugged repeatedly in the stomach and belly. Her face was swollen and shiny, the color ranging from bright red to darkening bruises. Her left eye was nearly closed. She had bled from the nose, which was now covered with a bandage, and her lower lip was split. The doctor's salve gleamed on her lip and on abrasions on her cheeks.

Ken Kane knelt before her and held her hands—a faintly ludicrous figure who had rushed from the theater in his white tie and tails, with his stage makeup still on his face.

"Miss Hodges, you should be at the hospital!"

Laura managed a little smile, and she shook her head.

Sir Alan was interested, too, in the condition of the flat, which appeared to have been ransacked. Drawers were on the floor, their contents strewn. Kane's posters had been torn down. Chairs were upset. Through the bedroom door he could see that the bed had been torn apart. Clothes, some of them torn, had been thrown onto the floor.

With a nod, Sir Alan ordered the uniformed officer on duty to accompany him into the kitchen.

"Putnam, sir," said the policeman, a graying man with a yellowish-gray mustache. "Sergeant Benjamin Putnam."

"What do you make of it, Sergeant?" Sir Alan asked. He glanced around the kitchen. It, too, had been ransacked. "Robbery? Rape?"

"Not rape, sir. The young lady says it wasn't that."

"The doctor agrees?"

Sergeant Putnam glanced through the door at Laura and the doctor. "I don't believe he's examined her for that, sir."

"What does she say happened?"

"Two men," she says. "She says they 'ad the idea she 'ad a lot of money on the premises. They searched for it, and when they couldn't find it, they beat her to make her tell where it was. But there was no money, she says, and they didn't get any."

"Have you spoken with the neighbors?"

"Yes, sir—them who are at home. Most of them are out. The man and wife downstairs say they heard nothing."

"Two men tore this place apart and beat Miss Hodges, and the neighbors downstairs heard nothing? Does that strike you as peculiar?"

"It does, sir. The couple downstairs don't like the young lady, though. Says she's too 'igh and mighty for their tastes. Besides, she's living with Mr. Kane there, and she's not married to him. They're Christian people, they say, and they don't approve of— Well, you know what they call it."

"Adultery."

"That's another word for it, sir."

"So no one saw these men, and no one heard them—and we have no idea who they are." Sir Alan sighed.

"That's right, sir. The young lady says she didn't recognize them."

"I'd like to speak to the doctor when he's finished."

Sergeant Putnam glanced at the scene in the living room, where Mrs. Roosevelt was speaking earnestly with Laura. The sergeant went out, spoke to the doctor, and the man came into the kitchen.

"I'm Senior Inspector Sir Alan Burton, Doctor. Can you give me a few minutes?"

"Of course," said the doctor. "We've worked together before, Sir Alan. Do you remember the 'dragon' murders?"

"Ah, yes," said Sir Alan. "You are Dr. Cuthbert Farrington."

The doctor, a heavy, elderly man with a great dome of a bald head and tiny silver-rimmed spectacles set in the middle of a broad, heavy face, nodded.

"Well, then, Doctor. You have experience with the pathology of crime. How would you judge what you have seen here?"

"A savage attack," said Dr. Farrington.

"No sexual abuse?"

"She insists there was none and declines to be examined for it."

"Permanent injuries?"

"I judge not," said Dr. Farrington. "I used a local anesthetic and stitched the cut over her eyebrow. That will leave a scar. Otherwise—"

"Painful, but not damaging injuries."

The doctor nodded.

"Yes. Well . . . Have you anything to add?"

"If I were investigating the case," said Dr. Farrington, "I should be curious about her vehement refusal to go to hospital. Unusual, that."

"I take note," said Sir Alan.

Dr. Farrington, back in the living room, stopped beside Laura to give her instructions. He left with her a small white envelope containing a dozen pills. Then, with a wave to Sir Alan, he left.

Sir Alan took a chair beside Mrs. Roosevelt, facing Laura. Ken Kane remained on the floor, holding Laura's hands between his.

"Two men, Miss Hodges?"

She nodded.

"Neither of whom you had ever seen before."

She shook her head.

"Descriptions, please."

"Oh, Sir Alan," said Mrs. Roosevelt. "She's described them for Sergeant Putnam. Can't you use—"

"I'm sorry," Sir Alan interrupted. "Very often, when a victim describes an assailant a second time, or a third, details come out that were omitted the first time."

"Two men," Laura mumbled painfully through

her cut and swollen lips. "Big. Ugly. Never saw them before."

"How did they speak?" asked Sir Alan.

"Low-class."

"How did they get in?"

"Knocked door. I opened. Pushed in."

"And they said they wanted—?"

"Money. Said they heard we kept money here. Wanted money. I said no money here—except little in my purse." She shook her head. "They say they'll find it. Start tearing up."

"And by tearing up the flat they found nothing?"

She nodded her head. "Then hit me."

"But no matter how much they hit you, you did not tell them where they could find money in the flat—because there wasn't any. Right?"

Laura nodded.

"Tell me, Miss Hodges, why did you refuse to go to hospital?"

She glanced at Kane. "Ken come home. I'm not here. Neighbors say I was hurt. Not hurt. Not that much."

"She loves Mr. Kane," said Mrs. Roosevelt.

"And I love her," said Ken Kane.

"Yes," said Sir Alan. "I think we would do you a service not to trouble you further tonight. I will ask you, Miss Hodges, to look at books of photographs at Scotland Yard. Perhaps not tomorrow. Thursday, perhaps, if you feel up to it. Since you are not working, it will not inconvenience you to come, will it?"

"Work," Laura mumbled. "Have to work. Soon as I look like it."

"Oh. You've found a stage job?"

"Chorus. Ken's show. Have to make a living," said Laura unhappily.

12

On Wednesday morning the sun broke through the clouds and London was deceptively peaceful. Of this day, General Sir Harold Alexander later reported to the Prime Minister: "This was the last occasion on which the enemy attempted to take the initiative." The Battle of El Alamein was won. Later, Churchill would write: "Before Alamein we never had a victory. After Alamein we never had a defeat."

Mrs. Roosevelt, now deeply concerned about the way suspects in the Brooke-Hardinge murder were being attacked and injured, arranged to complete her appointments by late afternoon. She told Sir Alan her mind was bubbling with ideas and that she wanted to give some hours to the mystery that evening.

She spent half an hour in the morning with General Eisenhower. She knew as well as he did that he was about to leave England to take up his duties as commanding officer of Torch, the invasion of northwest Africa; but both of them skirted the subject as if neither of them knew about it.

"Your son is under my command," said General

Eisenhower. "I've offered him a job behind the lines, but he won't accept it."

"What would the Republicans say?" she asked with an innocent smile.

General Eisenhower answered her playful question with a broad, guileless smile that she judged must be an element of his success. "He plays a fine game of bridge. Learned it from you, I imagine."

"Not from me, General. Or from his father. I've never quite found time for it. And his father prefers other recreations."

"Anyway, Elliott plays a good game. Sometimes when we have an hour to spare—"

"I imagine that's a rare event," she said.

"It's necessary," said General Eisenhower. "Now and again, a man just has to clear his mind for a little while."

"I constantly remind the President of that," she said. "I wish I could get him to believe it."

Harry Cross had no telephone, so Sir Alan could not reach him except by driving out to his flat. Which he did, the alternative being to wait for his call.

"Odd thing," said Harry as soon as Sir Alan was seated at his table. "Crowley backs out entirely. Says 'e couldn't get 'is 'ands on the Buddha. Says 'e don't know who's got it. Says 'e won't deal for it for any price. Says 'e don't want to talk about it no more."

"Changed his mind," said Sir Alan.

"Yas. Entire. Sorry, guv'nor. Afraid my wish to do somefin' for King and country has come up with nothin'."

"Not necessarily, Harry," said Sir Alan. "Not necessarily."

Harry nodded and seemed to be chewing his lips. "Uhm," he muttered. "Well. 'Ad a visit this morning from another gentleman interested in the death of Sir Tony Brooke-Hardinge. Larry Muldoon. You know 'im, the insurance investigator. Muldoon?"

"I know him, Harry."

"Yas. 'Ad a bit of jewelry, 'e did. Wanted to know if I'd ever seen it before. You know 'Arry; you know 'ow over the years I've developed an eye for valuable jewels, as you might say."

"Yes, Harry," said Sir Alan with a wry smile. "I am well aware of it."

"Muldoon knew I had some knowledge of the ways of items wot gets lifted from their rightful owners. 'E 'ad in 'and a bit that came on the market day before yesterday. In fact, Muldoon had just bought it for 'is insurance company. Seems it was the rightful property of a lady on Sloane Square whose 'usband 'ad insured it for a thousand quid. Muldoon 'ad bought it for six 'undred. 'E bought it from a gentleman wot's not honest, and—"

"Harry. Does this have some relevance?"

"Yas. I'd seen it before. Lovely piece, it is. Emeralds. Pretty green emeralds, set in diamonds. Necklace."

"*And?*"

"Sir Tony Brooke-Hardinge paid five 'undred quid for it about a month after it was pinched. Don't ask me 'ow I know."

"I *know* how you know . . . damn it!"

Harry shrugged. "So there you are. It was on the market again. Muldoon brought it around for identification, as you might say."

"Emeralds . . ."

"Yas. Now, says I, 'Did Sir Tony still 'ave it when 'e was done in,' or—?"

"Harry. Do you know anything more?"

Harry Cross lifted his chin and looked down his nose at Sir Alan. "Nice piece of merchandise, it is. Appears on the market again two or three days after—"

"Right. Two or three days after Sir Anthony was murdered."

"Muldoon doesn't plan to tell you about it," said Harry. " 'E doesn't want no interference with its being marketed by 'is insurance company. In fact . . . Well, I must be honest with you, Sir Alan. 'E wanted to know if 'Arry would buy it and market it." He shook his head. "I told 'im 'e'd be lucky to get two 'undred quid for it."

"But it's worth a thousand. I mean, it would be if—"

"If Sir T 'adn't been done to death by person or persons unknown," said Harry.

"What did the dishonest gentleman pay for it?"

"Sold it to Muldoon for six 'undred. So, of course, 'im or 'er wot pinched it got maybe three 'undred quid. Muldoon wanted six, said I could get eight. Could, too, except—"

"Except that Sir Anthony has been done in by person or persons unknown," said Sir Alan. "All right. Anything more."

"I supposed I'd told you a good deal," said Harry.

"You have, you old scoundrel," laughed Sir Alan.

"Do me a favor, then," said Harry. "Don't tell Muldoon wot I told you."

"Can it be done, Sir Alan? Is it inappropriate? Would it be considered—"

Mrs. Roosevelt had telephoned his office. He had never before heard her so fervid.

"I see no reason why we should not do it precisely as you suggest, dear lady."

"Well, it smacks of the melodramatic," said Mrs. Roosevelt. "Yet—"

"Mysteries are often solved in melodrama," said Sir Alan.

"Will you, then—?"

"I will make the necessary arrangements. It should be an interesting experience, at the very least. If it fails, we will go off to Chequers Friday and leave the problem of the murder of Sir Anthony Brooke-Hardinge in other hands—where, I dare say, it will be transferred in any case if we are unsuccessful tonight."

"I feel confident of the matter, Sir Alan," she said. "I've had less sleep than even *you* imagine, pondering on the subject. I really believe I know who killed Sir Anthony Brooke-Hardinge."

"So do I, dear lady," he said. "Let us see if we agree."

"Oh, Sir Alan! We will look such fools if we are wrong!"

"For me that will be no novel experience."

She sighed. "Nor for me, Sir Alan. Nor for me. Let us venture, then."

Midnight, almost. Mrs. Roosevelt and Sir Alan Burton had deferred the meeting until then, so Ken Kane might perform at the Prince of Wales and come afterwards to Buckingham Palace. They had assembled in Sir Anthony Brooke-Hardinge's apartment. The King himself had agreed the apartment should be opened, since Sir Alan had assured him this midnight meeting might solve the mystery of the murder of Sir Anthony Brooke-Hardinge.

Seated around a warm fire in Sir Anthony's living room, were:

—Lord William Duncan from the Home Office, Sir Alan's superior, sipping sparely of whisky from Sir Anthony's bar, attempting to affect an air of detachment and skepticism—and failing to do so.

—Alexandra, Countess of Stanhope, sipping vodka and nervously fingering the emerald pendant at her throat.

—Letitia, Lady Brooke-Hardinge, impatient to have been called away from Hertford Street, smoking intently and grumbling about the place and the hour.

—Laura Hodges, seated on the couch facing the fire, her bruises and swelling more grotesque than they had been last night, her body slumped from pain and fatigue.

—Ken Kane, sitting on the floor before Laura and holding her hand, stiff, apprehensive, and alert.

—David Desmond, on the couch beside Laura, still wearing his thick turban of bandages—he, too, looked exhausted.

—Jennings Duggs, apart in a chair, content and confident, curious about the meeting.

—Wen Yung, the Chinese houseboy, standing deferentially in a corner, watching the others with inquiring sharp eyes.

Sir Alan Burton entered from the library, followed by Mrs. Roosevelt, and took a stand before the fire. Mrs. Roosevelt sat on a leather-covered chair beside him and to his left.

"Ladies and gentlemen," said Sir Alan. "You will perhaps forgive us for summoning you here at this hour. All but one or two of you will forgive us enthusiastically when you hear you are no longer suspected of killing Sir Anthony Brooke-Hardinge.''

"Does that mean you *know* who killed him?" asked Desmond.

"Yes," said Sir Alan. "We know. We could have simply sent officers to make the appropriate arrests, but a confrontation seemed a better, albeit melodramatic, approach. Some of you may be able to contribute information, or corroboration at least, on some points."

"Are we to understand, too," asked Desmond, "that Mrs. Roosevelt has played a role in solving this mystery?"

"Mrs. Roosevelt *did* solve this mystery," said Sir Alan. "To my satisfaction, anyway."

"How long are we to be kept in suspense?" asked Letitia.

"No longer," said Sir Alan. "Let us review the facts. Along the way we will clear up some tangential points and dispose of some irrelevancies, so that all will be clear in the end."

"By all means proceed," said Duggs. "The hour is late."

"Very well," said Sir Alan. "Facts—Sir Anthony Brooke-Hardinge died of blows to the head inflicted with the poker from the fireplace in the library, while he sat on the couch. He was not killed by a stranger. He watched, unsuspecting, while someone picked up the poker, stirred the fire with it, and then stepped behind him and struck him. Apart from the difficulty of entering the Palace, no one but a friend could have taken the poker in hand, moved around behind him with it, and struck. Obviously, he made no move to defend himself until after the first blow landed. Why not? Because he trusted the person who struck.''

"He trusted none of us," said Letitia.

"He trusted you not to kill him," said Sir Alan.

"He was a fool, then," said Letitia.

The telephone in the library rang. "Forgive me," said Sir Alan, and he left the room to answer it. In a moment he returned. He smiled at Mrs. Roosevelt and nodded, then returned to his narrative.

"The autopsy showed that Sir Anthony drank a substantial quantity of whisky in the quarter hour before his death. His killer probably encouraged him to do that, to slow him down. Then the killer wiped the whisky bottle and the vodka bottle clean of fingerprints.''

"Which proves nothing, though, does it?" asked Lord William. "I mean, since the prints—"

"Actually it does prove something," said Sir Alan. "As we shall see."

"What of those grotesque phrases written on notepaper in Sir Anthony's handwriting?" asked Lord William. " 'Deadly Nightshade,' I recall, for one."

"Possible titles for a play," said Sir Alan. "Irrelevant."

"Go on, then."

"The person who killed Sir Anthony also stole the jade Buddha," said Sir Alan. "Stealing it would have been motive enough. It was worth ten thousand pounds—or, in Mrs. Roosevelt's terms, more than fifty thousand dollars. The murderer could not remove it from the Palace the night of the murder. So, he or she dropped it in the water tank above the toilet in the bathroom. The murderer—or someone working with the murderer—returned the next night, *with keys to these apartments,* and recovered the Buddha from the tank. By chance, Mrs. Roosevelt and I interrupted that endeavor. Even so, the person we encountered escaped from the Palace with the Buddha.''

"Then the killer is someone who had keys to these rooms," said Desmond. "Which, thank God, lets me out. Certainly I never had any keys—"

"I'm afraid it doesn't let you out at all," said Sir Alan. "This is a point Mrs. Roosevelt found especially interesting." He stopped and nodded at her.

"All of you, I am sure," she said, "have had the experience of looking at something quite familiar, vaguely noticing that something is irregular, and not immediately seeing what it is. When we examined the contents of Sir Anthony's pockets, we found a variety of items . . ." She paused for emphasis. *"But we did not find keys to these rooms.* At first we supposed—as you do, Mr. Desmond—that whoever returned for the Buddha had to be someone who could enter these rooms."

"Meaning me," said Laura.

"Not necessarily meaning you, Miss Hodges," said Mrs. Roosevelt. "You handed your keys to Sir Alan that night, at his request. But that was immaterial. Whoever killed Sir Anthony took his keys from his pockets, and used them the next night. The fact that you returned your keys, and the fact that Mr. Desmond never had any, are immaterial."

"Then we are all still suspects," said Alexandra resentfully.

"If you did not wish to be suspected, My Lady," said Sir Alan, "you might have acted a bit less suspiciously. For example—" He reached into his jacket pocket and pulled out a glittering necklace of emeralds and diamonds. "Selling this to a professional receiver of stolen property was not an innocent act."

"My God! Where did you get that?"

"Borrowed it from the insurance investigator who purchased it for his company—so that the company may try to recover a part of its loss. You *did* know it was stolen?"

She covered her blushing face with her hands and nodded. "I suspected . . ."

"Sir Anthony gave it to you, did he not?"

"Yes. I didn't *know* it was stolen, actually—but I had to suspect it." She sighed. "I knew, of course, the Turner was stolen. The painting. I knew the Buddha was. Tony loved beautiful things and had no scruples about how he acquired them. When he gave me the necklace, I—"

"Yes," Sir Alan interrupted. "He gave you this when he still hoped you might consent to marry him. You knew him well enough to know he bought stolen property. I suggest to you, My Lady, you did know the necklace was stolen. If you'd not known, you would have taken it to a legitimate dealer and obtained a far better price for it. Instead, you sold it to a fence."

"I needed the money."

Sir Alan spoke to her, but his eyes met those of Lord William as he said, "I believe if you pay over the money to the insurance company, no one will insist on prosecuting you."

She glanced up into his face. "Thank you," she whispered.

"What is more," said Mrs. Roosevelt gently, "you

will not be prosecuted for murder, Countess Alexandra. You did not kill Sir Anthony Brooke-Hardinge."

"If you knew that, Sir Alan, Mrs. Roosevelt, then why did you summon Countess Alexandra to this meeting?" asked Lord William.

"We asked people who have relevant information," said Sir Alan. "Also, to be entirely frank, we asked people who lied to us during the course of the investigation."

"As I did," said Letitia sharply.

"As you did," Sir Alan agreed. "Do you want to tell us where you went Saturday night?"

"Not here," said Letitia. "I didn't come here, to Buckingham Palace."

"Maybe not," said Sir Alan. "But if not, why did you lie about the hour of your departure from Hertford Street? You left about half past ten, as was established by the statement of the young woman in your employ, and confirmed by the statement of the American correspondent to whom you delivered her. You said you left an hour later. What did you do with that extra hour?"

Letitia raised her chin high. "I went to recover some property of mine," she said. "From the house in Belgravia that had been my home."

"Specifically . . .?"

"Specifically, when Tony divorced me he kept some things that were very personal to me: pictures, a Georgian silver cream pitcher, my mother's silver vanity set . . . Their value was not high. He did it to hurt me. I had keys to the house. He didn't know that, but I did; I had had copies made, and I kept them when I was forced to move out. Over the years I have been in and out of the house several times, recovering small items that were meaningful to me. I should have liked to set the place on fire.''

"And once he was dead, you went back—"

"To get things that were rightfully mine."

"A burglary!" said Lord William.

"I've been in the nick before," Letitia muttered.

"Oh, I doubt we shall prosecute for that, either," said Sir Alan. "Unless Lord William—"

"Never mind," said Lord William. "Never mind. Proceed, Sir Alan, Mrs. Roosevelt. Proceed."

Jennings Duggs walked to the bar and poured himself a small glass of sherry. He poured a second glass and carried it to Mrs. Roosevelt. She smiled and accepted it.

Sir Alan went to the bar and poured himself a splash of whisky. He returned to his place before the fire. "From the beginning," he said, "I was convinced that theft of the jade Buddha was the chief motive for the murder of Sir Anthony Brooke-Hardinge. I have focused on that motive—whilst Mrs. Roosevelt, fortunately, has focused on other elements of the crime. She and I have taken two approaches to the mystery. Either one might have solved it."

"And whose did?" asked Lord William.

"It was a joint effort," said Mrs. Roosevelt.

"But who—"

"Sir Anthony purchased the Buddha from a dealer in stolen properties," said Sir Alan. "And he bragged about it later. A number of you knew how he acquired it. Some of you even knew *from whom*. The murderer reached a decision to kill Sir Anthony quite independently of the possibility of stealing the Buddha. But having decided to kill him, the murderer decided to steal the Buddha. Why not? It was worth a fortune.''

"A fortune, indeed," said Duggs. "How many years does a breakfast waiter work for ten thousand pounds? How many years does an insurance broker?''

"Yes," said Sir Alan. "But who would buy it? Well . . . Why not the dealer from whom Sir Anthony purchased it in the first place? That dealer had made a profit on it once, and maybe he would like to make a profit on it a second time. So the would-be murderer went to Narberth Crowley, one of London's most infamous criminals—''

"This is speculation," objected Desmond.

"The murderer went to Narberth Crowley," Sir Alan continued firmly, "and offered the Buddha— omitting to tell him, however, that it would not be stolen until after Sir Anthony had been murdered.''

"Has Crowley confessed to this?" asked Laura.

Sir Alan ignored the question. "Narberth Crowley agreed to buy it. After all, since Sir Anthony had bought the Buddha as stolen property, he could hardly complain to the police if it were stolen *from* him. In fact, it all worked out better than the would-be murderer could have anticipated. Since Sir Anthony's death occurred in Bukingham Palace, we kept it a secret, for reasons of national security. When the murderer delivered the Buddha to Crowley, Crowley did not know that Sir Anthony had been murdered. Crowley took it and paid for it.''

"How much, do you suppose?" asked Duggs. "Surely nothing near its value.''

"I don't know how much," said Sir Alan. "Only a fraction of its worth, as you suggest. Several thousand pounds, however, we may be sure. But whatever he paid for it, Narberth Crowley had been fleeced. The murder made the Buddha all but worthless in the market for stolen goods.''

The Chinese houseboy had sat down on the floor now. With his legs crossed, his arms folded, he looked something like the jade Buddha must have looked. As Sir Alan spoke, Wen Yung nodded rhythmically, as if to express agreement and approval of every word Sir Alan spoke.

Sir Alan noticed him. "You know about all this, Wen Yung?'' he asked.

Wen Yung nodded. "Meeser Narberth Crowley, he sometime visitor, Belgravia house,'' he said. "Evil man.''

"Yes," said Sir Alan. "He didn't know Sir Anthony was dead—but I took pains to let him know. I made sure he understood the jade Buddha was evidence in a murder. He grasped the meaning of that, we may be sure—that he ran a grave risk even having the Buddha in his possession, much less trying to sell it.''

"Must've made him furious,'' said Duggs.

"Within thirty-six hours,'' said Sir Alan, "two of our suspects were physically attacked: Mr. Desmond and Miss Hodges.''

"You're accusing one of us!'' exclaimed Desmond angrily.

"I haven't yet,'' said Sir Alan coldly. "Mrs. Roosevelt has something to say.''

13

Mrs. Roosevelt remained seated, her little glass of sherry in her right hand, a sympathetic smile on her face. "I am most conscious," she said, "of being an intruder here. I should not have meddled in this investigation except that I am as interested in freeing the innocent as in convicting the guilty. I do apologize to you all for this . . . *session*. It was my idea."

"Her help has been invaluable," said Sir Alan.

"I have thought a great deal," she said, "about the remaining elements of the crime—the ones, that is, that do not focus on the theft of the jade Buddha. With your consent, I will review some of these elements."

"And announce a conclusion?" asked Lord William.

"The conclusion," she said, "remains for a British jury. Sir Alan and I are prepared to disclose the evidence and the conclusion we believe it leads to."

"Please," said Lord William.

Mrs. Roosevelt put the sherry—from which she had taken only one sip—aside. She folded her hands in her lap. "The evidence compels a conclusion," she said. "If anyone can review it and reach a differ-

246

ent conclusion, I should be happy to see how you do it. For me, it points to one person—distressingly clearly."

"Distressingly so," agreed Sir Alan.

"The murder of Sir Anthony Brooke-Hardinge was not committed on the impulse of a moment," Mrs. Roosevelt went on. "It was planned. The plan, unfortunately for the person who conceived it, turns out to be a trap. It often happens that the very device a criminal adopts to divert suspicion actually focuses suspicion—as it did here."

"Traps which of us?" Desmond asked aggressively.

"From the beginning," Mrs. Roosevelt continued, "I have found it implausible that Sir Anthony would hold a supper party at which he would assemble a group of people who hated him, who even had motive to kill him. That just doesn't seem . . . plausible."

"You didn't know Tony," said Letitia bitterly. "If you had known the man, you would understand how very plausible it is."

"I'm afraid I must agree," said Countess Alexandra.

"As must I," said Duggs. "That's the kind of man he was."

"He was very specific," said Laura. "He thought his invitation list was quite a joke."

"It is an oddly assorted list," said Mrs. Roosevelt. "Mr. Duggs and Lady Letitia had reason to hate him—as, for that matter, did Sir Alan Burton. But Mr. Desmond had no reason to hate him."

"But reason to kill him," said Laura. "Twenty thousand pounds' life insurance."

"Captain Gerald Exeter . . ." Mrs. Roosevelt mused with a frown.

"Tony seduced his wife," said Laura.

"Ah, yes," Sir Alan interjected. "But did Captain Exeter hate him?"

"Of course he did," said Laura. "And Tony thought it was funny. He bragged about it."

"To whom did he brag about it?"

Laura shrugged. "To anyone who'd listen." She looked at Desmond.

Desmond shook his head.

"It's very odd, Miss Hodges," said Sir Alan. "Captain Exeter says that Sir Anthony was one of his best friends and that Sir Anthony begged forgiveness for having had an affair with the captain's wife. Captain Exeter says he did in fact forgive him and that they remained the best of friends."

"He lies," said Laura. "If he now denies he hated Tony, it's because he knows Tony has been murdered."

Sir Alan shook his head. "When he received his invitation to the supper party, he sat down and wrote Sir Anthony a note, expressing his regrets at being unable to come. He wrote that note *before* Sir Anthony was murdered. I must tell you, Miss Hodges, it is a rather friendly little note, jocular in tone."

"I can't account for the attitudes of Captain Exeter," said Laura crisply. Her voice rose, and she added, "I'm beginning to think I am being accused."

"Another point, Miss Hodges," said Mrs. Roosevelt. "Why was the name Lionel Foster on the invitation list? Mr. Foster had been dead for some months."

"Obviously Tony didn't know that," said Laura sullenly.

"I'm afraid he did," said Mrs. Roosevelt. "He had been sending Mr. Foster checks every month for years, to buy his silence about a crime they had jointly committed but for which only Mr. Foster had gone to prison. When Mr. Foster died, Sir Anthony stopped sending checks to him and began to send checks instead to Mrs. Foster.''

Mrs. Roosevelt paused. She drew a deep breath as Laura Hodges stared at her, stiffening with apprehension. The others stared, too.

Mrs. Roosevelt shook her head and sighed. ''Oh yes, Miss Hodges,'' she said. ''Sir Anthony knew Mr. Foster was dead. But you didn't.''

''You *are* accusing me!'' Laura shrieked. She put her hands to her face. ''You are accusing *me!*''

''I am only reciting the facts,'' said Mrs. Roosevelt. ''You told us you prepared and mailed the invitations. It had to be you, of course, since no one else had access to Sir Anthony's letter paper and typewriter. But you did not address the invitations to a group of people he specified. Even if we are wrong about Captain Exeter, certainly he would never have sent an invitation to Lionel Foster. The facts suggest, Miss Hodges, that Sir Anthony knew nothing of the invitations, that *you* sent them entirely on your own initiative. Is there another explanation for the facts?''

''You may be sure there is one,'' said Ken Kane angrily. ''And I warn all of you—the wife of the President of the United States included—that you may have to answer before a libel court.''

''We accept that risk,'' said Mrs. Roosevelt placidly.

It was altogether too evident that the rest of the people in the room were relieved that the accusation had fallen on Laura Hodges. They relaxed visibly.

Laura Hodges had slackened, closed her eyes, and begun to cry quietly.

"I am a newcomer to this carnival," said Ken Kane resentfully, still clinging firmly to Laura's hand. "I assume you have explanations for all the elements of the mystery of Sir Tony's death."

"We do," said Sir Alan. "You may not wish to hear them, Mr. Kane."

"We will hear them," said Kane.

"Very well," said Sir Alan. "Where shall we begin? With motive? Or with means . . . ? Means, perhaps. An other element of the evidence against Miss Hodges: she knew—and unless I am in serious error, no one else in this room knew—that Sir Anthony's Chinese houseboy, Wen Yung, who had always lived with Sir Anthony and had been required to sleep on the floor in this suite, had recently been allowed to go home evenings. Anyone else entering this suite to kill Sir Anthony could not have expected to find him alone."

"Which proves nothing, if you'll allow me to say so," said Desmond. "Tony may have been killed while we were all assembled here in this room—and Wen Yung might have been in the kitchen."

Sir Alan nodded to Desmond. "Point well taken, Mr. Desmond. Suggestive evidence, not convincing."

"Nothing we've heard is convincing," grumbled Kane.

"Actually," said Sir Alan, "the evidence of the invitation list is *quite* convincing. What remains is to explain the remaining elements—as you asked us to do." He drew a breath. "Let us turn, then, to the events here last Friday evening."

"I had always supposed it would be pleasant to be invited to Buckingham Palace," said Duggs. "I hope I shall not be asked again."

"Miss Hodges could come in and go out as she wished," said Sir Alan. "She entered the apartments and waited for Sir Anthony, who was below as the state dinner began. When he returned, she went with him into the library. She encouraged him to drink some whisky. She herself drank vodka, because it would leave no odor on her breath. The other guests, arriving, would not suspect she had been here and drinking with Sir Anthony for some little time. She watched for her chance, saw it, and struck Sir Anthony on the head with the poker from the fireplace. The first blow so stunned and injured him that he could not thereafter defend himself, and she proceeded to bludgeon him to death."

"Horrible!" exclaimed Countess Alexandra.

Laura had stopped crying and sat shifting her eyes between Sir Alan and Mrs. Roosevelt, her cheeks flushed and wet with tears.

"It *was* horrible," said Sir Alan. "But not perhaps more than she had expected. His blood, which was splattered on the furniture and floor, was also splattered on her clothes. But this she had anticipated. She alone, of all of you, could have had other clothes hanging in Sir Anthony's closet. A few of her underthings remained in his bureau drawer, even though she no longer lived here all the time, so something of hers—a dress or suit—could have hung in his closet without his noticing particularly. I am inclined to think the item was a silk dress. His blood was indeed splattered on whatever she was wearing. She changed, from his bedroom closet. Then she burned her bloodstained clothes in this"—he nodded—"fireplace."

"I suppose," said Kane, "you have a laboratory

analysis of the ash from the fireplace, showing a quantity of fabric was burned there.''

"In fact we haven't, Mr. Kane," said Sir Anthony. "The analysis shows something entirely different. Our investigators did, however, find small globules of melted glass on the hearth. Buttons, Mr. Kane. In the hot fire, the glass buttons melted.''

"Proving nothing," said Kane scornfully. "If those globules were in fact buttons, they could have been anyone's.''

"And that brings us to the motive, does it not, Mrs. Roosevelt?'' asked Sir Alan.

She nodded. "I believe it does. You see, ladies and gentlemen, something more was burned in this fireplace Friday night. The laboratory analysis of the ash showed that a substantial quantity of paper had been burned in the fireplace. Paper . . .''

"Something was being burned!" declared Duggs. "Should have thought of that! Of course . . ." He swung around toward Laura. "The place was hot! Hot! And it was *you*, Miss Hodges, who kept feeding coals on the fire and poking them to life. All night you did it.''

"We may speculate," said Sir Alan, "—and I emphasize it is speculation—that the ash from the burned clothing simply went up the chimney on the hot flue gasses. The combustion products of thoroughly burned fabric, such as wool, are known to be light—silk, in fact, simply disappears, leaving no ash—whereas paper ash tends to be heavy.''

"So what was I burning?" asked Laura resentfully.

"*Star Blitz*," said Mrs. Roosevelt.

"*What?*"

"Your motive for killing Sir Anthony Brooke-

Hardinge," said Mrs. Roosevelt. "What you were burning in the fireplace was Sir Anthony's plagiarism of *Star Blitz*. You had found it in the apartment—or maybe he had actually shown it to you. In either case, you realized he was planning to produce *Star Blitz* as his own show, without you or Mr. Kane playing roles and without your brother's name as playwright."

"I'm afraid you're wrong about that," said Desmond. "The problem was not with Stanley Hodges and Ken Kane as playwrights; it was with Laura as lead dancer. We were still thinking of producing the show, if we could get Stan and Ken to drop their insistence on Laura. In fact, I continued to think of doing so after Tony was dead—which is why I was carrying a copy of the script with me to a dinner with Lucinda Bancroft when I was attacked in—"

"Lucinda Bancroft!" exclaimed Kane. "Are you saying Sir Anthony—?"

Desmond shrugged. "Tony would never have invested in a show starring Laura," he said. "In the first place, he didn't think she had the talent to carry a show like *Star Blitz*. In the second place, he wanted to keep her on a string for himself."

"In fact," said Laura bitterly, "he put that word around. My auditions were—"

"Farces," said Desmond.

"Well then Mr. Desmond what was *London '43?*" asked Mrs. Roosevelt.

Desmond shook his head. "I don't know what you are referring to, Mrs. Roosevelt."

"The title of a play," said Mrs. Roosevelt. "Sir Anthony's plagiarism of *Star Blitz*."

"What I am supposed to have burned," said Laura dejectedly.

"The typing service," said Mrs. Roosevelt, "made only one copy of *London '43*. It had earlier typed two copies of *Star Blitz* for Sir Anthony, copying from a script he provided. Later he returned to the typing service with the carbon copy of *Star Blitz*. He had changed it extensively, in pencil. He ordered the typing service to make one copy of the new play— *London '43*—which was nothing but *Star Blitz*, Sir Anthony's version. He ordered his own name typed on the title page as playwright."

"I swear I knew nothing of this," said Desmond.

"In spite of the fact that you were carrying the marked carbon when you were attacked in William the Fourth Street?" asked Sir Alan.

"In spite of that," said Desmond. "Yes, that was a revised version of *Star Blitz*—extensively changed by Tony. In fact, I was taking that copy to Lucinda Bancroft to see which version she would like—Tony's or the original. Tony said nothing to me of any intention to steal the play."

"But you can't deny that's what he had in mind, can you?" asked Kane angrily.

"God only knew what Tony ever had in mind," mumbled Desmond.

"And though he was dead, you were still carrying *Star Blitz* to Lucinda Bancroft?" Kane asked.

"Once it is established I did not kill Tony," said Desmond, "I shall receive twenty thousand pounds from his life-insurance policy. I shall use the money to produce a new show. It may be *Star Blitz*. I am looking at another play as well, but I may decide to do *Star Blitz*."

"With Lucinda Bancroft, I suppose," said Laura.

"That will require Mr. Kane's consent, I imagine," said Duggs. "An interesting problem in loyalty . . ."

"Actually," said Desmond, "the play belongs to Stanley Hodges. Ken Kane's name was put on it only because it was supposed that would help sell it. Stan has already told me—albeit reluctantly, I grant—that he will contract it to me for Lucinda if that is the only way he can get it produced."

"The bastard!" snapped Kane.

Desmond ran his finger down his nose. "Who, by the way, conked me on the head Monday evening? Surely you didn't really send Narberth Crowley after me, Sir Alan?"

"I must confess I had it in mind," said Sir Alan. "But all I gave Crowley, actually, was the word that Sir Anthony had been murdered. *He* knew who had sold him the Buddha. And he did pretty much what I expected him to do. He sent thugs to get his money back. I made an error. I surrounded you with police protection. I did not put protection around Miss Hodges, and Crowley's thugs attacked her and recovered the money."

"This is *utterly outrageous!*" yelled Kane.

"Your indignation rings false, Mr. Kane," said Sir Alan. "While we have been meeting here, some officers with a warrant have been searching your flat. They telephoned their results to me a short while ago. That was the call I took in the library. Do you want to tell us what they found, Miss Hodges?"

Laura shrugged. "Why not—since you know," she said dully, resigned and disconsolate. "They found the Buddha."

"Yes," said Sir Alan. "Where I had told them

they would find it. I thought it strange that you so
vehemently refused to go to the hospital last night.
Once Mrs. Roosevelt pointed out to me the facts
about the invitation—which is what tripped you up,
actually—I realized why you would not leave the flat
last night, why, in fact, you would not leave the
couch. The Buddha was under the cushion. You were
sitting on it.''

"The police arrived before I could hide it,'' she
said.

"You were stunned, hurt,'' said Sir Alan. "You
hid it in the only place you could.''

"Yes.''

Laura had begun to cry now, not hysterically, just
quietly, holding her lower lip between her teeth.
Mrs. Roosevelt went to her side and put a hand on
her shoulder.

"I believe,'' said Sir Alan, "that Lord William
will join me in saying to you that we will probably be
able to arrange a degree of leniency for you if you
will now give us the rest of the facts. You do understand, however, that anything you say will be used
against you in a court of law.''

Laura nodded.

"You did kill him, didn't you?'' asked Sir Alan
gently. "Very much the way we've said, and for the
reasons we have said.''

She sobbed. "I found the play,'' she whispered
hoarsely. "I saw what he had done. I knew he had
been scotching my auditions. Now I could see that he
meant to take our play away from us. I was furious. I
decided to kill him—even if I hanged for it.''

"Oh, my dear!'' Mrs. Roosevelt demurred softly.

"The supper party . . . It was as you suggested. I

thought I would assemble people who hated him and give them all an opportunity so they would all be suspects.''

"How did you know we would leave the room, one after another?" asked Sir Alan. "If all of us had simply sat here—"

"And drank and drank and never went to the bathroom?" Laura sneered. "Not likely. If you hadn't, I might have asked someone to go to the kitchen for some water or into his bedroom for a sweater for me—or something. Anyway, you did better than I could have asked. *All* of you left the room. I'd have been satisfied if two of you did."

"But he was dead when we got here, then," said Desmond.

She glanced around the room at the others. "Yes. He was dead when you arrived. I'd killed him about half an hour before the first of you came. I put my silk dress in the fire, just as Sir Alan says, knowing it would leave no ash. But the manuscript did. I kept putting in more coal and kept the fire hot all night. I played loud music to cover the sounds of a struggle in the library—that is, the struggle I hoped you would think had happened while you were all here and each of you was wandering off to the bathroom and so on."

"Why did you wipe the fingerprints off the bottles?" asked Mrs. Roosevelt.

Laura managed a faint, bitter smile. "That was clever of me, if you don't mind my saying so. It was to direct suspicion away from me. After all, why would *I* wipe my fingerprints off anything in this suite? I had lived here. I still came here often. My fingerprints are everywhere here. I thought by wiping

two bottles clean I would throw suspicion to someone
. . . I don't know who. Someone . . .''

"And you had been to Narberth Crowley, had you
not?" asked Sir Alan.

"Yes. As you said."

"You hid the Buddha in the water tank above the
toilet."

"Yes."

"And the next night you returned to recover it."

She lowered her head and nodded.

"She wasn't alone," said Kane quietly. "I came
with her. I was the one who was alarmed when you
entered the suite. I was the one who fell off the toilet
seat, where I was standing so I could reach down into
the tank. I—"

"I was waiting in the hall outside," said Laura.
"I saw you and Mrs. Roosevelt go in, Sir Alan, but I
couldn't do anything about it. When Ken ran out, I
locked the door to slow you down, and then I showed
him the way out."

"So, Mr. Kane," said Sir Alan. "I said your
indignation rang false."

"He had no part in killing Tony," said Laura
quietly. "He didn't even know I was *going* to do it."

"But I knew she did, afterward," said Kane. "She
told me, when she came home. And I came with her
to help her get the Buddha. She had told me where it
was, and I was afraid she wasn't tall enough to reach
it."

"I had just tossed it up and into the tank," said
Laura.

"Your brother supported your story that you were
with him at supper all that night," said Sir Alan.
"As, for that matter, did the restaurant owner."

"That's all that Stan had to do with it," said Kane. "Rick, at the restaurant . . . he accommodated us. He had no idea he was protecting us against a burglary charge, much less murder."

"And you took the Buddha to Narberth Crowley," said Sir Alan.

Kane drew a deep breath and stiffened his back. "You nearly got her killed, Sir Alan," he said, squeezing Laura's hand. "She told them she'd banked the money, didn't have it in the flat. They beat her until she told them where it was."

"And left the Buddha," said Sir Alan.

"Threw it at me," said Laura. "It hit me in the face."

"Well . . ." sighed Sir Alan. "A sorry matter."

"I'd still like to know who conked me on the head," said Desmond.

"I think I know the answer to that," said Mrs. Roosevelt. "Miss Hodges. And Mr. Kane. I'm afraid they meant to kill you, too."

Laura shrugged and shook her head. "What point in killing Tony and letting Desmond steal *Star Blitz?* That's what we supposed you meant to do, David. It was Ken's voice you heard. Then I hit you from behind. If that man hadn't come running, yelling—"

"And you danced in the chorus at the Prince of Wales that evening to give yourself an alibi," said Sir Alan. "That was another mistake, Miss Hodges. It was most uncharacteristic of you; you had made a considerable point of refusing ever again to dance semi-nude in follies-type shows."

"Anyway, I never had the least intention of stealing your play," said Desmond. "What is more, I don't think Tony really would have done it, either.

He had no scruples, but he'd have realized sooner or later that he couldn't get away with it. I think you killed him unnecessarily, Laura."

"I'm not sorry he's dead," she said sullenly.

"I'm not sure any of us are," said Sir Alan. "But it is murder, just the same."

Epilogue

On Friday, Mrs. Roosevelt, accompanied by Sir Alan Burton as her English bodyguard, left London for Chequers, the official country home of the Prime Minister, where she spent a weekend with the Churchills. After that, she began her round of visits to army camps and air bases throughout England and Scotland. Just before she returned to the States she visited the royal family once again, this time at Windsor Castle. Returning to the White House in mid-November, she learned that the President had been fully informed of her role in the solution of the Buckingham Palace murder mystery, and she found in her office a framed certificate—

ANCIENT ACHING ORDER OF
OFFICIOUS INTERMEDDLERS

BE IT KNOWN THAT,

Whereas Mrs. Eleanor Roosevelt has once again pursued her bent for sticking in her nib and doing her bit in the cause of justice; and

Whereas the said Eleanor Roosevelt has this time pursued her said bent within the ancient precincts of the United Kingdom of Great Britain and Northern Ireland; and

Whereas her officious intermeddling has once again resulted in the nabbing of the guilty and loosing of the innocent; and

Whereas the late Sherlock Holmes has no official successor in the United States of America;

NOW, THEREFORE, I Franklin D. Roosevelt, Commander-in-Chief, do hereby designate, create, appoint, and anoint the said MRS. ELEANOR ROOSEVELT official SHERLOCK HOLMES for and within the United States of America; and

I hereby confer on her all the rights, honors, dignities, perquisites, titles, and remuneration to the said office appertaining.

DONE at our City of Washington this fifteenth day of November in the Year of Our Lord one thousand nine hundred forty-two and of the independence of the United States of America the one hundred sixty-sixth.

FRANKLIN D. ROOSEVELT
Commander-in-Chief

Attest:
   HARRY HOPKINS,
   Master of Holmesiana

In London on January 20, 1943, Laura Hodges was sentenced to life imprisonment for the murder of Sir Anthony Brooke-Hardinge. She entered Holloway Prison the next day.

Ken Kane, convicted as an accessory in the murder, also of the assault on David Desmond, was sentenced to ten years' imprisonment.

Narberth Crowley was convicted of receiving stolen property, the jade Buddha, and of sending his thugs to attack Laura Hodges. He was sentenced to ten years.

Stanley Hodges was not charged, though technically he was an accessory after the fact in the murder of Sir Anthony Brooke-Hardinge.

On November 24, 1943, *Star Blitz* opened in London. Produced by David Desmond, and starring Lucinda Bancroft and Terry Bailey, it ran for 948 performances.

In 1946, Desmond produced another show by Stanley Hodges. Called *Twelve Nights,* it ran for 786 performances in London and more than 900 in New York. In 1949, David Desmond and Stanley Hodges co-produced *The Tempestuous*—play and lyrics by Stanley Hodges, directed by Stanley Hodges. It ran successfully and then was made into a motion picture.

In October 1955, Mrs. Roosevelt received an invitation from David Desmond to attend as his guest the New York opening of still another Stanley Hodges show, *A Dream.* At a dinner after the show she found herself seated beside Stanley Hodges. He was most cordial. She felt she could not but inquire after his sister, and he told her that Laura was still in Holloway Prison but hoped for a parole before long. He visited her every month. Ken Kane had been paroled in 1949, he said. Narberth Crowley had died in Broadmoor Prison in 1952, four months before completing his ten-year term.

Stanley Hodges smiled. "Laura still talks about starring in a show when she gets out. Wants me to write a part for her." He shook his head. "Irrepressible, Laura. Simply irrepressible."

ELLIOTT ROOSEVELT'S DELIGHTFUL MYSTERY SERIES

MURDER IN THE ROSE GARDEN
70529-X/$4.95US/$5.95Can

MURDER IN THE OVAL OFFICE
70528-1/$4.99US/$5.99Can

MURDER AND THE FIRST LADY
69937-0/$4.50US/$5.50Can

THE HYDE PARK MURDER
70058-1/$4.50US/$5.50Can

MURDER AT HOBCAW BARONY
70021-2/$4.50US/$5.50Can

THE WHITE HOUSE PANTRY MURDER
70404-8/$3.95US/$4.95Can

MURDER AT THE PALACE
70405-6/$3.95 US/$4.95Can

Coming Soon

MURDER IN THE BLUE ROOM
71237-7/$4.99US/$5.99Can